Hope

Passing Through

David Hartley

First published in 2022
by David Hartley

Copyright David Hartley 2022

David Hartley has asserted his moral right
to be identified as the author of this work

ISBN: 978-1-3999-2876-2

Printed by ImprintDigital.com, UK

This is a work of fiction. Names, characters, places and incidents
either are products of the author's imagination or are used fictitiously.
Any resemblance to actual events or locales or persons, living or dead,
is entirely coincidental.

PART ONE *Autumn 2005*

- 9   A Birder's Bird
- 19   Glen Gair
- 52   The Last Munro
- 61   The Plaque
- 74   The Jetty
- 81   Leonardo
- 91   The Prize-giving

PART TWO *Spring 2010*

- 103   Araucaria
- 121   A Change of Direction
- 131   The Snow-hole
- 144   A Good Example
- 164   The Plagiarist's Tale
- 176   Between the Showers

PART THREE *Spring–Summer 2016*

- 187   The Event Manager
- 194   The Old School
- 203   An Afternoon at the Reserve
- 211   People-watching
- 220   Doctor Emma
- 233   The History Student
- 260   Travelling with a Conscience

PART ONE

Autumn 2005

A Birder's Bird

I had noticed the man with the heavy backpack and the expensive-looking telescope when I was at the check-in desk. Obviously a bird-watcher. Orkney in the autumn is full of them. It's usually the rare migrants which bring them to the islands. My husband's aunt runs a B & B in Stromness, and she's always booked up at this time of year.

Once I had my boarding card, I went over to the café, collected a cup of tea and a scone, and sat down by the window. Kirkwall is the only airport where I look forward to waiting for a flight. It's a joy to look over the runway and watch the wading birds on the grass and the pools. The view on all sides is wonderful: open fields, big skies. I always have my camera handy, hoping that one day I'll capture that special Orkney light.

It's a friendly airport. No one rushes you, and the noise of the engines tells you when the planes are on their way. You can watch the island-hoppers landing and taking off, often with just one or two passengers. In the old days, security was just a quick check, and you shared a joke as you went through. Now, it takes longer, but it's still very relaxed. Like Orkney itself.

My Edinburgh flight wasn't due to leave until nearly six. I

put my passport and boarding card in the front pocket of my handbag and settled down to enjoy the wait. I had to smile when I heard the usual announcement warning passengers not to leave luggage unattended, but just as I was thinking that it was exactly four years since 9/11, I noticed a large item on the seat opposite. It took me a second to realise that it was the backpack belonging to the man I'd seen earlier. A bird-watching terrorist? Unlikely. A minute later, its owner returned from the window and sat down next to his luggage. He was carrying his telescope; that was clearly too important to be let out of his sight, even at Kirkwall airport. Then he looked over, smiled and said something about the good weather we'd been having. September was often the best month in Orkney, he reckoned. Nodding towards my camera, he asked me if I'd been photographing the birds. Not this time, I replied; I was on my way back from my cousin's wedding. He said that he was waiting for the Aberdeen flight. I half hoped that the conversation might end then and there, but he looked over to his telescope, willing me to show interest in his hobby.

So I asked him if he'd had a successful trip.

Yes, he had: short-eared owls, hen harriers, some rare warblers. Pretty much what he'd expected. Then he leaned over conspiratorially and said that he'd *got his Rumbold's on Sanday earlier in the week*. It seemed an odd thing to say, so, trying to keep a straight face, I asked him to repeat it. Yes, he'd *got his Rumbold's on Sanday earlier in the week*.

He was clearly expecting a reaction. So I asked him, is that a warbler, a bunting, or a...? He interrupted: it was a pipit. Rumbold's pipit. It wasn't the first time he'd seen one, he added, but it was still a special bird for him. I glanced at the screen: the Edinburgh flight was still due to leave on time. He saw which way I was looking, and said that he was going to buy a cup of tea, and that he'd tell me the story when he got back. It wasn't just about the bird, he insisted; it was more interesting than that. *Really?* I thought to myself. I was beginning to wish Kirkwall airport wasn't such a friendly place after all. But there was nowhere to hide.

* * *

His name was Ross McCormack, he said, as he put his cup of tea down. He looked to be in his early twenties, possibly a bit older. Tall and scruffy, his glasses patched up with Sellotape. I noticed that the straps on his backpack were badly frayed. He began by asking me if I knew the difference between bird-watchers, birders and twitchers. People start out as bird-watchers, he explained. Then, when they've really got the bug, they become birders. More serious, but not obsessed. The twitchers are the obsessed ones, the ones who rush off all over the country, abroad even, to see something rare. Sad people, the lot of them, in his view. Not interested in the birds; for them it's just a matter of adding another name to their life-list.

He wasn't a twitcher, he insisted.

It was the *Observer's Book of Birds* that had got him started. His grandfather had given him one for his birthday when he was very young. The format of the book was the crucial thing, he insisted. You didn't need an adult to hold it for you, and there was just enough information in it for a child to cope with. Pictures too, of course. It was a fair point. As a child I'd got a lot of pleasure from my Observer's books too, though for me it had been the ones about horses and dogs.

He'd started checking off the common birds in the book,

he said. I know quite a bit about birds, so when he confided that his first special bird had been a fieldfare, I had to say I was surprised: they're common enough, in the winter at least. Exactly, he said, that was the problem; you don't see them for a large part of the year, and waiting months to see a bird you've set your heart on, that was hard. He told me how he remembered hearing them call one Saturday morning in December, when he was out with his dad, and how it had made his day.

Then he asked me if I knew that there are some birds that get known as birders' birds. It was a silly expression, he admitted, but there was a point to it. A birder's bird is one that you've got to be a proper expert to identify: some birds are really tough to get right. I decided this was a good time to move the conversation on: the pipit, I said, it was obviously a birder's bird.

Yes, it was. Of course, he said, there are lots of other common pipits in the UK, meadow pipits, rock pipits, tree pipits. (I nodded: I had heard of them.) But until a few years ago, there hadn't been a single record of a Rumbold's in the UK.

He was starting to warm up now. He took out a field guide from his backpack and showed me a picture of his bird. Even for a pipit, it was a dull thing. He did have the grace to agree, admitting that it was a real LBJ (a little brown job, he informed me helpfully).

Then he stopped and gazed out of the window for a few seconds. I thought he must have seen something, but when he turned his face back to me, I could see there were tears in his eyes. He apologised, took out a tissue and asked me if I had ever had anything to do with people with Down's syndrome. That came out of the blue, and I didn't know how to react. No, I said, James – my husband – and I had been fortunate, our two children were both… I couldn't think of the right words. In the end, I think I said that they had never had learning difficulties.

He put his tissue away and explained that he had two sisters. The older one was called Karen. The younger one, Janice, had Down's syndrome. Naturally, Janice had to have a lot done for her, and took up a lot of his parents' time. He'd seen how his mother and father couldn't really have lives of their own any more. His mother loved dancing, and his father was a keen angler. I said I understood how tough it must be for them, that anyone who has had children dreads the thought of having to cope with any kind of disability.

Karen was clever, he continued, she picked up things quickly. But naturally she'd resented the extra attention her younger sister had got. She'd go upstairs and shut herself in her room for hours and yell at anyone else who tried to talk to her. I told him that she sounded just like our girls when they were teenagers, but he didn't react. He went on with his story. When Karen was in a good mood, he could have a proper conversation with her. She'd sometimes ask him to explain what he found so fascinating about birds.

I wondered if this was what he'd meant when he'd said that *it wasn't just about the bird.*

There'd been a big family row, he said, when he was in his teens. They had just moved from Aberdeen and were living near Fraserburgh. Ross's father was a joiner. He'd built him a hide at the bottom of their garden, where Ross could go bird-watching after school. One Saturday afternoon, he'd been on his way back from the local reserve when he'd seen smoke coming from behind his house. At first he hadn't thought much about it. It'd been hot for days and there had been heather fires on the hills inland. But when he got home, he saw his dad and mum rushing about in the garden, throwing buckets of water at what was left of the hide. Karen was leaning on the back wall of the house. She didn't seem too clear about what was going on. She had apparently been smoking something.

Soon after that his elder sister had left home and started living with her boyfriend in Dundee. His dad rebuilt the hide, and it was even better than before.

After a pause, he said that he wanted one last look at the waders before the light started to go. As he walked over to the window, I tried to remember what it was about his name that was niggling me. Then it came to me. *Albert Ross*. That was what they had called a solitary albatross that had spent years circling the Arctic Circle when it should have been in the Pacific Ocean. (Perhaps birders do have a sense of humour.) It had struck me at the time as a sad story. A bird thousands of miles from where it should have been, no chance of finding a mate, an avian *Flying Dutchman*. Most rarities are like that, really: lost, distressed, most of them unlikely to survive. But I didn't think my birder would see it this way.

When he came back, he got out his field guide again. As I was trying to see what the distinguishing features of his bird might be, he asked me if I knew that some birders are so expert that they can predict when a particular bird might turn up. He said he wasn't talking about the obvious ones, swallows, swifts, birds like that. No, these birders could tell when there was a good chance of such-and-such a rarity showing up in a particular area. They'd keep an eye on weather conditions, they'd know what had turned up where in previous years. So, say there was high pressure and easterly winds, and they knew there'd be a chance of a particular rarity turning up on the east coast, they'd rush off to try and find it, so they could be the first to see it.

I was wondering how long his story might take to reach its conclusion. I stood up and checked the departures board. No delays to the Edinburgh flight. Good, I thought, it won't be long now.

Ross insisted that he was getting to the point of his story. It had happened a few months after Karen had left home. That autumn all sorts of rare birds had been blown in on the northeast coast. Conditions were perfect: onshore winds and dull weather, which meant that the birds were less likely to move on once they did arrive.

One Sunday afternoon, it had brightened up, and he'd set off to check out his local patch. On the way, he'd had a look at an area of waste ground behind an industrial estate, with a rubbish dump in the corner. Waste ground can be good for birds, he said: it's often better than the reserves that you go miles to visit. When birds are hungry, they'll look for food anywhere, especially if they've just flown over the North Sea. But he couldn't find anything. Nothing unusual, at least. He was about to move on, have a quick look down at the shore and go home.

Then something had caught his eye.

I could see what was coming, and said something to that effect. It was perhaps a bit cruel, but he hardly seemed to hear. He was away, back in Fraserburgh with his special bird. He'd spotted it skulking in a bush over in the corner, he said; he could tell straight away that there was something odd about it. It was behaving like a bird that had just arrived. It wasn't one of the local birds, the regulars, the ones who know where they are. This one didn't belong there. It was lost.

He described how he'd managed to identify it. Rumbold's pipit wasn't in his own field guide, so he'd borrowed a more detailed one from the library, just in case. The bird he was watching was exactly like the Rumbold's in the book. He showed me the book again, pointing out the bird's pale eye-stripe, the tips of the primaries, details like that. I said I could see what he meant.

He knew what he had to do to get his ID of the bird confirmed. He was surprised how calm and methodical he'd been. He'd written it all down carefully, time, place, conditions. Drawn it in his notebook. Then he'd raced home, told his parents, and got his dad to phone a member of the local RSPB group, who had given him the number of one of the Rare Men for the area.

I pretended to be puzzled.

The Rare Men, Ross explained, are the ones who sit on the Rarities Committee, which does just what it says on the tin. You send them reports of rarities, and they have the power to accept or reject the sightings.

The member for his area was called Mr Martin. I said it was a good name for a bird expert, but again Ross didn't notice. He explained that when he rang Mr Martin, he didn't seem convinced by what Ross was telling him. I was tempted to say that I wasn't surprised, that the Rare Men must get lots of reports from people who get carried away. But I kept quiet. Ross said he knew he was right about the bird. He sent for the identification form, filled it in, giving all the details he had, and posted it off. He tried to make it sound as professional as he could, though he did lie about his age, he admitted. He'd said he was nineteen, not fifteen.

He became more agitated as he told me how his claim to have spotted the Rumbold's pipit had been rejected a few weeks later. He put on an English accent: "Sorry, Mr McCormack, but I'm phoning to say that the Rarities Committee is unable to accept your report of the Rumbold's pipit. Thank you for taking the effort, bla bla bla." He said it hadn't been a surprise, but he was still gutted. He reckoned he was as good a birder as the people who got their reports accepted. It was just that he was young, and didn't know anyone on the committee. He thought they'd decided that he'd copied his drawings from a book. He felt as though they'd patted him on the back and said "Nice try, son, but not this time."

I tried to think of something consoling to say. I asked him how his parents had reacted. His mum had been really supportive. He could remember exactly what she'd told him when he'd shown her the letter.

"You have to trust your judgement, Ross," she'd said. "If you're sure, that's all there is to it. When you see rare birds, sometimes you're certain about your identification, sometimes you're not. This time, you were certain. So it was a Rumbold's pipit."

I could hear my plane's engines as it approached. Perfect timing. But then he said that something had happened which proved he had been right. "A twist in the tale of my pipit", was how he put it, though I'm not sure he was trying to be funny. He had got a sort of corroboration in the end, he said. But I would never have guessed where it came from, would I? No, not another birder. About three weeks later, he'd got a letter from his sister Karen.

It was quite a surprise, he admitted. The letter hadn't said much, just that she was OK, getting by on casual jobs. She'd also sent an item torn out of the local paper, a report of a rare bird spotted on the coast near Broughty Ferry. The person who'd reported it wondered if it might be a Rumbold's pipit, and Karen had thought Ross might be interested. He'd been touched by Karen's effort; he supposed it was her way of getting back in contact with him, without losing face. He'd written to thank her and they'd met up in Dundee. Now his mum and dad and older sister were on good terms again.

Over the next few years, he added, Rumbold's pipits had started to show up fairly often on the north-east coast. So that must have been what he'd seen, mustn't it? And he'd been the first to see one, the first in the UK.

I agreed that had probably been the case, and that it was an impressive achievement. And it was good that his encounter with the special bird had allowed him to get back in touch with his sister and mend the broken family fences. Then I remembered what he'd said at the start, that he'd seen the bird again that week on Orkney. He seemed pleased that I hadn't forgotten. Yes, he'd seen another Rumbold's on Sunday. Ten years since his first one. He'd seen it really well, and it had brought it all back again. He thanked me for being such a sympathetic listener. I collected my handbag and camera, stood up and shook his hand. We wished each other a good day.

* * *

As I queued at security, I heard a cheer coming from the corner of the waiting room, where passengers were watching a game of cricket on the television. Then the sound of people singing *Jerusalem*. But before I could work out what that was about, the queue moved forward. As I went through the doors, I saw, out of the corner of my eye, Ross approaching one of the other passengers, presumably also waiting for the Aberdeen flight. I heard him commenting on the weather, and looking at his telescope.

Be careful, I thought. Don't get him started.

Glen Gair

The clock suspended from the station roof showed 17.14 as the announcer welcomed passengers to Glasgow Central and apologised for the fifteen-minute delay to the train from London Euston. Slowly, the crush on the platform thinned. Outside the ticket barriers, five passengers, surrounded by their luggage – four backpacks and one suitcase – greeted each other with more resignation than surprise.

"Well, Mike," said a slim, short-haired man, in a loud voice and an accent so estuarine that it turned a few heads. "What a surprise. Cunning bastards, putting us all in different carriages. And the train was packed. Has anyone the faintest idea of what we're supposed to do now?"

The other man, taller and bearded, shook his head and turned towards a smartly dressed woman, who shivered and said she had no idea either.

In turn she looked across to the other woman in the party, whose thickly padded jacket suggested that she at least had experienced the North British autumn before.

"What about you, Nicky?"

"No," came the answer. "Nobody told me anything. That just leaves you, Suresh."

The fifth member of the group was standing to one side, vigorously rubbing his calves as if the long journey was threatening him with cramp. He seemed about to speak, but paused.

"Ah, I've just got a text."

Seconds later, he was able to inform them that his instructions were to go to the travel centre and ask for the package that Markhams had arranged for them to pick up.

"Very cloak and dagger, you might say," he smiled. "Peter, Mike, let's go."

As the men joined the queue, the two women passed the time looking through the books and brochures displayed on the tables.

After a moment, the smarter of the two picked up a large volume with a picture of a snow-covered triangular peak on its cover.

"Christ," she said, handing it over. "All these books, all about Scotland. I'd never have thought…"

"Oh, there's some fantastic places. And some of the walking guides are great."

"Where is it that you and Mike go to climb all those Moiras?"

"Munros, Sandra. They're Munros."

"Whatever. They'd better not have sent us here to do anything like that. Oh, here they are. What joys have you got for us, Pete?"

"Oh, you're going to love this," their colleague answered, as he handed out four tickets from the envelope in his hand.

"We get the Fort William train from a different station, and we need to be quick. It leaves in half an hour. There's a shuttle bus at the front of the station. We're off to Glen Gair."

"Never heard of it. Is that a distillery or something?"

"You wish, Sandra. You wish."

Minutes later, as they climbed into the bus, a youth wearing jeans and a green and white hooped T-shirt emerged from nowhere and helped them with their luggage. He bowed low and looked up at them from under a grubby hood.

"Welcome to Scotland, my English friends. Mind how you go now."

"Pete, don't say anything," Sandra hissed, dropping her cigarette end in a puddle. "And for Christ's sake don't tell anyone we're bankers."

At Queen Street, they offered to pay the driver of the shuttle, but he waved them on, with a comment that none of them understood.

* * *

Once they had established that there were neither first-class coaches nor a bar on the Fort William train, they spent their time looking out of the window and sending bitter text messages to family members and bank colleagues. By the time the suburbs had been left behind, clouds had rolled in from the left and soon only the vague outlines of the hills could be seen.

After a while, Sandra began to fidget. She took a fashion magazine out of her suitcase, flicked through it and passed it across the table.

"Here you are, Nicky, can you see yourself in any of this stuff? I'd never get into it. Wouldn't be much use to us where we're going, I reckon."

Nicky shook her head and placed a well-thumbed book on the table in front of her.

"Listen, everyone. I brought this old guide to the Highlands with me when I set off. Thought it might come in useful. This is what it says about Glen Gair. 'An unmanned halt on the West Highland Line. A small, rather run-down hotel provides the only accommodation, but don't expect a Jacuzzi or satellite TV. Come prepared.' That's it."

"Come prepared for what, Nicky?"

"It doesn't say, Pete. We'll find out when we get there."

Sandra leaned forward to look at the book.

"I just hope we're not going to end up in some kind of outward-bound place. I'm not keen on the thought of spending the weekend with a bunch of thieving Scousers."

She was interrupted by the arrival of the ticket inspector, who explained that they were in the wrong part of the train. They decamped to the rear carriage.

After they had settled again, Sandra continued her complaint.

"A friend at Parkers West said they went on something similar to this last year. They all came back from the Lake District, frozen and hung-over. Bonded, of course. Bloody well bonded. Though he reckoned these things are very nineties."

She leaned over the aisle and whispered to the three men.

"Did any of you make sense of what that ticket collector was saying? I think it was something about the couple who run the hotel at Glen Gair, but his accent was so strong it could have been the price of haggis he was on about for all I knew. Mike, do you think our knowledge of the international currency markets will help us if the natives turn nasty?"

No answer came; no one seemed keen to continue the conversation.

The time passed slowly. The clouds lifted from time to time. At one point, the train slowly curved round the end of a flat glen, and then they saw steep slopes rising to their right, broken by gullies and patches of bracken.

"Beinn Dorain," announced Mike. "Fantastic hill. Still a while to go. Ours is a request stop. Presumably that's what the ticket inspector was talking about."

"So, just like London buses."

"Yes, Sandra. Just like London buses."

* * *

They were the only passengers who got out at the halt. They watched the train moving away, taking most of the light with it. Pete confirmed what they had suspected: there was no mobile signal. Over the footbridge, they could just make out a track leading to what they assumed was the hotel. Sandra began to shiver again. Her colleague rummaged in her backpack and handed her a jumper.

"There you are. Not this year's colours, perhaps, but it'll keep you warm."

"Thanks, Nicky, you're a star. Good job someone's been in this part of the world before. I know this is the bloody North, but I didn't think it could be this cold in September. What is the time anyway? It's not even nine. Feels like midnight. Let's go and see what they can do for us at the Ritz."

Inside, the light and noise drew them to the bar to the left of the hotel entrance. As they announced themselves, a tired-looking middle-aged woman behind the bar glanced up and smiled. She gave the impression that she was used to seeing people getting off that train and not knowing what they were supposed to do. She handed over three torches and the keys to a people-carrier, parked at the back, and a sheet of directions to a croft located five miles down a track behind the station. She wished them good luck.

They piled the luggage into the people-carrier. Pete volunteered to drive.

The track was wet and rutted, and the driver cursed as he struggled to keep the clumsy vehicle out of the ditches.

"What did she say? Turn right after a couple of miles, at the sheep fank, whatever that is. Ah well, no doubt there'll be canapés and cava waiting for us when we do get there."

After a while they saw a pile of stones on the right and decided that it must be a fank. They turned onto an even rougher track. When the headlights picked out the shape of the croft, the vehicle filled with nervous laughter and foul language.

They climbed out, switched on the torches and approached the croft. It was stone-built, single-storeyed. The path took them to a small porch at right angles to the building itself. The wooden door to the porch was open, but the door to the croft inside was locked. They went back outside. Hesitantly, keeping to the pools of light shed by the torches, and listening to the sounds of a generator coming from somewhere in the trees, they skirted the building, trying to find a way to get in. On the back wall they found a window, with some glass missing. They could see a rudimentary bathroom behind the window: if they could remove the whole of the glass, someone – Pete, wasn't he the slimmest? – could possibly squeeze through.

None of them was keen on a draughty bathroom, and Pete pointed out that breaking into the bathroom wouldn't mean they could be sure of getting into the rest of the building. But no one could come up with a better idea. They were searching for a rock to throw through the glass when Sandra produced a nail file and suggested that if they loosened the glass round the edges, with a bit of luck they might be able to put the pieces back later.

Nicky applauded.

"Didn't know you'd been in the Girl Guides, Sandra. OK, pass it over and I'll give it a try."

A few minutes later, Pete was opening the door from the inside. They entered and shone their torches on the interior. Once they had located the light switch, a dim bulb shone a dusty glow on their surroundings. In the middle of the room were a few threadbare armchairs and a table with more chairs around it. There was a fireplace on the opposite wall. To one side of it were piled five sleeping bags, still in their plastic packaging.

They looked around for any signs of life or comfort. On a shelf beside the fireplace was a pile of old newspapers and bits of wood. In the kitchen to the left of the entrance porch, they found mugs, plates, pans, an old camping gas stove and a cardboard box containing what they assumed were packs of food.

"Boys, get the fire going. Here's my lighter. We'll see what we can do with the food."

"Sexist, Sandra. Very sexist. But as you say."

It was some time before Mike could get the damp paper to light. After several minutes, as the fire at last began to burn, the women, now smothered in many layers of clothing, came in with tea, biscuits and…

"Please, Sandra, tell me what that is."

"It's porridge, Suresh. You'll love it. We all will. It's what there is."

Soon all five were sitting at the table, eating bowls of sticky gruel with broken oatmeal biscuits. After they had finished eating, there was an uncomfortable silence, finally broken by Suresh's voice.

"Thank you, Nicky, for introducing me to porridge. So, my friends, we have shelter, warmth and food for tonight. However, it seems to me that if Markhams cannot efficiently organise their bonding weekends – assuming that this is what we have been invited to take part in – then we should refuse them any further cooperation. Tomorrow, I propose we simply leave and catch the return train. This may even be what, in their perverse way, they are expecting of us. Now let us each find our own corner, make ourselves as comfortable as we can, and get some sleep."

* * *

"Good morning, and welcome to Glen Gair. I'm Frank Martin. Pleased to meet you all."

The speaker got up and pulled back the rough curtains. Sunlight flooded the room. Five bleary faces emerged from the sleeping bags. They peered at the newcomer sitting in front of the window, but his features, backlit by the low sun, were hard to distinguish.

They became aware of the smell of coffee and toast.

"On the whole, I'm quite impressed. Forced entry, not bad. But you could have tried to reseal the bathroom window. Do you know that a paste made of sheep droppings is as good as putty? Fire, passable. Though you're lucky one of you is a smoker. And you might have made more of an effort to keep the fire in overnight. Food and drink... well, you've survived. But oatcakes should be mixed with water, not powdered milk. And porridge tastes better with salt."

A mumbled response came from the other side of the room, but the speaker held up his hand and continued:

"Right. Today is Saturday, and it's 7.50 am. We're here till Monday morning. I'm away to collect some odds and ends from the hotel. I'll take the people-carrier and be back by half past nine or so. I've got the keys. Two things you have to do. One, get to know the place. Two, be ready to give a brief account of who you are, where you come from, what you do. Here are the boots and warm clothing you'll need."

Pointing to a large holdall in the middle of the room, he opened the door and left.

"Wanker!"

"Pete!"

"Sorry, Nicky, sorry. But who the hell does he think he is?"

No one answered. They climbed out of their sleeping bags, crossed over to the table and started to eat. There were also oranges, apples and more oatcakes. Hunger satisfied, they took it in turns to choose clothing from the holdall and then get washed and changed in the bathroom; if they were going to be here for the weekend, they decided, they might as well get as comfortable as possible. At first, they took care selecting their jumpers, trousers and fleeces, until someone pointed out that they were all going to look like prats, so there was no point in being precious about it.

There was awkward laughter as they tried on the woolly hats, and the five pairs of boots lined up on the floor, three large pairs and two size six. Choosing the right number of extra pairs of socks from the basket alongside the holdall meant that in the end they were all comfortable with what they had on their feet.

When, half an hour later, they were all together again in

front of the fireplace, they even congratulated each other on looking as though they spent all their weekends in the hills.

The warmer mood was broken by Pete's sullen voice.

"You realise we're stuck here now? That guy – what was his name? Yeah, Frank – must have walked here, but now he's got the keys to the vehicle. And what did he mean, 'get to know the place'? Doesn't look to me that there's much to get to know."

"You're right, Peter. It all looks pretty empty to me, but then I've never been to Scotland. Mumbai it isn't. But we know why we are here, don't we?"

"Of course we do." Pete's voice had even more of an edge. "It's the usual crappy team-building stuff, isn't it? To make us 'reflective practitioners', all that bullshit. So we'll be able to make even more money for Markhams. But I don't see why we should be treated like kids. We'll tell our friend here that we'll cooperate because we have to, but he'll have to change his tone."

"Oh, did you find my tone offensive? I'm sorry."

They spun round and saw Frank close the door behind him and stand in front of the window. The sun was now less dazzling, and they could see that the man who was addressing them was no more than average height, that he was wearing a nondescript outdoor jacket, worn trousers and boots. A full head of hair, heavy eyebrows.

But before they could ask him to modify his manner, he was speaking again.

"I know, I'm back earlier than I said. For once Susie had everything ready for me to collect; all I had to do was turn around and come back. Why don't we just start? I've put the kettle on, so if you'd like to sit down, we can make acquaintance. Let's sit round the table. I do apologise about these badges

– please pass them round – but I know next to nothing about you, just the fact that you all work in the same bank. By the way, don't forget the surgeon's knot."

He pointed to Suresh's boots.

"If you bring your boots here, I'll show you."

Suresh muttered that he thought he'd learned how to tie laces some time ago, but if Frank heard, he didn't let it show.

"There, you lace the boots up tight. When you get to the instep, cross the laces under and over each other, then finish off up your ankle. That way you might save your calf muscles. Now, who's going to...?"

"Pete Ancram, twenty-nine. Born in Romford, and don't laugh. Accountancy degree. Joined Markhams to get rich. Claim to fame: met that tosser Ray Mears in a pub once, spilt a pint of Guinness all down the front of his jacket. Accidentally, of course."

"Thank you, Pete. Now, who would like to...?"

"If I must. Mike Waterson. Born in Newcastle. Left school at sixteen, a couple of years stacking shelves, drifted to London, found I was good at selling things to people, especially if it promised to make them rich. Quite liked the idea of getting rich myself. Now I head up this little team."

"Excellent. Very good so far. And..."

"Sandra. Just Sandra, to you. Moved into trading last year. Before that, HR, which was the pits. I'm the North London Underwater Origami champion. That's all you're getting from me. Yes, more coffee, please."

"Nicola Price. I'm from just outside Ipswich. I suppose I'm not the normal Markhams type. I did a degree in comparative literature at UEA, and was planning to do an MLitt, but my father persuaded me to earn some money before starting. He got me a temporary post with the bank after I graduated, and I've been there two years now. I'm not sure what my long-term plans are. I've done a lot of hill-walking in Scotland over the years, sometimes with Mike, sometimes on my own. I don't know this area."

"Thank you, Nicola. And finally."

Before he spoke, Suresh stood up and looked Frank in the eye. He said his name was Suresh Mahendru, that he had been born in Mumbai and had come over to London with his family when he was eight years old. He had a first-class honours degree in maths from Cambridge. He'd joined Markhams as a trainee when they were establishing their IT section. He added that he was getting married later in the year, and that he played cricket for Blackheath.

"Just now, I'd rather be at the Oval, watching Shane Warne destroying the hopes of the Imperialists once again. And what about you, Frank?"

Frank ignored the enquiry. Instead, he took out a pile of maps from the backpack he'd brought with him and put them on the table.

He asked if any of the party knew how to read a map and compass. When Mike and Nicky told him that they could, he said that simplified matters.

"Two little groups, two little outings. I'll give you the maps and compasses in a minute."

First, he insisted, there were basic safety procedures to go through. Outside, warm clothing and waterproofs were to be worn, or at least carried. The hills may look benign at the moment, he explained, but the weather can change in a few minutes.

"Exposure can kill quickly."

"Too bloody true."

He ignored Sandra's comment and checked that no one had a GPS with them ("Just toys, and dangerous if you don't know how to use them"), and confirmed what they already knew, that mobile phone reception was non-existent where they were. He told them to watch out for adders.

As the two navigators were given their maps, Frank pointed out two summits marked on them. Each one was four or five miles from the croft. Their task was simply to get to the summit and pick up the small plastic bags they would find there, containing badges with GG on them.

"*GG* for Glen Gair. Now, Nicky, can you take Suresh? Second group: Mike, Peter and Sandra. Here are your day packs, and there are lunch boxes on the table there. Help yourselves. One map for each group. Any questions? Good, I'll see you about six."

The map-readers consulted their Ordnance Survey sheets and plotted their routes. They agreed that they couldn't see any serious problems, provided the weather didn't play any tricks, and calculated that they should be back by late afternoon.

* * *

Nicky and Suresh set off down a track behind the croft. It ran alongside a burn as far as a small loch, fringed with reeds. A family of mallards took off noisily as they crossed a plank bridge over the stream and set off up the hill. Nicky pointed out the summit they were aiming for, to the right of a low col at the head of the corrie. She looked again at the map and suggested that to avoid the corrie, which would probably be very wet, they should make for the ridge to the left of the col, and then walk over the col to the summit. As they started to climb, they noticed a stag standing on the ridge, silhouetted against the light-grey cloud.

"Impressive beast," commented Suresh. "Has he seen us?"

"Oh, he knows we're here all right. Even though we're a good mile away. Probably caught our scent. They can be pretty fierce at this time of year. We'll give him a wide berth."

She explained that there were too many deer, that they ate the young trees before they had a chance to grow.

"Bring in predators then."

Nicky laughed. That had already been proposed, she said, and it sounded fine in theory. But she didn't like the thought of being alone in the hills, perhaps nursing an injury and waiting for help, and hearing a howling sound in the distance.

"Though, of course, wolves would never attack a human being. So they say."

The conversation stopped as they climbed steeply to the crest of the ridge. Before setting off again over the col, they sat down for a few moments' rest. Nicky checked the map and pointed again to the cairn in the distance.

"There's where we're heading. Look, the map has the Gaelic name for the hill. In English, it just means Middle Hill. You know, I've always been disappointed when I've found out what the Gaelic names mean once they've been translated. Place names in another language always sound so much more exciting, don't they? But in the Highlands they often come out as The Grey Peak of the Bogs, Brown Hill. Something dull like that."

Suresh opened his lunch box, took out a packet of nuts and raisins, and said you had to be careful with people's languages. On one occasion when he'd gone back to Mumbai to visit his family, he'd been staying with his cousins and had told them how much he liked their Hindu shrines, how colourful they were. He'd especially liked the lettering that went with the pictures. He'd said he was glad he could hardly make out what it meant any more; he'd been away in England so long that everything in India was charming and exotic. One of the cousins had got quite shirty and told him not to be condescending.

Nicky thought for a moment.

"So someone born in India gets into trouble for behaving a bit like an English colonialist. Interesting."

Suresh looked at her and smiled.

The rest of the walk was easy enough, although the wind was stronger on the ridge. By the time they reached the top, it was starting to feel cold, and they could see shower clouds scudding over the hills to the north. The summit was marked by a fair-sized cairn. They looked for the plastic bags but couldn't find any. Suresh asked Nicky if she was sure they were at the right place. They checked the map: there were no other summits, and the map showed a cairn at that point. They searched again and removed some of the stones, but there was nothing. They ate their sandwiches, had a banana each, and drank the water they had been carrying. They decided there was no point in staying any longer.

"Perhaps our friend Frank has done it deliberately," said Suresh. "He wants to show us that it's the effort which counts and not the outcome, the journey not the arrival. You might call it an anti-incentive."

Nicky laughed.

"I can imagine what Pete's going to say about that."

As they set off down the hill, she asked Suresh what he'd made of Frank. She said she'd known that, at some point, there would have to be someone there to organise them, and she had formed a mental picture of what he'd be like. He'd be younger, for one thing. And a bit friendlier.

"Yes, you're right," her companion agreed. "He must be in his fifties. North of England accent, I'd say. It's clear that none of us has taken to him, but that appears to be part of his plan. He is in control, that's the point. I am sure we would all like to have our revenge on him. But we need him, and he knows this."

When they arrived back at the croft, it was clear that they were the first to return. Nicky checked her watch and found that it was just after three. Seven camp beds had appeared while they were away on the hill; they decided to take advantage of them while they could.

* * *

Their sleep was interrupted by the sound of a chair being kicked over.

"Up you get, you two. Sandra's putting the kettle on."

"Hello, Peter. Thank you. Did you have a good walk too?"

"Oh yes, loved every minute of it, man. Mike can tell you all about it. I just want to get these bloody boots off. Turned my ankle over on the way down."

Mike explained that their route had taken them along the track they'd come down the previous evening. Then they'd turned right, up a path leading through a plantation onto the open hillside. The path had soon petered out. It was one of those teasing Highland paths, he said, the ones which look as though they might lead you all the way, but then come and go and eventually fizzle out. They'd had to keep on trudging up the wet slopes. It had started to drizzle as they'd got onto the higher ground. Pete had had to stop to keep wiping his glasses, which had made him even grumpier than usual.

It was Sandra who'd seen the deer fence first. Eight feet high it was, stretching across the hillside. Pete had complained about Mike's navigation, but Mike had pointed out that it wasn't marked on the map. They had to get to the other side, and there wasn't a stile in sight. Eventually, they'd found a pile of broken bits of wood at the bottom of the fence and propped them up against it to see if they could get over it that way.

Nicky said she'd noticed that Mike was wearing an improvised bandage on his right hand.

"What's that, Mike? You didn't..."

"Yes, I bloody did. I didn't think it would be electrified at this time of year, did I? Well, it was. I felt like I'd been hit by a hammer. As I was getting my breath back, Sandra suggested we might be able to go under it, 'like in *The Great Escape*'. It seemed a daft idea to me, but it worked. The ground was soft, we found some stones to dig with, and were on the other side in a few minutes. We realised we needed to come back the same way, so we made the bits of wood into a pointer. When we got to the shoulder of the hill, the visibility wasn't great. I took a compass bearing just to be on the safe side. The route took us across peat hags, and we had to make detours to avoid the wettest bits. We weren't in the best of moods when we got to the top. We thought we'd collect our little badges like good boys and girls and be back in a couple of hours. Of course, we didn't find any. By this time, I don't think we cared, so we just turned round. How did two you get on?"

Nicky and Suresh outlined their less eventful climb. But no, there had been no little packages on their summit either.

Sandra passed round the biscuits, helping herself to more

coffee. She tried to untangle her hair in her reflection in the window but gave up.

"I tell you, it was even worse coming back. We thought we could cut the corner. But we ended up in all that long ferny stuff – yeah, bracken – and slopes of slippery rock, with millions of little puddles of brown water. There was nothing firm to put your feet on. I slipped and my ciggies got wet. I asked Mike what was the name of the hill we'd just climbed. He looked at the map and said something in a foreign language. Hill of the Flying Snot, I said, that's what it means. Then we had to cross a bog the size of fucking Ireland. And when we came to this stream, we had to throw rocks into it to make stepping stones, but they were slippery and that's where Pete fell in and sprained his ankle."

Pete tried to raise his swollen foot and groaned theatrically.

Sandra finished her account by saying that she'd kept myself going by thinking of the painful things she'd like to do to their friend Frank.

"But hey, we did see a couple of frogs and some deer, with those great bit horny things. This coffee's good."

"I hope you enjoy this as well."

None of them had noticed the activity in the kitchen. But as they turned to face him, Frank smiled and placed three bowls of soup on the table.

Pete raised both hands in mock apprehension.

"Stop doing this, will you? Creeping up on us."

Frank smiled again, returned to the kitchen and came back with two more bowls and a plate of roughly cut bread.

"Help yourselves to the first course. There's beer and glasses in that box under the table. I'll bring in the shepherd's pie in a few minutes."

They watched him go back into the kitchen, then pulled their chairs up to the table. Nicky helped Pete to sit sideways, his ankle resting on a spare seat. Mike began to open the bottles.

"I tell you, this man's spooky," he said, passing the beer round. "He's there when he's not there. But that's not a reason to refuse his beer."

The soup disappeared quickly. Frank brought the shepherd's pie in from the kitchen, together with a bowl of fruit and more bottles.

"Eat up. I've had mine. We'll de-brief when you've finished, then plan what we're going to do tomorrow."

The pie did not last long either, and most of the bottles were empty by the time Frank returned to take up his customary position in front of the window. Pete put his glass down and leaned over the table.

"Good trick, that, Frank."

Frank didn't reply.

"I said, good trick, that, Frank. The plastic bags, with no badges in them. Are you hearing me, Frank?"

"Glad you liked it," he said. "You all made it to the summits, then. Well done. The fact that you haven't got any packages doesn't matter. At least, as long as I believe that you made it. And I do. Please put the maps in a pile on the mantelpiece. What about the walks?"

The negative comments came from Mike's group: there were no proper paths, the footbridge across the stream had collapsed, the deer fence wasn't marked on the map. Frank told them that there weren't many easy walks in this part of the world, and that he was quite impressed with what they had achieved. Minor injuries were something to be dealt with appropriately, he added, nodding at Pete's raised leg.

"You're doing the right thing, though. RICE..."

"Yes, RICE. We're not stupid, you know," Sandra interrupted. "We've all done our first aid. It might seem strange to you, but accidents can happen in a London office."

Frank ignored her and looked across to Mike and his bandaged hand.

Mike shook his head, making it clear he was unwilling to explain.

Frank said he could see that they had had a full day, so he would delay tomorrow's briefing till the morning. He pointed to the bowl of fruit and said they should help themselves.

"The oranges are excellent. Think about them when you eat them. We might do something with the oranges tomorrow. I'll be back with breakfast at eight."

As he was going, Pete called out.

"Don't forget the salt, Frank. Porridge tastes better with salt."

Mike rose from his seat, intent on dragging Frank back into the room, but Suresh quickly blocked the door.

"We must not rush things, Michael. If we want to get our own back on this man, we need to do it properly. We are not in a strong position. We are five to his one, but we are unfamiliar with the area and the terrain. We have no transport of our own, and there doesn't seem to be a spare set of keys to the people-carrier. We are dependent on Frank for food. Has anyone got a good idea?"

No suggestions were forthcoming.

"It is dark now," Suresh concluded. "And we are tired. Let us sleep on it. I shall add some more wood to the fire. Who would like an orange?"

* * *

"Good morning."

Frank watched as five heads emerged once more from the sleeping bags.

"Good morning. The coffee's here. And the porridge is cooling in the kitchen. There is salt in it. It's just gone eight, and a lovely morning. You'll see the Highlands at their best today. I have no food for you for this evening. It's up to you to find your own."

Before any of the party could move, he had gone. They heard the wheels of the people-carrier crunching the gravel at the end of the track.

For a few minutes no one stirred. Then Suresh climbed out of his sleeping bag and fetched the bowls of porridge.

"We've been too slow again, my friends. Did anyone dream a master plan?"

As they pulled their chairs to the table, they noticed a note propped up against the milk jug. It informed them that there were biscuits and some chocolate in the kitchen, and spelt out in capital letters that the Glen Gair Hotel did not serve food, and that there were no trains on Sundays. "Good luck," it concluded. "I'll be back at 5 pm."

Pete crumpled the note and threw it in the hearth.

"He's got us again. We'll have to look for something to eat. We've not much choice. And while we're at it, we can think up how we're going to get our own back on the bastard."

After a few minutes' thought, Mike stood up and banged the table with his fist.

"Sheep," he said. "We all saw some yesterday, didn't we? Sheep or mutton, anybody know the difference? Anyhow, I don't see why we can't help ourselves."

"You're not serious?"

"Sure am, Nicky. We look for an injured one, a weak one. We must still have some hunting genes in us. I'll see if I've still got my ancestral ability to stalk, kill and dismember prey."

Pete clapped his hands and cheered.

"Great idea. Find an animal, tire it out until it just gives in and dies. You remember when we had to get rid of that dumb old bugger in charge of office equipment? Just like that. If the men hunt, can the women gather? I know it sounds sexist, but has anyone got a better idea?"

Suresh pointed out that Pete was not in a fit state to hunt. Pete decided that he'd stay in the croft, do some strategic thinking and sharpen some knives. He was sure he could hobble about and have a look around the croft; perhaps there'd be some fruit bushes somewhere. And hadn't they seen a field with turnips in it on their way back the day before? Nicky said she thought she'd spotted a boathouse near the bridge the previous day, when she and Suresh were setting off on their walk. Sandra agreed to go with her and see if there was a boat which they could use to catch something in the loch.

* * *

The two women set off down the track to the loch. Behind the boathouse, they found a rowing boat, attached by a long rope to a rock by the side of the track. The boathouse was unlocked, the old wooden door stiff and warped with damp. Inside, they found oars and rudimentary fishing rods. They went back outside and lifted some of the stones that lined the track, looking for worms for bait. They pushed the boat down the little jetty beside the boathouse, and Nicky rowed out into the loch. The water was still, glinting in the sun; they took off their fleeces and allowed the boat to drift gently away from the bank. They dangled the rods over the edge, but nothing took the bait. Nicky explained how she used to go fishing with her brother on the Stour, though she had to admit that they had never caught much. She leant back on the oars, eyes closed in the warm sun.

"Suppose by some miracle we do catch a fish, Sandra, what would we have proved? We all know this kind of thing's a complete waste of time, don't we?"

"Dead right. And one thing's dawned on me. If this was a real wilderness, we'd be completely stuffed."

They began to doze and woke as the boat nudged the grasses at the far edge of the loch. They rowed back, tried fishing from the jetty, but soon gave up.

As they trudged back towards the croft, they passed the remains of a township, which they hadn't seen earlier. Low walls covered by moss and ivy showed through the grasses, with the remains of a couple of gables. Nicky pointed out the patches of nettles, always a sign that the land had once been occupied. She explained that glens like the one they were in would once have been full of small settlements. Not just farmers, but brewers, cobblers, tailors. The croft they were staying in had obviously been a family home. She told her that late last summer she had been walking back to the car after a day in the hills with Mike, when they'd passed a croft where the family had clearly been living until quite recently. The garden wasn't overgrown yet and the paint on the doors and window frames hadn't faded. There had been a child's tractor abandoned in the front garden, and a climbing frame that was leaning over.

"Funny how some images stick in your mind, isn't it?" she said. "That one always makes me feel uneasy. Guilty, almost."

"I know, it's a beautiful country. But it does seem so empty. I couldn't live here, could you?"

"Oh no. Mind you, on a day like this, it does have its appeal. But you're right. None of us could live here. We can't even catch a fish."

Back at the croft, Pete was sitting on a stone bench, enjoying the sun. In front of him was a large saucepan with a lid on.

"Just look at what I've got," he said with a grin. "Enough to feed us all."

The two women walked over and lifted the lid. At the bottom of the pan there was a handful of rotten gooseberries, with grubs climbing all over them.

"Nice work, Pete. And the turnips?"

"Ah, what I thought were turnips, Sandra, were in fact stones. No wonder no one lives here. What about you two? You don't look as though you've caught a lot."

Before they could answer, Mike and Suresh arrived, likewise empty-handed.

It had been quite entertaining to start with, Mike said, trying to round the sheep up. But they were always too quick, running off up the hillside, jumping over the walls if necessary. He'd pretended he had a dog, whistled and shouted 'Shep, come by, Shep', but the more they chased the sheep, the faster they got.

It was Pete who suggested making a sheep trap. He asked Suresh if he'd ever had to catch an elephant in India, but Suresh said he objected to racial stereotyping, and anyway there were only leopards in Mumbai.

They decided to dig a ditch near the corner of the smallest field, between the croft and the stream, cover it with bracken and try to get some of the sheep to funnel into the corner. They found spades and shovels in the porch. The two able-bodied men picked out a ragged group of eight or nine sheep, climbed the hill to be above them, and drove them down towards the croft.

Eventually five or six of them were forced into the small field and were herded towards the trap in the corner. At the last moment, they swung frantically to the right, outflanked the men and disappeared.

They decided that it was too hot for hunting. Better to sit in the sun at the side of the croft.

It was Sandra who woke first and eased herself out of her chair.

"What's that smell?"

They turned to see Frank walking towards them, a bottle of wine in his hand.

"Who's hungry? Lamb casserole. Susie's special."

* * *

Inside, the table was laid, and there were two more bottles of red wine opened. As they sat down to eat, Frank served the casserole and proposed a toast: "To the Markhams Five." He congratulated them on their collegiate attempts to feed themselves but admitted that there wasn't much food to be found in the area around the croft: the old vegetable patch was a mess and there was very little fish in the loch. But had they thought of using the gun, for the rabbits? There was one in the corner of the porch.

"You can make a good soup with nettles," he went on. "And there's watercress further upstream. But there's not much fruit around at this time of year."

As they tackled the casserole, he said that he owed it to them to explain how he'd come to be at Glen Gair, and how they'd come to be there too.

He began by saying that he had always been an outdoors person. He was well known in bird-watching circles, and for a long time had managed to make a living from conducting bird surveys for organisations like the RSPB and checking reports of rare birds. Great work if you're young and fit. But as he'd got older, he'd needed to find something else. And he had to build up his pension fund. It was another birder who had suggested running bonding weekends, or Professional Development Events, as he'd been told to describe them. He'd moved from Yorkshire to Scotland, which seemed to offer the best locations. Wilder, more remote. Now he was making reasonable money. So far, most of his clients had come from local government, retail, industry, NHS management, that sort of thing. This was the first time he'd put something on for a group of bankers; he'd tried to make it a bit special.

"You're really my guinea pigs," he added with a smile. "I hope you don't mind."

Sandra put her plate down on the table.

"OK, but just don't come out with any of the usual anti-banker crap, Frank. Yeah, Markhams make plenty, and we earn plenty. But you say you've got a pension. Where do you think your pension fund's invested? We're doing all this shitty stuff so that you can retire and live comfortably. Remember that."

Frank showed no sign of rising to the bait.

Soon the casserole was finished, the bottles of wine empty. Nicky and Suresh were collecting the dirty plates and glasses when Frank produced a bag of oranges.

Pete pretended to be drunk.

"Bloody hell, Frank, you can't expect us to eat oranges, not after all that red wine."

Frank ignored him. He began to throw the oranges, giving easy catches.

"Think about it, please. Oranges, they look the same, but they're really all different. People, employees, customers – you might think they..."

He looked at Suresh.

"The cricketer. Ought to make it a bit harder for you. Slip catch."

He threw an orange hard and low, to Suresh's left. Suresh leaned forward, caught it, held for a split second, and hurled it back, viciously. It just missed Frank's head and smashed into the door behind him.

Mike was on his feet in a second.

"I've had enough of this."

He leapt behind Frank's chair and hooked his arms under Frank's, holding him there, his own hands grasping the back of the chair. Suresh took two quick strides across the room, grabbed Frank's feet before he could react and held them tight against the chair legs.

"You should have noticed I was left-handed, Frank. Come on, the rest of you. We can't hold him for long."

Sandra ran into the porch and came back with a dirty washing line.

"Never thought we'd get chance to use this."

They tied Frank's ankles together, then pinned his hands behind his back and tied them too.

Frank didn't seem inclined to put up much of a fight. He laughed and said that they had made their point, that the clients he dealt with often felt angry. Mike gagged him with a tea towel which he picked up from the table.

Pete insisted that Frank should be taken into the kitchen while they decided what to do with him. Mike and Suresh lifted him, still on his chair, and took him into the kitchen. Mike searched his pockets and found the keys to the people-carrier. They returned to the rest of the party.

Pete got awkwardly to his feet.

"Before we untie this clown, there are some things I want to say. We've been made to look complete bloody fools these last two days. We were dropped off at a place none of us had ever been to and forced to break into a freezing, uncomfortable house. Then we were sent on a series of fool's errands. And we've just played along. We haven't protested, even though we could all see how stupid it all was. We've been mugs. We've been like the sheep we've seen wandering round the croft. Heads down, with droppings hanging from their arses. Looking for a bit of juicy grass. And what's the point? There isn't one. We're all 'reflective practitioners' already, or we wouldn't be paid what we're getting. I don't see why we should take it lying down."

Nicky said he'd made his point, and that they should untie Frank. She went into the kitchen for a knife to cut the rope, but Sandra got there before her and stopped her opening the drawer.

"It's not his fault, really. He's just doing his job," Nicky insisted.

"No. I'm not having that. It was his choice to do this."

Nicky proposed that they ought to make Frank comfortable but keep him under their control. Then they could release him the next morning, once they were ready to leave for the station. Pete wanted to leave with Frank still tied up.

"If he's so resourceful, he'll find a way of getting free."

Suresh said he had a better idea. Lowering his voice, he said that the thing he had enjoyed about the weekend – the only thing – was the navigation, the map-reading. All the rest was nonsense. But the map-reading had appealed to him. It was a form of problem-solving. He liked the idea of matching what you saw with your eyes to what was on a piece of paper in front of you. Pete said get on with it, they hadn't got all night. Suresh said they could turn the tables on Frank by giving him a navigational problem. Take him somewhere, leave him there to find his way back to the croft. But – and he smiled slyly as he said it – it would be more taxing if he didn't have a map.

"So we blindfold him, drive him somewhere, release him, and leave him to it."

Pete rubbed his hands.

"Now, Suresh?"

"Why not? It shouldn't be cold tonight. We had to sort ourselves out on Friday night, now it's time for Frank to make a shelter, keep warm, get some food. Then he can find his way back here when it's light. It's only one night."

Mike wondered if Frank might complain to their line managers about his treatment, but they agreed that this was unlikely; he wouldn't want to admit that a group of London bankers had got the better of him. Nicky was concerned that he might not have enough to eat, but Pete pointed out that no one had given a toss about what they might eat when they got off the train.

Suresh asked if anyone had any other ideas. No one came up with anything.

"We're agreed, then?'

Nicky and Mike took one of the maps from the pile and

started to work out a route. They found what looked like a suitable track. It turned left before the loch, went over the ridge and finished at a shallow dip in the next glen. There appeared to be a small quarry in the dip. They could leave Frank there and drive back to the croft. The quarry was about twelve miles away. That was good: they didn't want Frank to be able to work out where he was and get back to the croft before they left the next morning.

They lifted Frank into one of the back seats of the people-carrier and strapped him in, still blindfolded. Pete's ankle was still swollen, so Mike drove. As the track zigzagged up the hillside, the vehicle lurched from side to side, and they had to keep propping Frank up.

The quarry was a shallow hollow dug out at the side of the track, a source of stones and sand. They lifted Frank out and put him on the ground. Pete slackened the blindfold and the ropes on Frank's hands and made sure that he was lying near some sharp stones.

"He'll be all right," he said. "He'll soon get free. Time to go."

Nicky asked if they were sure they were doing the right thing.

"What's the worse than can happen to him?" Pete answered as they turned back to the people-carrier. "He might have a cold night, get hungry. Tough. It's no worse than what we might have had."

"Bye, Frank," he called. "Been good to know you. Remember us."

Back at the croft, they packed and crept into their sleeping bags. The following morning, they ate the last of the oatcakes, drank their coffee and drove back to the station. Sandra took the keys to the people-carrier and walked to the hotel to drop them off. Pete distributed their tickets for the 12.40 Glasgow train.

* * *

It was raining steadily as they reached the platform. In the shelter, Mike checked the timetable.

"We've got half an hour to wait. Look, there *is* a train on Sundays. Leaves at 12.30. The lying bastard."

Pete spotted a large brown envelope in a waterproof sleeve, placed under a stone on the bench.

They picked it up. It was addressed to *The Markhams Five* and contained a single sheet of handwriting.

Frank hoped they'd found the weekend enriching. He'd been impressed with their resourcefulness. Given their successful collaborative efforts, it was clear that they had become more aware of the need for teamwork. He was sure they'd grown in self-confidence and hoped to see them again one day.

They passed round the sheet of paper, glaring at its contents. Pete tore it up and threw it on the tracks. No one wanted to be the first to admit that they had failed. After a while, Suresh walked to the end of the platform, returned and shook the rain off his jacket.

"We should give him credit," he announced. "He must have got free, worked out where he was, and walked here overnight, in order to make sure we knew we hadn't got the better of him. Remember how bright the moon was last night on our way back, and he knows the area well. He was much too clever for us. So he wins the last match, and just when our hopes were high."

The signal rose with an echoing clank, and a few minutes later they were climbing into the train and hoisting their luggage onto the racks.

As the train moved away, Sandra pointed through the window.

"Talk of the devil."

Frank was on the footbridge. He didn't wave, but raised his right hand, palm open.

"Bugger me," said Pete. "He looks like Chairman Mao."

They watched as Frank walked jauntily down the steps of the footbridge and set off in the direction of the hotel.

* * *

At Crianlarich, they had to wait for the connecting train from Oban. By the time they were approaching Glasgow, they were an hour late.

Nicky broke the long silence.

"I've been thinking about what you said, Suresh."

Reluctantly, the others turned to listen.

"You remember, that first night? You said that if we just turned round and went back to the station and got on the train, that might be what Markhams were expecting us to do. Maybe you were right. But what's bothering me is that we ended up playing the game according to Frank's rules, even when we thought we were being smart. Even when we thought we were rebelling."

"Sorry, you're not making sense."

"Look, Mike, until last night, we'd done pretty well. I think so, anyway. We were still acting as individuals. We never bought into the idea of getting our own food, did we? Sandra and I didn't try very hard to catch any fish. Then there was Pete and his gooseberries. And we weren't ever going to catch a sheep and kill it, were we? I reckon you were wrong, Pete. Sorry, but we weren't acting like sheep. Not then. But last night we spoiled it all. We thought we were getting our revenge, but we ended up doing something we didn't all agree with. We did it as a team, not individuals. What was the phrase Frank used? When he was congratulating us on our efforts? *Acting in a collegiate manner*, that was it. That's what we did. But last night, not before. That was when we acted in a collegiate manner. Stupid us. And that must have been what Markhams were looking for when they set the whole thing up."

Pete disagreed, saying Frank deserved everything they had tried to do to him, that it wasn't their fault he had more outdoor skills than they had. Suresh wondered if their attempt to get their own back might have been part of Frank's plan all the time. No one seemed inclined to take the argument further.

Soon, the train was slowing down as it entered Queen Street station. With a cry, Suresh slammed his phone down on the table in front of him.

"Damn. Damn. Damn. England did make a draw of it. Kevin Pietersen, of all people."

Pete leaned across to look at the screen.

"Oh, the cricket. Never mind, mate, only a game. And you wouldn't have wanted to miss this weekend for anything, would you?"

They collected their luggage and, once on the platform, headed for the exit.

"Talking of petty revenges," said Sandra. She put her hand into her jacket pocket and took out a bunch of keys. Unobtrusively, she dropped them into the next litter bin and continued towards the ticket barriers.

"I wonder if Frank has a spare set of keys to that bloody van. Hope not."

The Last Munro

It was no good. He had to get up for a pee.

As he crawled back into his sleeping bag, he looked at his watch: nearly five o'clock. He'd forgotten how cold nights could be in the Cairngorms in the autumn. What was that story about a couple dying of hypothermia in the Lairig Ghru in July? Just now he could believe it. And it would be some time before any daylight found its way into the glen. He dozed off again, and it was half past seven when he emerged from his tent.

He was pleased to see that his brother had the tea ready, though he felt a bit ashamed. Despite being older, Paul seemed to be coping better with the cold conditions.

He produced what he hoped was a brave smile as he was handed a mug. The two men looked up the side of the mountain, and the path they would have to take; the smile disappeared.

His brother looked concerned.

"It's bloody steep, isn't it? More than I thought. Are you sure you're up for it, Alec? What about your shoulder?"

"It's OK. I'll manage. We can take our time. We'll leave the tents up and use the day packs. Then come back here. That'll make it easier. It'll be worth the effort, Paul. It's a great hill, the Angel's Peak. A good one to finish on."

His brother leaned over the gas stove, filled two plates of porridge and passed one over.

Alec took his plate, blew on the porridge and began to eat. After a few mouthfuls, he fetched a fleece and a woolly hat from his tent and walked a few yards up and down the track to get his circulation going. He refilled his mug, took a cereal bar from his backpack, but it was cold, too hard to bite into. There were bananas in his tent, chocolate too, but he didn't fancy them.

He hadn't slept well.

It hadn't just been the cold. He'd kept waking up, fretful, thinking about the Test Match at the Oval. The whole series, and it had come down to the last day. He'd done the calculations: England would have to bat into the evening, to be sure of the draw. It would be a struggle; Australia had to be favourites. Warne, he was the danger man. And if they couldn't get through till tea, that was it. Australia would keep the Ashes. Again.

His brother seemed to sense what he was thinking about.

"I am sorry I messed up the cricket. I didn't realise it finished today."

"Don't worry, I'll be able to find out the score when I get back to Braemar. Maybe earlier. Probably best I haven't been able to watch it. Too stressful. All summer, and it comes down to the last day of the last Test. Bloody Aussies, they'll probably nick it."

"How many do England need?"

"It's not that. Like I said, they can't win. They just need to bat all day, or most of it. Easier said than done. But you never know."

He put on his boots, sorted out his day pack. Told himself to forget about the cricket. He'd have to be patient; there would be no mobile signal for ages. At least they'd been able to get yesterday's close of play score from Fiona before the phone reception had disappeared. But it was frustrating. If he'd been at home, he *would* have watched it, despite what he'd said. But he knew Paul wasn't keen on going into the hills on his own after that time he'd slipped coming down Beinn Eighe. And he couldn't turn his brother down when he'd asked him to go with him on his last Munros.

"You ready, Alec?"

"Let's go."

* * *

It was a hard climb all right. Two thousand feet of it. A good track past Corrour bothy onto the ridge. Then the long slog over the boulders, past Cairn Toul. But the views from the summit made it worth the effort. Ben Macdui across the pass. Braeriach to the North, over the Great Moss to the Glen Feshie hills in the West.

And best of all, a dram. You have to celebrate your brother's last Munro.

Then two thousand feet back down. Worse in some ways; by the time they were back at the tents, his knees were sore as well as his shoulder.

He checked the time: it was nearly three. It would probably all be over by now.

They took off the day packs and sat down to eat the remaining sandwiches. The older of the two men looked back at the ridge and smiled.

"OK, Alec, that's it. Mission accomplished. Thanks a lot. Look, I do appreciate it. We'll have a bloody good party to celebrate. I'll check dates with Fiona when I get home. How long will it take you to Linn of Dee?"

"Good couple of hours. What about you?"

"More like three. It's a long slog. It'll be getting dark by the time I get to Aviemore. I just hope my car starts."

"Me too. We'd better get on with it."

As they packed up the tents, Alec noticed the clouds building up behind the ridge they had climbed. The forecast further west was not good. With a smile, he thought of the party of five he'd seen at Queen Street station on Friday, on his way back from Tyndrum. Getting onto the West Highland line, and some of them had looked unprepared and apprehensive. They'd probably had a good soaking somewhere.

If only it was raining at the Oval.

They checked that they had left nothing and prepared to get going. They'd agreed that as soon as one of them had mobile reception, they'd get the result of the Test Match and try to pass it on, though Alec knew that his brother didn't share his obsession, that he was humouring him.

"I hope England manage to save it, Alec. You'll be able to watch it when you get back, won't you? Presumably Marie-Louise is recording it?"

"Should be. If she's back in time. I don't know where she was going over the weekend, she wouldn't say. Left Sophie with her mum. She'll be home by now. She was very mysterious about it, said she'd explain it all tonight. Well, it was a good walk. It's been a great few days. And congratulations. You can do the same for me when it's my turn. Love to Fiona."

"Thanks again. Love to Marie-Louise."

They eased the heavy packs onto their shoulders and set off, one to the North, one to the South.

Alec looked at the sky; for the moment, the rain was holding off. His thoughts started to wander. Wouldn't it be great... Don't get your hopes up; it's happened before... Flintoff, it has to be Flintoff. Or Pietersen.

Think about something else.

OK. It had been a funny summer all right. Bad start. The accident on the rig, and the fortnight's lay-off. But then meeting Marie-Louise, the best physio in Scotland – was it really only four months ago? Really hitting it off, the two of them. Moving in with her and little Sophie. Starting to learn French, for God's sake. Everyone on the rig taking the piss. Then Paul saying that he fancied tackling his last few Munros. So they'd done Ben Lui and Beinn Dubhchraig on Friday, and today the Angel's Peak. All good hills, and the weather had been dry. Tiring few days, though.

But it had been an Ashes summer. Always special. In the end, Lords had been disappointing. But there'd been good signs. Harmison and Flintoff roughing them up, Pietersen looking as though he could turn a match. Then that amazing first day at Edgbaston. And all the rest of it.

He sat down, ate the last of his chocolate and forced himself to look at the scenery. What was the point of being in the hills if you didn't take any notice of what was around you? It was like mobile phones. Now that everyone had one, people were using them all the time in bars and restaurants, instead of talking to the person sitting next to them. But he'd been in the Cairngorms so many times before; the hills were almost too familiar. Still, the landscape was dramatic enough, especially the black triangle of the Devil's Point ahead. He smiled when he remembered Paul explaining what the name meant in Gaelic, and how the Victorians hadn't liked the literal translation. Not that he'd ever seen a penis that shape.

Carn a'Mhaim on his left. His first Munro. Twenty years ago? No, more. His dad had watched him rush across the plateau to the cairn, and then deliberately let him set off down in the wrong direction, to teach him that you've always got to look out for points of reference on the way up. That was Dad, a bit pompous, but it was a good point.

"*Un bon point?*" No, that didn't sound right. God, French was hard. But Marie-Louise was a great teacher. He laughed out loud, thinking about the tricks she had for getting him motivated, and the reward she'd come up with when he'd finally got the hang of the perfect tense. Alarmed, he looked around, in case there was anyone else on the track, hearing him laugh. But there was no one there.

Might as well check the phone.

No reception. Nothing. *Rien.*

He looked ahead, tracing the path as it contoured round the slopes of the hill to where the Luibeg Burn came down from the left. It must still be a couple of miles away, but it was a good track; he could stride out. Then another half an hour to Derry Lodge. He should get reception there. He eased the pack onto his shoulders and set off again.

Insane to be playing a Test Match in September. Should have started the series in May, when the Aussies wouldn't have liked the conditions. Why do we always make it hard for ourselves? Come on, come on. It's only a game. Doesn't really matter.

A group of walkers was approaching. Probably doing the Lairig, he thought, south to north. Good luck to them, it's a tough walk. He wondered about stopping them and asking if they knew the cricket score but decided against it. The game was a bit of a minority taste in Scotland. Though this summer, it had been different. Everyone seemed to have got involved.

Like the walker he'd met as he was setting off on Friday. Broad Glasgow accent, but he was into it all right. Not the usual banter. Will the clouds stay off? Which one are you going for? No, it was "Let's just hope for some good English rain."

Worth trying the phone again?

Yes! Two bars, three bars. He dialled Marie-Louise's number, fingers trembling. As the phone rang, he suddenly realised that if Sophie was there, her mother would only speak in French. Christ, he didn't have the right words!

"Allô. Alec? C'est toi? Alors, c'est bien passé? Paul t'a quitté maintenant?"

"Er... oui, Marie-Louise. Bien passé. Très bien. Alors, le cricket, tu sais comment...?"

"Attends. Je vais voir. Il paraît que ..."

"Marie-Louise? Marie-Louise? ... Oh fuck."

He cursed his phone, cursed Orange, cursed whatever it was that had lost him the signal. He'd just have to wait.

A heavy shower caught up with him. He stopped to put on his waterproofs. He was still hungry and managed to find another banana in the pocket of his backpack. The shower came and went, but he kept his waterproofs on.

An hour later he reached Derry Lodge and took out his phone once more, ignoring pitying looks from two cyclists who overtook him.

I know, I know, he thought. You shouldn't be sending texts when you're out in the hills. But this is different.

Yes, it was ringing, and there was the familiar voice answering.

"Allô, Marie-Louise. Oui, c'est Alec. Mon signal a revenu."

"Est revenu, Alec. Mon signal est revenu. Perfect tense, you remember?"

"Oui. OK. Est revenu. Marie-Louise, le cricket..."

"Justement, je regarde la télé. Oui, le monsieur dans la blouse blanche, il vient d'enlever les deux morceaux de bois..."

What was she talking about, *morceaux de bois*? Bits of... what? Wood, that's it. Ah, the *bails*. That was it then, it was all over, Australia had won. He thought hard to find the right French words.

"C'est fini? Australie a gagné?"

"Non, non, je ne crois pas. Attends. L'Anglais, le grand, il semble très heureux."

"Le grand? Ah, Flintoff? Freddie?"

"Oui, oui. C'est lui. Très heureux. Les autres aussi. T'es content?"

"That's fantastic. Ah... oui, très, très content. Merci, Marie-Louise. Je marche à Linn of Dee, je serai à la maison dans... plus tard."

"Parfait. A tout à l'heure, Alec. Alors, je te prépare quelque chose."

"Merci. Au revoir, Marie-Louise. A tout à l'heure."

* * *

So they'd done it! It didn't matter how; he could find that out later. What a relief. And it was probably a good thing that he'd not been watching it. How many miles to go now? Two, three to Linn of Dee and the car? He wished it was longer, just to enjoy the moment.

Another group of cyclists came round a bend in the track. Alec smiled, tempted to pass on the good news. But they were soon past, heads down, into the wind.

He realised he'd forgotten to ask Marie-Louise if she'd

recorded it, though she was pretty good at indulging his requests. And he'd have had to ask her that in French.

When he arrived at the car park, he was still wearing his waterproofs. The car park was starting to empty. He noticed a young woman with a dog, sending a message on her phone.

He switched his on again. There were more messages than he'd ever had. From work colleagues: "KP What a man Celebration next Saturday BYOB No Fosters", "Wow! Haven't felt so good since Thatcher resigned." From Paul: "Great result Great trip Thanks again." Even one from his dad: "You missed a wonderful day's cricket, though I'm sure the walk more than made up for it."

And from Marie-Louise: "Oui, je l'ai enregistré. Bises."

It looked as though she had recorded it. He'd never really doubted that she would. He switched his phone off, sat on the wall and loosened the laces on his boots. He looked at his watch; he'd be back in Aberdeen before nine.

The Plaque

*   *   *

Now I will tell you where I went to this weekend, Alec. I am sorry I was vague about my plans. I was going to explain it all last night, but when you got back, you were so happy that I did not want to spoil the mood.

What did I do on Saturday and Sunday? It was all to do with my father. Let me tell you his story. Now that we know each other well, it is a good time to tell it, though it is not a happy story.

* * *

I do not think you know much about my father, do you, Alec? Only that he is no more. You may have heard my mother refer to Jean-Pierre from time to time, but it is true that we do not talk about him a great deal.

He was called Jean-Pierre Navez. He was born in 1942 in Northern France, the part which British tourists drive through as quickly as possible as they rush south to Paris or the Midi. In Papa's eyes, however, they were wrong to neglect the area round Arras where he lived. He believed that the area was the source of his country's prosperity; it was no accident that this rich soil had been fought over for centuries. His grandfather had been killed in action in 1916, and his father had been a prisoner of the Germans from 1943 until the end of the war. As a consequence, Papa was a keen student of the history of the two world wars. He believed that he owed it to his ancestors to take his country's past seriously. At school he was known as a *bûcheur*. You would call him a swot, I think.

After he left school, he worked for some years in the coal mines. But these closed, little by little. Happily, Papa was able to use the knowledge he had acquired of the war of 1914–18. He found a post accompanying groups of British schoolchildren around the battlefields and the cemeteries. He quickly learned enough English to enable him to do the job. He was passionate about it. He was delighted to see the transformations in the attitudes of the British youngsters. At the beginning of the tour, they were often bored and irreverent. By the end of the visit, they were frequently in tears at the deaths of so many individuals only a little older than they were.

He was twenty-nine when he married my mother, Geneviève Wardenski. She was from a Polish family. Many Poles had arrived in France earlier in the century, to work in the mines. In many ways they were a contrasting couple. Papa was quite heavily built, with dark hair. He had very big feet. It's funny the things you remember, isn't it? I can still see his enormous shoes by the back door. Papa was... distant. No, that's not the right word. Reserved, that's better. He was rather intense; he never seemed to be quite at ease. As you know, Maman is very different. She's fair, more slightly built. Very vivacious. You know her habit of looking at you out of the corner of her eyes, with a playful smile on her mouth. She always seems pleased to see people. When I was a child, my friends would love to come round, and we would spend hours with Maman in the kitchen, making *crêpes* and chocolate cake.

Well, once he was a married man, Papa needed a larger income. He followed courses at the *École des Mines* in Douai. He obtained a diploma in geology; this allowed him to find employment in local government, advising on the siting of things like motorways and housing developments.

Then I arrived, on 3 May 1976.

But Papa desired above all to have a son. Of course, all these things I learned later, from Maman. She told me that Papa sometimes talked about the absence of his father during the early years of his life. She wondered if this had left a gap in his life that could only be filled by a close bond with a son of his own. Maman was over thirty when I was born, and the birth had been a difficult one. She would have gladly tried to avoid further pregnancies. However, in France at that time, contraception was perceived as a matter for the husband, and state subsidies still encouraged the *famille nombreuse*. So Maman accepted that the Navez would persist in their attempts to procreate. She used to tease Papa about his name. Navez, you see, sounds almost the same as the French word for turnip. Mother would say there were already enough turnips in the fields of Northern France. But Papa didn't see the funny side.

Well, I was three years old when Maman found that she was going to have a baby. For the next few months, even I noticed anxiety in my parents' behaviour. Maman often remained resting in her room. Papa would come and go, constantly asking her if she needed anything. I even recollect Maman, the gentlest of people, losing her temper with him, telling him to stop fussing and leave her alone.

Philippe Navez was born on New Year's Day 1980. He

soon became the centre of the family's attention. He was a bright child. I'm sure Papa dreamed about how, in later years, Philippe would enrol in the *École nationale supérieure* and win all the glittering prizes. Papa inspired in him his own love of the landscape. Even while Philippe was still very young, father and son went on geological expeditions. By the time Philippe started at primary school, he could identify some of the rocks in his father's collection. But Philippe was less at ease away from his adoring family, however. His teachers commented, as tactfully as they could, that he could be sullen, occasionally aggressive towards his classmates.

When I was ten and Philippe was six, we moved to Scotland. At that time, new oil fields were being developed in the North Sea, and French companies paid good wages to geologists willing to relocate to Aberdeen. Papa seized the opportunity, delighted that Philippe would have the chance to learn English in an English-speaking environment. He would become a bilingual polymath; all doors would be open to him.

In Aberdeen, we were impressed by the splendid granite buildings, especially on majestic Union Street. But we had to work hard to adapt to our changed circumstances. At the beginning, the language was very difficult. I had already begun to study English at school, and Philippe was a quick learner. But we all struggled. I can still remember the delight in my mother's face when she returned from the shops one day and announced,

"Marie-Louise, I understand it now. This Ken they all mention at the end of questions, he is not a person at all."

And the local dialect, the Doric! Many of my school friends said they could not follow it either, which was a consolation for us.

We had to get used to the climate too. Yes, the winters were less cold than in our Artois, but they seemed to go on for ever, and when it did become warmer, the haar would roll in.

Initially, it was Maman who felt the isolation most keenly. During the week, she would meet the other French-speaking 'petrol wives'. They would lament the absence of good restaurants, of cultural life, of everything, in fact. Even as a child I could detect the snobbery in their attitude. Maman was much more open-minded than most of them. She soon understood that she should try to integrate herself. She joined a local history group; she tried to cook traditional Scottish food. She enjoyed helping at Philippe's primary school, taking optional French classes in the lunchtime. Here she became known as 'Miss French', much to her amusement. I am sure her attitude was the right one. There is nothing worse than people who come from abroad and who constantly find fault. Like me, Maman believed that we were guests in this country.

Once we had lived in Aberdeen for a while, we found that there were so many things which delighted us. Though Papa worked long days, we spent our weekends together. We went for walks in the parks, we explored the coast. In summer, the long, light evenings were a great source of joy. We could appreciate the quality of British television. Papa took Philippe to see the city football team playing, telling him that he was lucky to be watching a team that had recently been one of the best in Europe. Of course, these outings were not for me.

At home, with Papa and Maman, we spoke mostly French. At Papa's insistence, however, we attended Scottish schools, not the *lycée française* we could have gone to. It was a good decision. What is the point in living in a country, and being educated as if you are living in another? The teaching we received was much less rigid than the one we had known in France, and I appreciated this. However, the lessons were not always stimulating. The Scottish system is too democratic, too egalitarian. And I'm a French woman, so a belief in equality is supposed to be in my blood! But the most intelligent pupils had to work at the rhythm of the lazy. Even for Philippe and me, the lessons were easy, our homework was quickly done. But my brother's personal problems increased. He was a spoiled child and did not like to be ridiculed. 'Wee froggie bastard', that was the least of the insults he endured. His aggressiveness became more marked; he was often in fights.

One of the best things about our school was the range of sports we could do after school finished, and the clubs which teachers arranged. We had never come across anything like this in France. We were taken on expeditions into the Scottish hills. We learnt rock-climbing, abseiling, kayaking. Philippe became more... *ancré*. What's that in English? Settled, I suppose. When the whole school party was outdoors, responsible for themselves, they seemed to have no time to bully him.

In the summer, Papa and Philippe would go on their own camping and walking trips. For Papa, this was ideal. He could spend his free time with Philippe, developing his son's interest in the landscape, teaching him what it could tell us about the past, and so on. Sometimes I accompanied them, but these trips were not for Maman. She had a horror of the things which delighted us. She would have hated the steep ascents, the exposed crests, the frisson which came from dramatic changes in the weather.

* * *

This happy period of family life lasted for some years. Then, when I was nineteen, I went away to university in England, leaving my parents and my brother behind. On returning home at Christmas – this was 1995 – it was evident that all was not well in the Navez family.

What had changed? It was difficult to know. Philippe was now nearly sixteen. He had let his hair grow long. This displeased Papa, though Maman was unconcerned. Philippe had made new friends, this time from his school. With them, he listened to music, chatted. As for me, I was happy to see my brother again, and my parents, of course. But I had made new friends too, especially Nick. We had met in London, where I was studying to become a nurse. Philippe and I were beginning to go our own ways. It happens all the time; it's quite natural. Maman understood. She had found a job as a teaching assistant, and seemed happier in her skin, as we say.

It was Papa who seemed to have changed. The serious side to his nature had become more pronounced. He spent more time in his study. Evidently, Philippe's conduct annoyed him. I tried to treat it all lightly, but it's true that our family conversations were becoming tiresome. Papa was short-tempered. The slightest thing irritated him.

You are perhaps thinking that I am hard on my father. But when a child is aware that one of her parents prefers her sibling, this can be painful. Of course, Maman knew this, and tried to make up for it. That is no doubt why we have always been so close.

Let me tell you about one incident which had happened in the summer before I left home. It might help you to understand the kind of person my father could be.

It had been unusually warm. Warm for Aberdeen, that is.

I had been sunbathing in the back garden. It was one of the rare occasions when I was able to wear my bikini. I needed a refreshing cold drink. As I passed Papa's study, I saw that he and Philippe were sorting through the collection of geological specimens. I smiled and said something flippant about it being too sunny to be inside looking at rocks.

Philippe laughed and put his tongue out. But Papa scowled, looked hard at me and said:

"Va t'habiller, petite garce."

It was a shock. He was telling me to put some clothes on, and he called me *une garce*. It means slut, or worse. It is not the kind of word a father should use towards his daughter. I ran to my room and slammed the door. I was glad I was leaving home in a few days' time.

That Christmas, as I said, Papa was difficult to live with. Perhaps there were problems at work, I thought. The only activity that seemed to interest him was planning expeditions into the hills, which he hoped to take with Philippe once the winter was over. I could see that these plans appealed less to Philippe than they had done in the past. On one occasion, I remember Papa asking his son to come and have a look at maps of Sutherland which he had spread out on the table in his study, but Philippe made some excuse and left him to it.

We all tried hard to laugh Papa out of his dark moods, but we didn't succeed. As you might have guessed, he did not have much of a sense of humour. When I spoke to Maman about my concerns for our family, she appeared convinced that things would improve.

"It's just his age," she said. "In a few years, he'll become a friendly human being again. You were just like him before you went away to university."

I told her it wasn't Philippe I was worried about; it was Papa.

So when I left Aberdeen in January, I was on bad terms with my father. How I wish now that we had made up.

Back in London, I tried to forget about these little family difficulties. I had asked Philippe to come and visit me during his mid-February break. Philippe got on very well with Nick, and my boyfriend and I enjoyed showing him some of the sights of the capital. We spent a whole day in the Science Museum; I couldn't help wishing that Papa had been there too. Other places that we visited would have appealed to Papa less, however: Soho and Brixton, for example. I suppose Nick and I did take some pleasure in trying to shock my brother, but he was not as naive as I had perhaps expected.

Naturally, Philippe and I talked about Maman and Papa. Philippe said he was very fond of Papa, he respected all that he had done for him, but now he found his company a little boring. He preferred to spend his free time with Gregor, Gary and the others. When Philippe said that he had decided to stop going into the hills with Papa, for the moment at least, this worried me. I was very conscious of the importance for Papa of these days spent walking with his son. But Philippe was firm. He had other things to do with his weekends, he said, and days alone with Papa were long when they had little to say to each other. I pointed out how much suffering this would cause Papa, all the more so since I wouldn't be there at Easter; Nick and I planned to go travelling in Italy. Just before Philippe went back, I had a brilliant idea.

"Promise Papa that you'll go on one more expedition with him," I said. "And that he can choose the area and the route. I'm sure he'd love to go back to Torridon. You know how much he loves the geology of the area. And tell him that it most likely won't be the last time, as you'll probably want to start again one day." He promised.

In April, Nick and I went to Italy as planned. At the end of the fortnight, we were spending our last night, in Florence. When we returned to our hostel that evening, the warden gave me a message. I had to phone home urgently. When I finally succeeded in speaking to Maman, I learned that Papa had had an accident in the mountains. She was not sure exactly what had happened, but it appeared that he had taken a few days off work, and left home for the Highlands, alone, two days earlier. Then at some point he had fallen from the ridge, into a remote corrie. He was in hospital, gravely injured.

I went straight back to Aberdeen. But I was too late. Papa had died in hospital. Maman was distraught, unable to understand what was happening to her. I tried to comfort her, and also get to the bottom of the incident. Why had Papa gone off alone? Hadn't Philippe promised to go with him? When I spoke to Philippe, he explained that he had decided to spend the weekend with Gregor and his parents. They owned a timeshare in Edinburgh. I was angry with him for breaking his promise to me, but he didn't want to speak.

* * *

Did we ever know the complete story? Not really. In Philippe's absence, Papa had set off on the Thursday evening. Before leaving, he'd told Maman that he wanted to follow the ridge that he and Philippe had planned to take, before Philippe had changed his mind. He had driven to Kinlochewe and stayed in a bed and breakfast, phoning Maman that evening to say that all was well, that he had listened to the forecast, which was good.

Maman was not too concerned when she did not hear from Papa on the Friday evening. But by Saturday lunchtime, she was beginning to worry. She contacted the bed and breakfast, seeking information. The owner could not help. Papa had not booked in there for Friday evening, which was surprising. Maman made efforts to reassure herself. Papa was experienced. He had all the equipment necessary. The weather had been fine, not too cold or wet. There was no doubt an explanation. But eventually she got in touch with the police and the mountain rescue services. She told them Papa's route. At last, that evening, they rang her to tell her that they had found someone at the foot of a corrie below the ridge, and that his description resembled that of her husband. The individual was unconscious, with fractures. He was transferred by helicopter to the hospital in Aberdeen.

He never regained consciousness. He died of injuries to his back and his head, and of internal bleeding. Of course, there was an inquest, which was traumatising for all of us. The verdict was Accidental Death. No one could say for sure how or why he had fallen. Maman asked the rescuers if they could explain the accident. They hesitated, saying that these were mountains which required care, but no, where Papa had fallen was not a notorious spot. An accident can happen anywhere, of course, Papa was, after all, fifty-three years old. But the conditions on the mountain were good, even though the path Papa was following was rather eroded. Where he had fallen, that was the only exposed part of the ridge.

For the funeral, all our little family gathered in Aberdeen. Maman's sister came over from Paris. Two colleagues from Papa's company helped with the administrative side. They were wonderful. We placed announcements in the local paper and in one that serves the Arras area. And then... we had to go on living. But it does not ever finish. There are thoughts with no direction, questions which have no answers.

That was nine years ago. For a long time, there was little joy in our family. Philippe, for his part, suffered for a long time on account of his father's death. He found it difficult to forgive himself for his part in the accident. He believed he had acted selfishly. Of course, he wished he had known what was going to happen. It was not easy to know what to say to him. Maman eventually brought him some peace by persuading him that what we do is self-regarding most of the time. Only sometimes we are unfortunate, and our acts have tragic results. I'm sure she was thinking of her husband as well as her son.

Now, things are much better. Maman is happily remarried. As you know, Simon made a lot of money from buying and selling property in the north of England. He says he fell in love with Scotland when he went to the West Coast with school friends after leaving school and always wanted to go back when he was rich enough. I sometimes smile when I think what Papa would have made of Maman being married to a right-wing businessman. Papa had been a member of the French Communist Party when he was a young man. This was not unusual in the sixties. But as Maman says, you don't need to approve of a man's politics to help him spend his money. They are good for each other. Simon's grown-up children adore their French stepmother, and my Sophie loves to go and stay with Maman and Simon in their big house by the river in Strathdon.

Last summer, Philippe completed his master's degree in geology. I think his choice of subject reflected a desire to please his father, posthumously. He is more content with his life now, though I feel that he would perhaps like to return to France one day. And I... but of course you know my story, or most of it.

At the celebration we held for Philippe's graduation, Maman said that she had decided that she wanted to do something to commemorate Papa's life. She had the idea of placing a plaque where Papa had taken his last walk in the hills. We had the plaque made, and on Saturday, I met Philippe at Inverness and we drove to Torridon. At the start of the track which climbs to the summit, we found a place for the plaque. We'd brought a battery drill and some screws and managed to find a flat enough rock to attach it to. I know by heart what it says:

> *A la mémoire de Jean-Pierre Navez,*
> *qui trouva la mort près d'ici en avril 1996.*
> *Amateur de montagne, et père de famille.*

I'll translate for you:

> *To the memory of Jean-Pierre Navez,*
> *who died near this spot in April 1996.*
> *A lover of the hills, and a father.*

As Philippe left to go back to Edinburgh, he told me that he had got a job with Gaz de France. He will be working off the coast of Brazil, where they are looking for oil and gas. Maman is delighted with the news.

So now we have three things to celebrate, Alec. Philippe's job, Paul's last Munro – and your cricket match. Do you think it will be warm enough for a barbecue next Saturday? I'll get in touch with Fiona.

The Jetty

The battered pick-up slowed and pulled into a passing place as the low rays of the sun glinted in the rain-filled potholes on the road ahead.

A middle-aged couple got out, the woman tall and wiry, the man shorter, stocky. Both weather-beaten, dressed for the outdoors. They looked around and, after a moment, crossed the road and looked at a run-down building on the far side of the field.

"This is it, Sal. Must be. But it's sad. Look at the grass on the roof and the broken windows."

They walked down the short, overgrown track. Beyond the building, low hills emerged from the lifting cloud, brown bracken winning the battle with the purple of the heather.

The door to the cottage was open. They looked at each other and went in. The floor was covered with bits of soggy wool; sheep were clearly using it as a shelter. In the main room, something scurried across the floor and disappeared in the fireplace.

"It's ages since anyone's lived here, Sal."

"I know. It is sad. Look, there's a hole in the floorboards. It wasn't exactly luxurious, was it, but it suited us fine."

They walked carefully up the stairs and into one of the bedrooms, laughing as they saw the marks on the floor where the beds had been.

"Remember when Jeff and Simon were arguing about the double bed? Threatening to wrestle naked in front of the fire to decide who got to sleep in it. Then you and Marguerite saying OK, as long as you got to take the photographs. That stopped them."

"Silly boys. But they were good times, John, weren't they?"

They went back down the stairs and turned into the kitchen. A dirty wooden table with an empty bread bin on it, and two chairs that looked close to collapse. They looked around at the walls and began to rummage among the shelves, but all they found were cobwebs, a couple of broken mugs, empty mousetraps.

They swept the years of dust off the chairs and sat down carefully.

"I suppose this was where it all started, wasn't it? I mean, for you and me, Sal. I remember thinking, that first night, looking out to the islands, I can't imagine living in a city again."

"I know, I was the same. But I never thought that we'd still be out here, making a living from it. And still loving it. But you know what, it's Simon I still can't get over. Coming back to Scotland after all these years."

"Landed on his feet. Always did, our Simon."

With a last look round, they got to their feet and shook the dust off their fleeces.

"Come on, Sal. We'd better be going. Before this place falls down."

* * *

"Bloody Scots – they can't even build decent roads. Americans can put a man on the moon, but here you've still got country lanes with cow shit down the middle."

The shorter of the two young men laughed and handed over a lighted cigarette. They looked over to the cottage, where unpacking was in progress. The journey had certainly taken much longer than they'd expected. Three hundred miles, they'd calculated. Nearly eight hours. It hadn't been too bad at the start, mostly motorway, but then ages on the A74, 'Scotland's Killer Road', as they'd learned from the newspaper they'd picked up at Gretna. And at the end, thirty miles or so on a single-track road. No wonder the driver was grumpy. His companion gave him a playful thump on the shoulder.

"You're right. But we made it. Come on, Si, let's get the rest of this stuff shifted. Before the others start complaining."

Inside the cottage, tea and coffee were already stacked on the kitchen shelves, with the beer and crisps, soups, Vesta curries, packets of Smash. On the low table in the lounge ("I suppose we'll have to call it a lounge," someone had scoffed), board games and jigsaws had appeared. Cases and holdalls, together with six sleeping bags, were piled up at the bottom of the stairs; no decisions so far on who was sleeping in which bedroom.

The accommodation was basic, they could see that, but it was more than big enough for the six of them. And it was very cheap; that was the main thing. It was a long way to come for four days, but you have to do something to celebrate the end of grammar school.

Someone commented on how warm it was. They'd been told that Scotland was always wet and cold, even in July. They were amazed that it was still daylight at ten o'clock, even allowing for the distance they'd covered since leaving Manchester. And where were the biting insects everyone had warned them about? The man at the petrol station had told them with a smirk that the *madges* preferred English visitors, especially virgins, though he admitted that the breeze would keep them away for the moment.

Someone switched on the television ("It's black and white!"). In the kitchen, the aged kettle began to wheeze away. At the third attempt, the gas oven was lit, and the six ready-made meals were heated up. Cans of beer and a bottle of red Hirondelle were opened.

Once they'd finished eating, there wasn't a lot of washing-up to do, just knives and forks, beer mugs, six wine glasses. They decided against reusing the plastic plates: there were plenty more in the polythene bag. They switched the television on again, but reception was poor. One of the party went up the creaking stairs to explore the bedrooms, but he was called back.

"Cluedo! Compulsory Cluedo!"

The game was set out on the table; four participants chose their identities. The two who declined to join in settled down in a corner, the man opening a one-inch map, the woman looking through some of the leaflets left for guests.

After a while, she stood up and explained that she wanted to have a look around outside; even though it was nearly eleven, there was still enough light.

The man looked up from his map as she passed him on her way to the door, and then got to his feet.

In front of the cottage, a path led through low grass to a gate in a tumbled-down wall. They were careful not to tread in the sheep droppings. Through the gate, the path turned to the right and took them to a small bay, invisible from the cottage.

A broken stone jetty, clearly unused, led into the water. Beyond, broad stretches of sea, then mountainous islands, their outlines just visible. The man passed the map over.

"That's Eigg, Sally, the one with the cliffs. I think the other one must be Rum."

"What brilliant names! I've never seen a view like this. This is what we came for, isn't it?"

"Yes. Some of us, anyhow. I want to get to Skye if we can, that's supposed to be the best of the lot. There's a ferry from Mallaig, but I'm not sure if it takes cars."

They stood gazing over the sand and the seaweed to the rocks at the mouth of the bay.

The young woman sat down on a flat rock at the edge of the path, her long arms hugging her knees.

"There aren't the words, really, are there? Especially on a night like this."

"No, it's fantastic."

The breeze was dropping. A few late midges began circling.

After a while, the woman turned to her companion.

"You're definitely going to Peru, John?"

"I think so. I'm not sure what I want to do. And they seemed quite keen to have me."

"I'm sure they are. You've always been really practical."

"Thanks. Don't know how I'll make out building a school on the Altiplano, mind."

He paused.

"Why don't you come, Sal? You know you said your mum was happy with it. It would be great if you could. You don't have any plans, do you?"

"Not really. I'll let you know by the time we get back home, John. Promise."

A drunken shout reached them from the cottage. They laughed, looking back along the path they had taken a few minutes earlier. They began to retrace their steps.

But before they reached the gate, the woman stopped, turned around and walked to the end of the jetty. There, she took off her sandals, T-shirt and jeans, then removed her underwear and jumped into the water, swimming strongly into the bay.

A few minutes later she was about to emerge from the water when she felt a hand gently touch her shoulder.

"Oh, John, I thought you were going back."

* * *

They went out through the open door, trying without success to close it behind them, and walked across the wet grass towards the pick-up. Then, without saying anything, they left the path and headed towards a gap in a wall. Beyond the wall, they reached the shore of a sandy bay. To the west, the sun was beginning to slip down towards the islands, accentuating the jagged lines of the mountains and cliffs.

The woman noticed her husband looking towards the end of the stone jetty.

She laughed and slipped her arm in his.

"No, I don't think so, John. We're a bit old for that now. But it was a lovely idea of yours, coming back to look at the old cottage. Funny we've never been back after all these years. It meant a lot to us, didn't it?"

They reached the pick-up, kicked the mud off their boots and climbed in. The clock in the pick-up wasn't working.

"What's the time, Sal?"

"Just after six."

"That's OK. Fort William won't be too bad. Should be back in plenty of time to get the climbing stuff out for tomorrow."

As they drove away, they both turned around for a last look at the cottage. It almost seemed that the bracken had covered more of it since they'd crossed the field half an hour earlier.

Leonardo

Jake was one of those annoying individuals who seem to be good at everything.

An only child, he had been the sole focus of both parents' love and attention. The family lived in the West Midlands, where his father, a lawyer specialising in labour relations legislation, was much in demand in the seventies and eighties as the motor industry shed most of its workers. His mother had been a primary school teacher; she took time out of her career to raise her son, who knew his alphabet before he was three, and the names of all the dinosaurs in his book by the age of four. His father would tease him by pretending to correct his pronunciation.

"It's Diplódocus, Jake."

"No, Dad, it's not. You know it isn't. It's Diplodócus. Diplodócus."

He was big for his age too, which helped him to shine on the sports field. He was captain of his junior school football team when it won the Birmingham and District Under-12s competition in his last year at primary school.

He won a scholarship to a boys-only public school a few miles from home. Here he coped effortlessly with the various challenges he faced, personal or academic. He took a leading part in the activities offered at the school: drama, the literary society, sport. Some of his teachers were slightly in awe of the range of his intellect and his willingness to give forceful expression to his views. Most of his peers looked up to him, and the breadth of his abilities earned him the nickname of Leonardo, although there were probably some who used it ironically.

Rather than taking a law degree like his father, he announced that he intended studying French and German at university, and that he was turning down the chance to go to Cambridge, in favour of Edinburgh. His mother suspected that he knew that there would be too many stars at Cambridge, and that he preferred to be the centre of his own bright universe. She was touched when, the day before he moved north, he came to thank her for the perfect childhood his parents had given him. Jokingly, he then chided her for not providing him with any misery which he could turn to account once he started to write his novels; how could he be expected to produce a story of angst and regret if the worst memory of his early years was the death of his goldfish? Besides, he'd been told by a cousin who had left home a few years earlier – and whose upbringing had been anything but contented – that young people of his age blossomed once they had escaped the grey repression of home, but that a happy childhood meant university could be a disappointment.

Despite his disadvantage in this matter, he informed her, he fully intended to flourish in Edinburgh.

Once there, he soon made a name for himself. He acted, he wrote, he partied. In the late seventies and early eighties, the cry was "It's Scotland's Oil", and to exploit the comic potential of the nationalist cause, he created for the student review a monstrous Scottish stereotype, Sandy McVitals. Sandy would try to convince his audience that everything worthwhile had been invented by a Scot. He would get cheers initially, when he mentioned steam power, television, golf, whisky, the usual things. Then he'd get more outrageous – Scotch tape, Scotch Corner, Scotch eggs. "All great Scottish inventions," he'd bawl at his audience. "Don't forget it. And then there's Scott of the Antarctic, Jockstraps. Oh, beam me up, Scottie, beam me up!"

Sandy's enemy, of course, was the Englishman. "If an Englishman wishes you a Merry Christmas, you check your diary first, don't you?" He took a delight in misfortunes visited on the English. And not just sporting disasters, that was too easy. For Sandy, floods in Sussex were proof of the existence of a benign deity. Traffic jams in the West Country showed that English drivers lacked sense. Sandy claimed that once, on a flight to London, he'd asked an air steward what happened to the contents of the plane's toilet, and that afterwards he always waited until he was sure he was over the border before relieving himself. He would finish his stage performance by singing all the verses to Loch Lomond, loud, lachrymose and very flat, getting more and more entangled in a grubby tartan flag, which by the end had all but strangled him. Of course, there were members of the audience who saw this as insulting, and sometimes he was heckled. It was puzzling. Why couldn't they see that it was just an act?

In his final year, one of Jake's girlfriends – there were several – shocked him by saying that it was a pity things came to him so easily. She was worried that he was in danger of spreading himself too thinly and leaving university disappointed; a reputation as an entertaining partygoer would be no compensation for a poor degree. He took her advice, stopped performing and concentrated on preparing for finals. After he graduated, with his first-class degree, he told her how grateful he was for her help. Now he needed a new challenge, he said. He was moving to London, where he had got a job working in PR.

At Waverley, as he kissed her goodbye, he was surprised to see the tears in her eyes. Waving from the train, he promised to keep in touch.

Why did he choose PR? Probably because it was another kind of performance; the truth of what you said, or what you wrote, mattered less than the way your material was delivered and the impact it had on others. To be successful, you had to possess the ability to detach yourself from what you were doing, and he had always found it intoxicating to stand to one side and observe his own conduct. On stage as an undergraduate, he'd loved it when audiences had laughed at his jokes. He could see things with their eyes, in a way doubling his own personality. For a moment he was the-man-who-told-the-joke and the-man-who-heard-the-joke at the same time. When he got a bad reaction from his audience, it was the mismatch between the two that he found hard to comprehend.

He had been in London for seven years when he announced, to the surprise of his family and most of his friends, that he was getting married.

Sheila was a work colleague, a few years older than him. She had been briefly married already, to someone she had been at school with. "Too much haste, very little repentance," she said. Jake and Sheila were well suited, hard-working and sociable. After a while they moved to Islington. A good move; the area was starting to become desirable.

Three years later, Sheila and a male colleague set up their own company. Sheila had to deal with the accusation that her new company was stealing business from Jake's old firm, but they seemed to smooth things over pretty well in the end. Sheila and her friend specialised in PR for young celebrities; her husband's firm was more traditional, working mostly with publishers and pressure groups.

They had been married for more than ten years when Jake began to imagine that Sheila was having an affair. It was only to be expected that she would spend a lot of time talking about Piers, the friend she'd set up in business with, but it was another colleague, André, whose name came up more and more when she recounted her working days. They had taken André on as they expanded, and he was clearly something of a star. There was nothing wrong with that, of course; his own office was full of clever people, men and women, and he always had plenty to say about his dealings with them. But it was the way Sheila talked about André that he started to notice. André was the one person in the office who seemed unaffected by the glamour – if that was what it was – associated with their clients. André was always the one who knew when Sheila needed a lift, a bit of flattery or a laugh; he never had moods himself, apparently. Her voice quickened when she mentioned his name. He told himself that he was wrong to react the way he did, and he never revealed how he felt. He could even see, when he analysed the situation dispassionately, that Sheila had just as much cause to feel mistrustful towards him. He had spent weekends away with Pamela, his PA, hadn't he? He had once returned from a trip to Copenhagen with her, and he knew how excited he had been at the deal they had done. He had talked and talked about it, until he realised that Sheila could easily misconstrue his behaviour, though he knew she would have had no cause.

So he tried to forget it, but he was never able to set aside his working habits, what he called his office mind. His suspicions moved from the in-tray to the pending tray, and then to the bottom of the filing cabinet, but they never made it to the shredder. Though his IT skills were more than adequate for his job, on one occasion he had become convinced that he had deleted a day's work by mistake. He was relieved and surprised when a colleague managed to retrieve it all for him. "Things are hardly ever completely wiped," the colleague explained. "There's usually a way of getting them back." It was reassuring in a way, but he wished things could be properly deleted when he wanted them to be. He felt that he needed to know the truth, or rather to be reassured that his suspicions were imaginary; if he didn't ask Sheila, he would go on indefinitely in this state of emotional irritation. He felt stupid and miserable, especially when faced with Sheila's reluctance to discuss any long-term plans. Beyond their planned summer visit to Costa Rica, she didn't seem interested.

What prevented him from raising the subject wasn't just the fear of forcing her into saying something he couldn't bear to hear. It was the realisation that he would have to use all sorts of ridiculous clichés, the ones they'd pointed out to each other with scorn while watching a television drama or a film. They called it Separation Cliché Bingo. "Is there something I should know about?" Tick. "We've always been honest with each other, haven't we?" Tick. "You would tell me if...", and so on. He couldn't bear to imagine himself in the role of the jealous husband, speaking in such an unimaginative way. There had to be a more satisfactory way of asking the question, but he struggled to find one.

Relief from his anxiety came in the most unexpected way. Sheila and André were away for a weekend, setting up some ridiculous stunt for an up-and-coming footballer and his current girlfriend. Before she left, he had asked Sheila jokingly why they couldn't take the photos at Littlehampton and save themselves the expense of the trip to Spain. Her clients, Sheila had explained, wouldn't have liked it. Proper publicity required proper locations; the glamour had to appear genuine. Marbella it had to be.

By now, his work colleagues were mostly family men; their drinking sessions after work on a Friday were a thing of the past. At home, he'd eaten his pasta, finished the bottle of wine from the previous night and checked the television schedules. There was a Polish film on just before midnight, but he wondered if he'd still be awake by then. He was loading the dishwasher when he heard something come through the letterbox. He laughed when he saw that it was the local free newspaper that had been delivered on Fridays over the last few weeks. He and Sheila had often smiled at the pettiness of its contents, though they usually managed to find an item involving someone they know. The crime reports were the best, though recently these had become predictable. "Why can't they do something more original?" Sheila had asked. "Steal some garden gnomes or something? Have a domestic row in church instead of always in the supermarket or the pub?"

The other bit they read, for their own amusement, was the agony column. They had plenty of contacts in newspapers and knew that even in national dailies, when the paper was short of spicy copy, some of the letters had to be invented by office staff. They would amuse themselves trying to guess which letters were genuine and which were fake. The requests for help in the free sheet were usually concerned with acne, adolescent urges, crushes on young teachers. Very occasionally there might be something from a reader uncertain about his or her sexual orientation. 'Aunty Pamela' would counsel caution and point out the social difficulties which might affect the future lives of same-sex couples.

This week's letter wasn't from the usual adolescent, but 'Arthur, 45', and it asked for guidance on how to save his marriage. Arthur suspected his wife was having an affair. Arthur wondered if his fears were in fact groundless, though his wife had certainly been acting differently in recent months. She still loved Arthur, she insisted, but he thought she had become withdrawn and rather forgetful. She mentioned a male work colleague more and more. But Arthur thought that it was probably nothing; perhaps it was just the 'change of life', something like that. But he'd taken to following his wife once or twice when she left the house on her own, but it was only to go the chemists; she had always suffered from migraines.

Arthur came across as self-obsessed, pitiable. Aunty Pamela's advice was clear-cut. Arthur should get the whole thing out of his head, or, if he was really anxious, find a way of talking to his wife about it, ideally through a flippant or humorous remark.

He put the paper down and laughed out loud. He tried to image 'Arthur, 45' finding a witty way of airing his suspicions to his wife, but couldn't. What a loser! And what an idiot *he* was, with his absurd suspicions. He realised that he'd been playing a new role, that of Othello, but failing to draw the obvious conclusion. Desdemona was innocent, for God's sake. That was the whole point, wasn't it? Sheila was innocent as well. She had to be.

For the rest of the weekend, he was happier than he had been for a long time. He had no one to share his delight with, and was too restless to stay in the house. So on the Sunday he took the tube and the DLR to Greenwich, and tramped across the park, over Blackheath, and treated himself to a pub lunch. He returned to the flat and made a chicken casserole, Sheila's favourite. He placed a bottle of white Rioja in the fridge, sat down and waited.

As it was getting dark, he heard the taxi arrive. Sheila seemed to take a long time paying the fare. Eventually, she came in, locked the door behind her and entered the sitting room. He rose to greet her, they embraced. He asked her how the weekend had gone.

"Fine," she said. "Very successful." She took the gin and tonic he offered her and sat down. "It went really well. Everyone was in good form. Oh, chicken casserole sounds good."

When he came back into the room after switching on the oven, Sheila had still not removed her jacket. She was sitting on the sofa, twisting the wine glass in her hand.

"Listen," she said. "I'm sorry, but there's something we need to talk about."

* * *

Sheila and I got divorced four years ago. I've hardly spoken to her since.

It was obvious that it was my own story I was telling, wasn't it? It's just that I found it easier to tell it like this, as if it was happening to someone else. That's how I am. And anyway, if owning up to being the first-person narrator of something you've told in the third person was good enough for Camus in *The Plague*, it's certainly good enough for me.

The break-up wasn't easy. Especially as I'd just convinced myself that everything was going to be all right. It was the loss of self-esteem that was the hardest part. I'd be lying if I denied that. I felt diminished. There didn't seem to be any role for me to play. All the excitement went from my job; it suddenly seemed shallow. Seeing people who had known us as a couple became too painful. Friends tried to make helpful suggestions. I shouldn't blame myself. I should see it as an opportunity to change. I was not yet fifty. And so on. More clichés.

I nearly went under. At a friend's suggestion, I tried a Buddhist retreat, but it was too passive for my tastes. I did spend a week at an outdoor centre somewhere near Fort William, run by a couple from Manchester, and that was more successful. Nothing alternative, no yoga, no meditation. Lots of walking, some fairly tricky scrambling on the Aonach Eagach, wild swimming, building walls. Very different from Islington, but it was the new mental landscape that mattered. You do feel differently when you realise there's nothing between you and a thousand-foot drop except your own concentration and the encouragement of the guy above you.

I've also changed jobs. I now work for an Edinburgh publisher. It's a small outfit, but quite ambitious. I enjoy the work, though there's a lot of networking and glad-handing involved. I am starting to get some of my confidence back. On the whole, it's been a good move. I'm more content in Edinburgh. Fortunately I've yet to meet anyone who remembers Sandy McVitals. Tomorrow we have our annual prize-giving: fiction, non-fiction and short story. I've been asked to officiate, which will be a new departure. It should be OK, though one of the listed titles is by someone I used to know, and that concerns me a bit. We'll have to see how it goes.

The Prize-giving

From his table at the back of the room, Anthony peered at the screen, hoping that his poor eyesight might have confused him. The words came back into focus: *Chairman of the Judges' Panel: Jake Marquand*. No, his eyes hadn't let him down. He put down the glass of white wine and the plate of smoked salmon they had given him at the door, and moved towards the front of the room, squeezing past a couple of people who nodded as if they knew him. In front of the screen, he removed his glasses. There it was, black letters on blue: *Douglas and Ford Short-Story Competition. Edinburgh, Monday 12 September 2005. Chairman of the Judges' Panel: Jake Marquand*. He recognised the names of the first two judges, a well-known novelist and a Tory MP who wrote romantic fiction. The third, he decided, belonged to a children's TV presenter. But his eyes came back to the name at the top.

He cursed himself for not having checked the judges' names when he'd received the email telling him his story had been shortlisted. For some reason, he'd been uneasy at the prospect of his effort being read by someone famous, like the novelist. He'd never thought that it might be assessed by someone that he'd been to school with. It had to be the same

Jake Marquand; he'd always been the literary type. And now here he was, *Commissioning Editor, Poetry and Fiction*. He'd done well for himself.

He turned to the other display, *Shortlisted Titles*. He still hadn't got over his surprise at having his story accepted. But it was there all right: Anthony Barlow, *The Boy in the Garden*. It wasn't the punchiest title, he had to admit, and there were bound to be better efforts than his, but at least there were three prizes, so he had a bit of a chance.

He returned to the back of the room and chose a table in the corner. Looking up, he saw that according to the clock above the platform, it was ten to seven. He'd arrived early, as he usually did. The announcement of the winners wasn't due until half past. He could see that more tables were now occupied, probably by other authors congratulating each other on making the shortlist. He took out his mobile phone, pretended to send a text and closed his eyes.

Would he recognise Marquand if they met? He tried to remember what he'd looked like all those years ago. Taller than most of the others in the class. A black greatcoat, not parkas like just about everyone else. Long hair too, that was part of the image. Some sort of fancy headgear...

Jacksie, that was it. *Jacksie* Marquand, that was what they'd called him, those who weren't in his little clique. Not to his face, of course. It had been one way of getting back at him, since most of the rest of the school had been under his spell, teachers as well as boys. He'd been so well read for a teenager. His copies of the A-level texts had been dog-eared, and he'd made sure you noticed it. There'd been that class on *Godot*; even Mr Lowe had stopped talking and listened. Liked to be the centre of attention. Same with sports. Captain of the football and cricket teams. Couldn't understand why others found things hard. Anthony shuddered at the memory of that catch he'd dropped, and Marquand's scornful reaction. What else? Of course, he'd edited the school magazine. Most of the content had been contributed by the editor; Anthony had always thought of it as *Marquand's Miscellany*. Some of it was pretty good, no question about it; he'd had a way with words. He was fine if you showed how much you were impressed with him. Then you were made welcome, you could share in his aura. But he could be scathing if someone else tried to get stuff into *his* magazine. *What's this, Barlow? Fancy ourselves as a poet, do we?*

Anthony's mobile buzzed. He started and looked around, hoping no one had noticed. He smiled: the text was from his wife. *Good luck A. Never mind glory, £2000 would be useful. Love J.*

She was right. The new kitchen was going to be expensive.

There was another text waiting. From his older daughter, also wishing him luck, and saying that she had picked another two kilos of courgettes, and that the news from the Oval was good.

Before he could finish his reply, a short middle-aged woman appeared from nowhere and, after looking around at the other tables, asked if she could join him.

"Yes, please do," he said. "No, you're not interrupting. I was just turning my phone off. Nice to meet you. I'm Anthony Barlow."

As she sat down, she introduced herself as Charlotte McBain. Anthony noticed the quality of her trousers and jacket; her hairstyle looked expensive too. Then he remembered reading something by C. McBain in one of the weekend supplements and immediately felt uncomfortable.

Before he could think of anything to say, she began to ask

him about his story. He mumbled something about gardening, and said no, he'd never been shortlisted before. This was the first time for him; he blushed at his choice of words.

"Yes, the competition is always strong for the Douglas and Ford. Still, one never knows, does one?"

He had started to ask her what her story was about when he heard a man's voice calling his name.

"Tony! Tony Barlow!"

They turned and saw a tall, balding man moving towards them, hand outstretched. Anthony recognised him immediately, then realised he had to introduce him.

"Er... Charlotte, this is, er... Jack... Jake Marquand, the chairman of the panel. We know... we both went to..."

"Burnham Park, Charlotte, Burnham Park," the chairman interrupted. "A minor though rather pretentious public school in the badlands of Birmingham. My pleasure, Charlotte. Yes, Tony and I go back a long, long way. Twenty years? More? It's so good to meet again, Tony. You see, Charlotte, Tony and I had the mixed fortune of attending one of those schools that aimed to make men of their charges by beating irregular French verbs into them. Yes. Made us who we are. Can you believe it, they actually made us learn things by heart! The monsters! Tony here was the star linguist. No one could handle French subjunctives quite like him. And now he's a writer! That *Gardener's Tale* of yours is a little gem, Tony. I always knew you had talent, back in the days of the Monday afternoon lit soc, and Friday night gigs with Slasher Morgan and the Transplants. Oh, weren't you in the group? That's funny, I have a vivid image of you on bass guitar. Well, the memory plays tricks, doesn't it? Isn't it wonderful to be here in the land of the thick black cloud, in the city of Boswell and

Hume, Stevenson, Spark and... and... oh so many others. Look, I'd better move along. We have one last judges' meeting before the announcement. Though the deed is done, of course. Well, fingers crossed, everybody. Catch up with you later."

Anthony saw Charlotte suppressing a smile as the chairman left them.

"Oh my word, what a performance! 'Fingers crossed, everybody.' He made me feel like a sixth-former. I must admit I've never heard of the school he mentioned. Were you really in a rock group?"

"No, of course not. It was a different Anthony. He was just looking for things to say."

"I rather thought so. You don't look the type, if you don't mind me saying so. Listen, Anthony, I need some more wine, and so do you. I'll be back in a minute."

Anthony watched Charlotte move towards the front of the room, but his eye was caught by the sight of Marquand shaking hands and sharing a word with just about everyone, then disappearing through the door at the side of the platform.

When Charlotte returned with the refilled glasses and another plate of salmon, she put them down and leaned over the table.

"I've just realised that I met Jake Marquand last night. He obviously didn't recognise me just now, but as he said, we all forget faces. It was a different gathering; there were lots of publishing people there. He's entertaining enough, I suppose, but a little of him goes a long way. Were you really in the same class, by the way? He looks older than you."

Anthony laughed.

"We're the same age. They always said I looked young for my age. Jake was always clever, good with words. Ambitious as well."

"And a bully."

Anthony was taken aback.

"I suppose so. How could you tell?"

Charlotte took a drink from her glass and looked around before answering.

"I was watching your reaction. You did seem rather uncomfortable. He gave me the impression that he was trying to be extra friendly toward you, making up for the past perhaps. It was all a bit forced. That's how it appeared to me. I suppose you start to look for this sort of thing, don't you? If you're trying to work people out, seeing if you could turn them into characters of your own. I haven't read your story. I avoid the other offerings, even after they have appeared online. I'm always a bit afraid of what the opposition has come up with."

Anthony forced a smile.

"I'm sure you don't need to. I think I read a piece of yours not so long ago. In the *Scotsman on Sunday*, wasn't it?"

"Did you? That's good. Have you had anything...?"

Anthony shook his head and looked away and towards the platform, where the chairman was showing the other judges to their seats. Charlotte followed his gaze.

"From what our chairman said, your story must be about gardening."

"In a way. But the gardening's only a framework, really. It's always been a thing of mine. I've always loved growing things. My daughters are keen too. When I was a kid, some people thought it was odd. I used to get stick about it."

"From Jake Marquand no doubt. He was probably envious. People like that seem to resent it when the person they're bullying has something they have no control over..."

"Another glass, Charlotte? We've just got time."

"That would be nice. The Mâcon, please."

Returning with their glasses, this time Anthony had some difficulty negotiating the spaces between the tables. He could see that some of them were not going to be occupied: the short-story competition clearly had less prestige than the other ones, whose prizes had been handed out earlier.

Charlotte sniffed the wine before tasting it.

"Mm, not bad. Incidentally, do you ever wonder how the judges choose the winners? Sebastian, of course, he knows what he's doing. They were very lucky to get him. Have you read his latest? Really very good indeed. But you can't say the same for our MP's efforts. Banal and pretentious at the same time, which is quite an achievement. And I really have no idea what Deirdre Petersham's qualifications are for sitting on this panel. She can just about manage an auto-cue on a good day. Ah, I think the firing squad is mounting the stage."

They turned to see the spokeswoman for Douglas and Ford testing the microphone and introducing the chairman and judges as they took their places on the platform. Each name was greeted by polite applause. Anthony finished his glass and leaned over towards Charlotte.

"What's your story called, Charlotte? Then I'll know when to clap."

"*Never Talk to a Writer*. Seriously. Do you have your winner's speech ready?"

Anthony lowered his voice.

"Ladies and gentleman, I'm delighted to receive this prize from Jacksie Marquand, who was an absolute shit as a schoolboy and, judging by the conversation I've just had with him, hasn't improved much these last twenty-five years. I'd like to tell you about the time..."

Charlotte laughed.

"No, that won't do. You don't want to make enemies. Not yet, anyway. And why Jacksie, for goodness sake?"

"That was his nickname at school. If you didn't like him, you'd mutter *Up yours, Jacksie*, behind his back. Oh, people are looking at us. Here we go."

The chairman thanked everyone for coming and explained that, in a break with tradition, he was going to start by announcing the winner of the first prize. As he outlined what the judges had found so compelling in the winning entry, Anthony could tell from the phrases he was using – *acute social awareness... language of the street... a voice for the voiceless* – that he wasn't talking about *The Boy in the Garden*.

Charlotte scowled, folded her arms and looked straight ahead.

The announcement of the second prize was no more encouraging – *inter-generational conflicts... multicultural challenges...*

After the applause had died down, the chairman explained that, in contrast, what the panel had liked about the story which had won the third prize was its more traditional content, its celebration of – dare he say it? – bourgeois values. Anthony felt his cheeks flush as he heard how they had been enchanted by a simple little story depicting one boy's hobby, and the way it had enriched his family's life. He wasn't sure what the chairman meant by the paradigmatic function of the act of gardening, but sorting that out could wait. He'd won third prize!

Hearing his name read out was unnerving, much more so than he'd imagined. Charlotte patted his arm; he could see that she was trying hard to be pleased on his behalf.

As he got clumsily to his feet, he heard her whisper.

"Remember, no insults. Wait till you're famous to get your revenge."

Mustn't fall over, he kept telling himself as he made his way between the tables. Thirty seconds to make up his mind. Surely it would be churlish to be uncomplimentary to someone who was giving you a prize? But wouldn't it be wonderful to tell everyone what Jake Marquand was really like!

He took the chairman's outstretched hand, felt the friendly arm on his shoulder.

"Congratulations, Tony. That is a fine story you gave us. Ladies and gentlemen, I ought to say that Tony Barlow and I attended the same Neanderthal educational establishment, back in the days when I still had some of my own hair and before the verb *to be like* had become a synonym of *to say*. Yes. But we survived. And we seem to have prospered, in our separate ways. But I can assure you that there have been no favours repaid, no backs scratched. *The Boy in the Garden*, Tony's delightfully understated story, is a worthy winner of our third prize. Many congratulations, Tony; I do hope there will be more stories to come."

Anthony pocketed the envelope and forced himself to look the chairman in the eye.

"Thank you very much. I'm... I really wasn't expecting to have to say anything today, but of course I'm delighted to have won the third prize. As Jake says, we were at school together many years ago, so it's especially pleasing to receive this prize from him."

The two men shook hands again. Anthony leaned a little closer to Marquand's ear, away from the microphone, and whispered, "Yeah, thanks again, Jacksie."

He retained Marquand's hand just long enough to feel it

twitch as it was withdrawn. And as he watched the other man's face, he saw a glimmer of discomfort. It was enough.

Returning to his table, he looked at Charlotte for her reaction.

"Nicely done. I don't know what you said at the end there, but I definitely saw a wee squirm. But no real damage done, I'd say."

"Thanks, Charlotte. Look, let me buy you something to eat. To celebrate. There's a bistro a couple of doors along. I'll just phone my wife and tell her the news. I need a bit of air. See you in a minute."

The room was beginning to empty. As he made his way to the door, a few of the other authors stopped to congratulate him. He wondered if he'd ever have the chance to get used to this. But he was relieved to see that on the platform, Marquand had his back to him, in eager conversation with the MP.

As he stepped outside into George Street, he saw that it was getting dark and that the drizzle had set in. He took out his mobile. Despite several deep breaths, his fingers were still trembling as he dialled.

There was no reply, so he sent a text:

Small glory. £500 towards new units. Love A.

PART TWO

Spring 2010

Araucaria

The three shoppers looked through the doors of the garden centre, towards the trees and shrubs displayed outside. Peering over her glasses, the older of the two women spoke quietly but decisively.

"I think your father's ready for home."

The young couple with her – the woman visibly pregnant, the man with a protective hand on her shoulder – agreed. They'd had to flatter him into joining them by saying how much his advice would be appreciated. After just half an hour looking at decking and garden furniture, he'd wandered off on his own.

They collected one last set of brochures and walked over to where he was bending down inspecting the bushes. He straightened up and attempted a smile.

"Did you get what you wanted? Enough information?"

"We've got plenty, Dad. You look as though you're past your boredom threshold."

"Yes, Jonathan, I think I am. Mind, they do have some nice things here. Some lovely forsythias. But have a look at this before we go."

He led them past the potentillas, the dogwood, the daphnes, towards the bigger trees. Among the acers and cherries, he pointed to a strongly growing bush with stiff twisted branches and glossy leaves.

They bent down to read the label. The younger man's attempts to pronounce what it said were cut short.

"It's an araucaria."

"Is that what it is, Dad? Funny-looking thing. Are you saying it would look good at the front of the house?"

"No, no. No idea why people want to grow them up here. It's hardly a tree for Perth, is it, though you do get some in the big Scottish estates. South America, that's where it comes from. It's the national tree of Chile. Not exactly native. And look at the price."

"Come on, Dad. We've got the message."

They were making their way back to the car park when the younger man, pleased for once to be able to show some gardening knowledge, broke the silence.

"I've just remembered. I was looking at one of those trees the other day. There's one in a garden down the road from us. The chap who lives there did tell me its proper name, but he said most people call it a monkey puzzle tree."

Half an hour later, they had reached the newly built suburban house, with its front garden containing nothing but piles of stones and muddy rubble.

The younger couple got out of the car and offered tea and cake.

The older woman smiled but shook her head.

"It's kind of you, but we won't come in this time, Jonathan. I've got a lot to do."

"OK. Well, thanks a lot, both of you. We've got some ideas, now. And Claire really likes the idea of raised beds. You know, for herbs and vegetables. Just need a bit of dry weather."

They unloaded the supermarket shopping from the boot.

"See you on Sunday, then. You haven't forgotten, Dad, have you?"

Jonathan grinned as he saw his father scowl. He knew he pretended to hate celebrating his birthday, but secretly liked to be the centre of attention once in a while.

"Come round about one, if that's OK. Claire's got some Stella in especially for you."

"She's got some *what?* I hope you're joking."

"Of course I'm joking. We stocked up at Inveralmond yesterday morning. We know how to look after you."

"Thank goodness. Well, see you on Sunday. I hope you voted the right way."

* * *

The overnight rain had made the front garden boggier than ever. The smell of coffee still made his wife feel nauseous, so he put the kettle on for tea. He'd fetch some fresh bread once he'd had his shower.

Peering out of the kitchen window, he tried to imagine how it might look. They had been told how patient they would need to be. At the same time, he knew that this first summer would be important. They wanted to make as much progress as possible before the baby arrived. Some roses, a hedge down the side, decking at the back... Yes, decking, despite what the old man thought.

He switched on the television. They had both become bored with the endless election campaign. At least it was over now. The only time they'd really paid attention was when the talk was about the NHS. Claire was particularly anxious, though they knew that the Royal had a good reputation.

When Claire came down for breakfast an hour later, they tried to make sense of the election result.

A sleepy-looking commentator was standing in front of a pie chart made up of different colours: mostly blue and orange, with some red. The message seemed to be that no one knew exactly what was going to happen next, except that Gordon Brown was on his way out.

"Can't say it'll make much difference to us up here. But Dad won't be pleased. You know what he thinks about Cameron and his rich friends."

His wife grimaced.

"God, that was a big kick. This baby doesn't approve of the Conservative Party."

"Takes after his grandfather then. Or her grandfather. Bread, cereal, bananas – anything else? I'll be back as soon as I can."

It was nearly an hour later when he returned. Claire was still lying on the sofa with her feet up. The morning sickness had gone on and on; she was only back at work three days a week.

"Sorry I took so long. You'll never guess. I got talking to the man with the monkey puzzle tree again."

He explained that he'd seen their neighbours working in their garden and they'd started to chat. The husband asked to be called Ernest; he said his full name was too complicated. He hadn't caught his wife's name. He hadn't been able to get away. That was why he was late. He'd complimented Ernest on his garden; it was so neat and tidy, with daffodils, tulips and other bulbs he hadn't recognised. But just to show that he wasn't totally ignorant, he'd said he now knew the proper name for the tree in the middle of the lawn. The funny thing was that when he said this, his neighbour seemed to shake a bit, and needed to steady himself by leaning against the fence. But he'd pulled himself together and said yes, that was the Latin name for it, and it was the national tree of Chile. Then he'd said that once the spring bulbs had finished flowering and he'd had time to sort them out, he'd be happy to hand over any spare ones; it was always a pleasure to help someone who was just starting out.

"Nice guy. Seemed pleased to have a chat. Shall I toast this bread?"

* * *

"Cheers. Happy Birthday."

"Cheers. Thanks, both of you."

They looked at the spread Claire had put together on the kitchen table, mostly, she'd admitted, from the local caterers.

"And don't look so glum, Dad. The Tories don't look like they'll have a majority on their own."

"Get him a beer, Jonathan. That should cheer him up. Claire, love, how are you...?"

Claire made a vomiting gesture.

"Just mineral water, please. No, it is getting better, slowly, but things still don't seem to taste right. Let's eat, anyhow."

"Thanks, Claire. It's good of you to ask us over. And think about it. Next birthday, we'll be grandparents. And your garden will be starting to show some colour. It won't rain all summer."

"You haven't unwrapped your present, Dad."

The sixty-five-year-old removed the paper from the flat, cylindrical object. The others tried to keep a straight face.

He forced a laugh when he saw what it was.

"Well, that's great. Chicken manure. How much...? Five

kilos. Perfect. I'll get on with spreading it tomorrow if it's fit. Proper gardening. Much more fun than decking. Thank you very much. Now, let's start on those samosas."

A couple of beers, family news, some photos of the Saga tour to Austria: a quiet afternoon. They were careful not to tire Claire. As they were getting ready to leave, Jonathan remembered what had been at the back of his mind.

"Oh, I forgot to say. You know the man I told you about, Dad, the one with the tree…"

"…the araucaria…"

"That's the one. I got talking to him again. Ernest, he's called. Not local, speaks with a bit of a foreign accent. Anyhow, I was saying what a lovely garden he had, and he promised me some of his spare bulbs, once they'd finished flowering."

Jonathan's mother collected her belongings.

"That was good of him. People do like to share their plants. Your dad and I got some lovely things from my parents when we first came up here. Not all of them survived, mind. They'd no idea how much colder it is up here. Remember that camellia, Mark?"

"Never stood a chance. But you're right, it's a nice thing to do. This chap, you said he had a foreign accent. Did he tell you where he's from? How old, would you say?"

"Not young. Sixty? Maybe more. On the frail side, even a bit shaky. Friendly guy. I'll probably be seeing him again. I'm not offshore for another couple of weeks. Why…?"

"Just curious. It is an unusual tree for a garden, in these parts. Or it was before gardening got trendy. Well, we'll pop round later in the week to give you a hand, if it clears up."

* * *

It was only half an hour later, as Jonathan was loading the dishwasher, that the doorbell rang. On the step, he found a stocky elderly woman, nervously rubbing her hands together. As he tried to place her, she looked up and said:

"Ernesto is ill. He has had..."

She rolled her eyes and rocked backwards. Jonathan leaned forward, fearing she would fall. She steadied herself and repeated her words:

"My man, Ernesto, has had a..."

Ernesto, he thought... right, the wife of the man with the tree. He'd had a stroke, was that what she was trying to say? But why had she come here?

The woman was already rushing back down the drive to the road. Jonathan started to follow but pulled up.

"Just a minute. I'll have to tell my wife."

Two minutes later, the woman hurried him through her front door and into the kitchen at the front of the house. Ernest was slumped into an armchair but seemed able to focus on the new arrival. Jonathan tried to remember his first-aid drill. He asked Ernest his name and got a clear reply: that was good. Ernest could open his mouth and show teeth on both sides. He could raise both arms.

"Right, Ernest. If it is a stroke, it doesn't look like a bad one, though I'm not an expert. We'll have to get you to the Royal to make sure. I'll just pop back and get my car. It'll be quicker than an ambulance; it's only ten minutes from here. Perhaps your wife could..."

The old man interrupted, shaking his head and trying to get out of the chair. It wasn't what Jonathan had expected. He looked at Ernest's wife.

"He does not like hospital. Bad memories."

She then said something in a language that Jonathan didn't understand, though he thought it sounded like Spanish. Her husband seemed reassured, even managed a weak smile, nodded towards his wife.

"Go for your car, please. I'll get ready."

As they drove the two miles to the Infirmary, Jonathan kept hoping that there wouldn't be long delays at A & E. The receptionist was friendly and efficient. Ernest and his wife were made comfortable and promised that a doctor would see them as soon as possible. They thanked their driver. Jonathan wrote down his phone number on a bit of paper, handed it to Ernest's wife and asked them to get in touch; he really had to get back to his wife.

* * *

The rain had stopped, and a weak sun was already above the roof of the next house in the street.

"Yes, thanks. I did sleep much better. You know what, I fancy a cooked breakfast."

"Really? What have we got? There's some bacon..."

Before they could decide, they were interrupted by the phone ringing in the hall.

By the time Jonathan returned to the kitchen, Claire was filling two coffee cups.

"That was Mrs... Ernesto's wife. I still don't know their surname. Anyhow, seems it wasn't a stroke. Might be a sign of diabetes, she said. They're doing tests, but he should be out by this afternoon. Sounds like good news. Can I have some bacon even if I'm not pregnant? I'll put some more on."

They sat down at the table, added milk to their coffee. Claire picked up her mobile to check for messages, then switched it off.

"Well, you certainly did your good deed yesterday. Proper Good Samaritan. No, I don't mean... and it's always useful to know the quickest way to the hospital. But I still don't see why she came here."

"I don't think they know their neighbours all that well. According to Mum, these houses are changing hands all the time. Ernest knew where we lived because I'd told him about the garden, and... well, that swamp out the front is pretty distinctive, isn't it? I'll see what I can do now it's brightened up."

By early afternoon, he was up to his ankles in mud, loading a barrow with clay, broken bricks and odd bits of wood. He looked up when he heard what sounded like his name being spoken from the pavement.

"Mr Amritage..."

"Sorry?"

Then he saw that it was Ernest's wife, peering at the name on the number plate of their house.

"No, it's Armitage. But I agree, could be clearer. How's Ernest?"

Ernesto was much better, she said. Resting at home. He had an appointment for the end of the week. She said how grateful she was for the lift to the hospital.

"Not at all. Glad to be able to help. I'm pleased it doesn't sound too serious."

He could see she was wanting to say something else and was going to ask her in to meet Claire, when she said that she and her husband would like them to come round for a bit of food, to thank him for his help.

"That's very kind. Yes, it would be nice. Only thing is, Claire is five months pregnant, and she's not finding it easy to get the right food."

"Ah, I understand it. But I can find some of my Chilean dishes which are tasty but also very easy for digestion."

"Thank you. I'll tell Claire. When..."

"Will you be free on Wednesday? Come around at about four o'clock of the afternoon, if you can."

He thanked her; they were about to shake hands until she saw how muddy he was. She smiled her goodbyes. He went to the front door, removed his boots and went inside.

* * *

Ernest's wife named the cakes as she served them.

"This we call 'Arm of a Queen'. It's a caramel cake. And this is 'Heart of Coffee'. It's like a boat, no? I hope you like tea. Chileans drink a lot of tea. You British do too."

They were sitting in the room at the back of the house, overlooking a neatly landscaped garden, invisible from the road. The room was traditionally furnished: three-piece suite, coffee table, bookcases either side of a gas fire.

Claire accepted another cake. Perhaps her appetite was returning at last.

Confusion over surnames proved a good ice-breaker. Jonathan explained that, no, Armitage wasn't a Scottish name. His father came from Derby, where he'd met his mother when she was there on a training course. Then his father had got a lecturing job at Dundee, and they'd moved north, intending to stay for a couple of years, but they'd found a house in Strath Earn and really got to love the area. They'd never gone back, though he knew his mum sometimes missed the warmth of the south-west of England. Claire was from Dundee; she and Jonathan had met at the local football stadium, of all places, when St Johnstone had been playing Dundee United. (He thought he saw Ernest wince: what was that about?) He added that Claire was a McDougall, which was a proper Scottish name.

There was a pause, then Claire patted her belly and said, "So if I have a girl, she might be Emma McDougall Armitage. We sometimes use the mother's maiden name as a middle name."

Ernest smiled.

"That's a nice idea. If you think that's complicated, you know how it is with Spanish surnames?"

Blank looks.

"Well, you take your father's name and then your mother's, with a hyphen. I'm Ernesto Calderon-Quiroga."

"And I'm Juanita Vincente-Gonzalez."

Jonathan laughed.

"I can see why you said Ernest was easier."

Claire thought for a moment.

"And your children, Mrs..."

"Please call me Juanita. So... if we had had children, it might have been Jaime Calderon-Vincente. But..."

An awkward pause. More tea was poured. To break the silence, Claire asked about the photos on the bookcase. The ones in the formal clothing were of parents and relatives, explained Ernest. They had died long ago. The other photos were of younger people. These were friends; sadly, many of them were dead too.

After a pause, Jonathan asked the question that had been at the back of his mind for some time.

"What made you come to Scotland? It wasn't the climate, I'll bet."

Ernest looked at the photos again and seemed about to bring some over to talk about them. But he hesitated and the moment was gone. Then he explained that they had left Chile in 1975, during the period of military dictatorship. His eyes sought a reaction on their guests' faces but found little. There had been a military coup, he continued, then a time of repression. The enemies of the regime had been persecuted, rounded up, tortured. Many had been killed.

Suddenly, Jonathan found a way into the conversation.

"I remember something now. Wasn't there an old Chilean president in England a few years ago? Didn't he get arrested or something, and then Margaret Thatcher took his side. Why was that?"

"Yes, that was Pinochet. The dictator. Mrs Thatcher supported him because he had helped her with the Falklands invasion."

Jonathan wondered what he meant by *invasion*, but as he leaned forward for Juanita to refill his cup, his eye was caught again by the photos. He hesitated.

"Were you...? Did your friends...?"

For a while there was silence. It was Juanita who answered. Taking her husband's hand, she told them that they had been lucky, they had managed to leave. Many of their friends had not been lucky. The photos helped to keep their memory alive.

Neither guest could think of the right thing to say. The pause lengthened. Jonathan looked at Ernest, now staring through the patio doors into the garden; he thought he suddenly looked much older. He caught Claire's eye.

Yes, she said, she was beginning to feel a bit tired; perhaps it was time for the two of them to be heading back home?

Ernest insisted on rising from his chair. He and his wife

said how much they had enjoyed having someone to visit them, and that they looked forward to the next time.

Once Claire and Jonathan were on their feet, they could see how much effort had gone into the landscaping of the back garden. From the patio doors, steps led down through a wooden arch and across a lawn to a summerhouse at the far end. Despite the cool weather, late bulbs provided colour everywhere; tall bushes with different coloured foliage hid the walls of the gardens on either side.

Jonathan thought of a way to compensate for his embarrassment.

"Your back garden is really something. Look... would you mind... my mum and dad would love to see it some time. Could they come and have a look?"

"Of course. Just let us know; we're here all the time. Apart from my hospital appointment of course. That's tomorrow."

They went through to the kitchen and Ernest unlocked and opened the front door. He and Juanita stayed in the doorway as their visitors stepped outside, Jonathan taking Claire's hand as she negotiated the step. They turned and waved.

"Thank you again. We both really enjoyed the afternoon. I'll phone my dad and get back to you. Take care."

* * *

Sitting in easy chairs by the patio doors, Claire and Juanita watched the three men inspecting plants, picking up the odd bit of debris, making their way towards the summerhouse.

Claire helped herself to another cake.

"I'm really pleased that the hospital hasn't found anything seriously wrong with Ernest. He's looking much better. The men certainly seem to be finding plenty to talk about, don't they? Mark and Janet – that's Jonathan's mum and dad – they're both terrific gardeners, you know. Janet's really sorry she can't come, but she's been asked to fill in at the CAB in Stirling again. They always seem to be short-staffed there."

She saw the puzzled look on Juanita's face.

"The CAB, that's the Citizens Advice Bureau. They help people who have problems... debt, personal difficulties, that sort of thing."

"Do they deal with refugees?"

Claire was not sure, but said that she thought they did. She decided to bring the conversation back to gardening; it seemed the easiest topic.

"You know, it's funny watching Mark and Janet when they're working in their own garden. They both get on with their own jobs. Then they'll sit down and look at what the other one's done, and occasionally say something complimentary. But they keep out of each other's way. They think we're impatient with our garden plans. Probably right too. But we would like to have something done before the baby comes. I'm sorry we left a bit suddenly the other day. Jonathan is always fretting that I'll get too tired. And I'm afraid we don't know a lot about your country, and what you must have..."

"Don't worry. We understand."

"Jonathan's dad is much better informed than we are about that kind of thing."

As she spoke, her husband opened the patio doors, carefully wiped his shoes on the mat and came into the sitting room. He beamed when he saw how many cakes had disappeared from the plate.

"Well, you'd have thought those two had known each other all their lives. It's great. I couldn't get a word in."

They looked through the glass doors, but the garden was now empty. The two older men had disappeared into the summerhouse and were deep in conversation, leaning forward on the wooden bench.

Before Juanita could refill Jonathan's cup, his mobile rang. He walked towards the kitchen, and when he returned, his face was clouded.

"Sorry, I... I've got to go offshore tomorrow. It wasn't supposed to be till next week. Some problem on the rig. Still, it means I should get back home sooner. I'd better go and tell my dad. If you'll excuse me."

Juanita put a hesitant hand on his arm.

"Perhaps you could leave the two of them to talk a little longer? Ernesto sometimes likes to... what is it you say? Unburden himself, I think that's it. He doesn't get many chances now. I promised to show some recipes to Claire. Not your cup of tea?"

Jonathan laughed.

"Not really. But I'll tell you what, I'll pop home, do a bit of packing and come back in an hour. That should give them enough time?"

"That would be perfect, Jonathan. Thank you."

* * *

"It was a bloody awful time they had, the two of them. We really can't imagine."

Jonathan had checked the train times and found that to get to Dyce in time for his helicopter flight, it would have meant leaving just after five. So he'd gladly accepted his father's offer of a lift to the airport. The Kingsway around Dundee had been slow, but now they were making good time, dropping down the hill towards Forfar, the Angus glens on their left shining in the morning sun. At the start of the drive, his father had said little: nothing unusual in that. But after a while, he'd begun to relate what Ernest had told him in the summerhouse.

Ernesto and Juanita had been members of the Socialist Party of Chile, he said. The party had come to power as part of a left-wing coalition in 1970. Ernesto had explained that the coalition had won less than 40% of the votes, but they were the largest group, and they decided to do what they had promised to do.

"He said they were right to do what they did, even without an overall majority. That was their system. It was like ours. And if it works for parties of the right, why shouldn't it work for parties of the left? I agreed with him."

The new policies had been unpopular with the middle classes, who had most to lose. The country had been destabilised, with strikes and financial problems.

"Hang on a minute, Dad. Just let me check the flight details."

Jonathan deftly flicked the screen on his phone.

"OK, no problems. As long as we're there by ten. Go on, Dad."

"Well, there was a coup. Organised by the Americans, the CIA. President killed, military rule. No one was surprised. But what followed was more brutal than even the Americans had expected. Ernest gave me some of the details. A lot of it I knew already. They rounded people up, using football stadiums. There was the story of the singer, a protester. They broke his fingers one by one, then killed him. Ernest saw it. He said he'd been trying to hide in Juanita's parents' house after the coup, but they'd found them both, taken them to separate camps. That was the worst, he said, not knowing what had happened to each other. In the end, he'd been released. Just like that. Juanita too. They'd met up at her parents' house again. Some strings had been pulled. Juanita's father had been quite high up in earlier governments. They got out. Paris first, then Berlin. Then someone found Ernest a job teaching Spanish at Perth Grammar. They'd been made so welcome that they settled here. Ernest retired a couple of years ago."

"Christ. I'd no idea what had happened to them. When we were talking about the photos on the shelves, they said they were of friends who'd died. Ernest and his wife, they were ones who got away, then."

"Yes. But it can't have been easy for them either."

"I know. Survivor guilt, I suppose. We got a lot about that when they were giving us counselling after the helicopter crash."

Approaching Stonehaven, they were stopped by roadworks. As they waited for the green light, the driver took his hands from the wheel, sighed and spread his hands.

"You have to feel sorry for them. Ernest seemed to want to talk, but at the same time kept holding back. But you know what was worst? When Juanita was taken in, she was pregnant. They beat her up so much she lost the baby."

The traffic started to move. An hour later, queuing at the traffic lights at the entrance to the terminal, Jonathan's father leaned over and picked up a small packet from the rear seat and handed it over.

"There were a couple of other things Ernest said. The monkey puzzle in the front lawn. They brought it over from Chile, as a seedling, kept it growing in Paris and Berlin. Then brought it to Scotland. Apparently other exiles did the same. You can understand why, can't you?"

The car was moving forward again.

"Yes, it must help them a bit. What was the other thing?"

"This book. Ernest asked me if I'd read it. I have. It's about Chile, about those times. But about other things too. The writer came from the same family as the president. Why don't you take it offshore with you?"

They pulled in to the drop-off point. Jonathan got out and opened the rear door, picked up his holdall and slipped the book inside, glancing at the title: *The House of the Spirits*.

"Thanks, Dad. For the lift and everything. I'll look at the book tonight, once I'm sorted out. There's always plenty of free time. Well, see you all in three weeks. Look after Claire."

A quick embrace, and the younger man marched off to the terminal. His father watched him go and drove away, keeping out of the bus lane until he reached the traffic lights where he turned towards Aberdeen and the South, wondering if his son would read the book he'd given him.

A Change of Direction

Right. I'm Dave Henderson. You know you said it'd be good to talk. I hope you're right. Because this is going to be bloody embarrassing for me. Probably for you as well. Anyhow, you've all said your piece, told everyone why you're here. And it's my turn now, so I'll have to get it off my chest.

About six months ago, I was accused of inappropriate behaviour towards two teenage girls.

Thought that might shake you up a bit. I can see from your faces. You're thinking, I didn't realise we'd get people like that in the group.

But don't worry. I didn't do anything.

You all reckon you've got really stressful jobs, don't you? Estate agents, teachers, fund managers, whatever that means. And it was the stress that got to you, that's why you're here. Well, I used to be an HGV driver. No stress in that, is there? You just keep on down the motorway, everyone gets out of your way. You listen to the radio to avoid the jams, stop for your greasy spoon. Keep the weekends free for the family if you can. If you've got to stop overnight, there's always entertainment on offer if you know where to look for it.

I bet that's how you see it. Maybe it was, once. But it's not like that now, I'm telling you. Deadlines are getting tighter all the time, and if you want decent money, you've got to flog your guts out. Your company'll tell you they've got to match the competition, and sorry, but you'll do your fifty, fifty-five hours, without a bonus. You do it, but it's no joke. Maybe this new government will deal with all the immigrants we've got, taking our jobs. Half the truckers are Poles or Lithuanians.

It was last spring when it all started to go wrong for me. I'm not from this part of the world. You've probably guessed. I was brought up in Stevenage, north of London. But Marie – that's my wife – she's Scottish. We met on holiday in Alicante ten years ago and we lived down south for a bit, but Marie always wanted to come back to Stirling, so I got a job here. Can't say I miss Stevenage.

I'd been working for this firm for five, six years. Up and down the bloody A9. Starting at Kinross, then Perth, Inverness. Sometimes up to Wick. Six days a week usually. Pay was good, but it was all starting to get to me. I wasn't nice to be with. Marie was glad to see the back of me when I set off in the morning. Anything would get me rattled – motorway repairs, wind and rain, dozy drivers. I know what you're thinking. Typical bloody lorry driver, doesn't give a toss for anyone else on the road. But I'm telling you, when driving's your job, and you've got delivery times to meet, and there's some daft pillock blocking the middle lane... I swear there are some drivers that don't even know HGVs aren't allowed in the outside lane. And don't get me started on caravans.

It wasn't just the roads either. The transport caffs got to me as well. I hated the food there. It was all Scotch pies, haggis and stuff. I could never get a proper cup of tea either. I'd got all ratty, and if anyone tried to push in front of me in a queue, they'd get a mouthful. Then someone'd tell me to piss off back to England. I was even threatened with being barred at one place. Can you imagine that, being barred from a bloody transport caff?

I ended up in trouble, didn't I? Should have seen it coming. Funny thing was, I'd started off in a good mood for once. Nice dry morning. I even had a weekend off to look forward to. I'd pulled in at Newtonmore to get some sandwiches for lunch, and I was ready to get back on the dual carriageway. This car was blocking the exit – the driver was just sitting there. I waited a bit, then hit the horn. The truck behind me did the same. Nothing happened. In the end, I got out, shouted at him to get a move on. Anyway, seems this guy was having some sort of attack. Just my luck, a police car rolled up. The copper got out, asked what was going on. Like a fool, I started arguing. He took my name, told me to watch my language and stuff. Then the ambulance rolled up. Well, I got off with a warning, but when the news got through to my boss, he jumped at the chance to get rid of me. Suited them fine. Part of their down-sizing policy, they told me after. Thank you very much.

Obviously, we couldn't afford to keep the car. Marie has to get the bus to work. Takes her nearly an hour each way. She works at the hospital, in admin. Loves it, she's really good with people. I could never do her job. Bet that doesn't surprise you.

At first I quite enjoyed having a lie in. Marie would bring me a cup of tea before she left. But soon I was starting to stay in bed later and later. Sometimes Marie would come back, and I still hadn't got going. There didn't seem to be anything to get up for. It'd have been different if we'd had kids, but it was starting to look like we wouldn't be able to.

Eventually, Marie had to bully me into doing normal things

like getting dressed, shaving. She'd force me to go out, send me to the shops. She was worried I'd get into trouble again; she could see I was getting all aggressive. After a few months, she said she couldn't stand it any longer. She said, Dave, you're going to have to see someone, get some help. We went to the medical centre, talked to the GP. He said he'd get me an appointment at the Lawrence Institute.

Christ, I knew what that meant. The white-coat brigade. That put the wind up me. At the centre, they gave me this form to fill in. What were my hopes for the future, crap like that. I wanted to put what about a driving job and less idiots on the road but thought I'd better not. You had to say if you'd ever thought about a different career. I'd wondered sometimes about being a teacher. I'd always got on well with kids, used to take my sister's kids fishing, to football practice, that sort of thing. But having to go with no pay when I did the training, that had put me off. When I went for my first appointment, they made a big thing of it, said it might be worth applying to do teacher training. There was always a shortage of teachers, apparently. I said I'd think about it.

Listen, I am getting to the point. About the girls, I mean. I just thought you ought to know what happened before.

At the Lawrence, they also said I ought to take up walking. They said it would be good for me, regular activity, change of routine, all that. I've never liked people telling me what to do. Walking seemed bloody pointless. I'd spent all my working life behind the wheel, hadn't I? But Marie said to give it a go. She was right, as usual. It was hard getting started, but what I really liked, once I'd got into it, was planning a route, working out the best way of getting there and back. It wasn't that different from the driving. Except there weren't as many pillocks to spoil it for you. It was something I could control. At first, I just went round the estate, past the sports centre, called in at the shops if there was something we needed. I got some funny looks from the kids hanging around. They were lippy, but hell, they were in the same boat as me, bored with no jobs. One or two of them even joined me sometimes. But then a couple of them started throwing stuff at me, just clods of earth mostly. I threatened to lamp one, but then thought better of it.

I decided I'd better change my route. I started getting a bus to the edge of the city, then walking back. A couple of hours. More sometimes. I liked to come back different ways; I even kept a log of my routes. Old habits. Christ, I wish I hadn't done that.

It went OK for a time. I was certainly a bit more cheerful. Then one day – some time in October, I guess – I missed my bus home. I ended up walking round a reservoir, with ducks and seagulls on it, then getting a different bus. But instead of being home by two as usual, it was going up to four. The road to our house goes past a secondary school, and the kids were just coming out. So were some of the teachers. They didn't half look knackered, and I wondered if I'd ever be able to do their job.

I was crossing the park, nearly home, when a couple of the girls from the school caught up with me. They'd be... fourth, fifth year? I'm hopeless with ages. They asked where I'd been, seemed to think it was weird to be walking on my own. It's not an area where you choose to go walking, I suppose. I didn't want to explain – you wouldn't, would you? I told them I was trying to get fit; I was planning to do a walk for charity. They could see I was carrying a backpack, so I guess they believed me. They were nice kids, real friendly. We just chatted. One wanted to spend a year in India, then go to university. The other said her mum was on her own and not well. She and her sister had to help out at home.

I started coming back that way two or three times a week. There were lots of birds on the reservoir. I took an old pair of binoculars with me and a bird book and was getting quite good at telling them apart. I wrote the numbers down in a log. I liked keeping track of what I was doing. It was like being back on the road.

You can see what's coming, can't you?

When I went that way home, the two girls sometimes joined me if they were coming out of school, giggling a bit, and getting daft comments from their friends. But they were good company; they seemed happy to have someone different to natter to about their teachers. Lisa and Deirdre, they were called. Lisa was the pretty one. She'd lovely green eyes.

I was starting to think about applying for jobs. Marie was dead keen. It wasn't easy living just off her wage and my benefit. None of you will know what it's like, I'll bet. But I wasn't sure I was cut out for teaching. There were haulage firms in the area, of course, but there was bugger all in the way of jobs.

It must have been two or three weeks later. I was washing up the breakfast things when the cops came knocking at the door. A sergeant and a woman constable. They wanted to speak to me about something serious. I thought it must be about what had happened at Newtonmore and was getting a bit ratty. That was supposed to be all finished. But it wasn't that. They said certain allegations had been made against me. I'd have to go to the station with them. When I got there, it was all waiting about, filling in forms. What they said didn't make any sense. I'd no idea what they were on about. In the end, they told me they were investigating reports of inappropriate behaviour towards two girls. They asked me if I knew anyone from the secondary school, so of course I told them about Lisa and Deirdre. They said they'd be round to the house later in the week, and that I shouldn't leave the area.

How the hell was I going to tell Marie? That was the hardest part. She knew about my walks; she'd always encouraged me. I'd even mentioned the two girls. She'd laughed, said I'd have to watch myself, but I didn't think anything of it. When I got back from the station, I just sat there trying to work out what the hell was going on. It had to be Lisa and Deirdre, hadn't it? Who else could it be? I'd told the police that I'd talked to them, told them about my routes. I might even have mentioned the birds on the reservoir. I didn't know what I was supposed to say. What the hell would you have said?

When Marie got back, I should have had something for her to eat, but I was just sitting there in the kitchen when she came in. She was dead tired as usual. I tried to tell her what had happened, but I don't think I made much sense. She said yes, it must have been the two girls. But of course I'd done nothing – just chatted, a bit of company, for them and me. I said it must be somebody's idea of a sick joke.

I had to go back to the station on the Monday, but they said they couldn't tell me anything new. I asked if I should get a lawyer. The guy on the desk laughed and said yes, that would probably be a good idea. But where was I going to get a lawyer? Let alone pay for one? We were only just keeping up with the mortgage.

Next day, when she got back from work, Marie said she'd spoken to her union rep about where you get a lawyer if you need one, and you're not earning much. She'd not said what it was about, of course. She'd spun a story about family difficulties, how we were having to deal with things we weren't used to. The rep had said something about legal aid, and Marie had stopped off at the Citizens Advice Bureau on her way home. I used to pass it on my way to the depot, hadn't really paid it much attention, except to wonder what was the point of it.

We went there one morning the following week. Marie had to tell a pack of lies to get the time off. They put us in this room round the back, closed the door and windows so no one could see us. I kept saying I hadn't done anything, but the woman we spoke to said there was nothing much we could do for the moment. She asked me if I had any previous convictions. Conviction for speeding, I said. No, she meant any previous convictions in connection with minors. That made it worse, as if she was expecting that I'd been doing whatever it was all my life. The main thing, she kept on saying, was not to go anywhere near the secondary school. That had to be where the complaint had come from.

Next day, the cops came round to the house. They wanted to know if I had a computer. Of course I didn't have a bloody computer. Did they think we were made of money? They asked me again about the school, why I came back that way. I explained about the walks, how I was trying different routes. To prove it, I showed them the log book. Wished I hadn't. One of them took it from me, giving the other one a funny look when he put it in his bag. They took the binoculars too.

Just try and think what it was like, can you? I knew I hadn't done anything, but I couldn't prove it. But you start thinking you must have done something, don't you, even when you know you haven't. And why had the girls complained? And what if I got sent down? I'm not stupid. I've seen the programmes on the telly.

That was Thursday. Then, Friday afternoon, there was another call from the police. The allegations had been withdrawn. No explanation, but I got them to repeat it, just to be sure. I phoned the hospital to tell Marie, then just sat in the chair, crying.

That night, after we'd finished our tea, there was a knock at the door. This woman said she was Mrs Christie, Lisa's mother. I noticed she was walking with a stick and seemed to have problems getting her words out sometimes. She'd got my name from Lisa and had come to apologise for what had happened. I was going to tell her what she could do with her apology. But before I could start, she said that it wasn't her daughter who'd reported me. It wasn't Deirdre either. It was another girl, in the same class. Apparently, this girl had told her father she'd seen this guy walking back with Lisa and Deirdre, and he'd had a backpack and a pair of binoculars, and so on. She'd invented stuff. Must have thought it would be a bit of a laugh. Seems she'd had a falling-out with Lisa. This girl's father had told the cops. They'd spoken to the three girls, told them they'd look into it. The cops must have had me followed, then knocked on my door that first morning.

In the end, Lisa had got worried, had a long talk with her mother, told her how it really was. Her mother had spoken to the police, and then asked around until she'd worked out where I lived. Quite brave, I suppose.

She sounded really sorry, Mrs Christie. I said it was OK, I was just relieved it was all over and thank you for coming round. She apologised again and said her daughter had told her she'd really enjoyed the time she'd spent in my company, walking back from school, though she realised this wouldn't make it any easier for me.

You'd have thought I'd have got an apology from the police, wouldn't you? Nothing doing. When I went to collect my log books and binoculars, they looked at me in a funny way, as if they still didn't believe me.

I should've got over it by now, shouldn't I? That's what you'd think, isn't it? But it's not that easy. I can't sleep, I'm still ratty with everyone. Then, in the New Year, Marie said we had to go back and see the GP again. To cut a long story short, that's how I got into this group. I suppose it does help, listening to other people who've cracked up for some reason. And going over what happened to me, maybe it'll show me it wasn't my fault.

There's not much point in me applying for teaching jobs now, is there? And there still aren't any driving jobs on offer. But a vacancy came up at the hospital, so I'm working as an orderly. At least it brings in some money. It's pretty boring, but every other week, when we work the same shift, we have some time together. I've tried to persuade Marie to get out more, come walking with me, but no luck. Can't blame her. She gets very tired, likes to take it easy when she's got time off.

I can't believe the whole thing only lasted a couple of weeks. You know what's the hardest bit? It's the fact that I don't know who set me up. Even now, if I see a girl that age when I'm out on my own, I can't help thinking, it might be her. She might be laughing at me behind my back. And when I'm doing the shopping, I think, it could be the girl on the checkout, the one stacking shelves, the one who gives you the free biscuits and things.

It could be any one of them.

The Snow-hole

As the two men emerged from the room at the side of the bar and closed the door, the sound of voices faded behind them. The younger of the two moved to a table by the window; his companion walked to the bar and peered at the impressive range of malts behind him.

"Tamdhu. Two, please, Gordon."

The barman poured the whiskies, with possibly a bit extra for good luck.

"There, Jack. Good to see you again. Doesn't seem like a year. Did you have a busy winter?"

"Not too bad. Enough to keep us going. But no fatalities, thank God."

The barman nodded and looked over to the table by the window.

"Who's the guy with you? Don't think I recognise him."

"Neil... Neil... Christ, my memory. Just joined, good lad. Saunders, that's it. Neil Saunders. How's trade? You're quiet at the moment."

"Oh, it's good enough. Mind you, it's always good when your AGM comes around. Went well?"

His customer rolled his eyes and paid for his drinks, then picked up a small jug of water and joined his companion.

Once seated, they gently swirled the liquid in their glasses, sniffed and took a sip.

"Now, Neil, I'm not telling you. You've got to guess."

"Oh, I'm no good at this. Speyside?"

"OK, right area. Go on."

"I don't know. Balvenie?"

"Close, but no, not Balvenie. Tamdhu. Cheers."

"Cheers, Jack. Much appreciated. Ah, that's a good one."

"Is there another kind? I've never had one."

The younger man looked around the almost deserted bar and took another sip.

"Me neither. I'd better go canny, though. It's still a bit early in the day for me. For whisky anyway. Nice to finish the meeting in good time. I must admit, I loved the way the chairman..."

"Stephen."

"Stephen. I loved how quickly he got through the business. Means I'll be able to get the bus back to Bridge of Allan in good time. I didn't realise Callander was so close."

"Yeah, no distance. Stephen's been doing it for ages now. If he'd really tried, we'd have had time for a quick trip up Ben Ledi."

"Not sure about that. It would have been pushing it a bit."

They drank some more of the whisky. The younger man picked up the sheet of paper on the table, folded it and put it away in his pocket.

"You decided to come off the committee then, Jack?"

"I've had enough of committees. Someone else's turn. As long as I can pull people off the mountains, I'll keep on doing that. Some people like committees, some don't. But that wasn't a bad meeting, as AGMs go. At least you had a chance to get to know the others."

"Sure. Mind you, I'd met some of them before. Jason, though, I didn't know him. Knows his stuff, doesn't he? You wouldn't want to get on the wrong side of him. Wasn't he on the television a while back? Can't remember what it was about now."

"He was. Winter before last. He'd just joined us. Been on the Glencoe Rescue for years. The time you're talking about, Jason had organised a rescue on Ben Cleuch. They got the woman down just in time. She'd had to spend the night in a snow-hole. Made the *Stirling News*, no less. Must have been the snow-hole that got people interested. Anyhow, Jason made sure we got some publicity out of it. In fact, it was me who called the team out."

He waited for the reaction.

"You called them out?"

"Yes, I knew the woman. Quite well. That's why I let Jason do the PR side. And there were things we didn't want said. Do you want to hear the whole story?"

"Go on then. Another dram?"

They looked at the almost-empty glasses.

"OK. Your round."

As his companion got up to order the drinks, the older man moved his chair to get a better view of the bar and watched carefully. When his glass was handed over, he raised it to the light, sniffed, sampled the whisky and paused.

"Got it. Islay. Bowmore?"

"I'm impressed."

"Lemon and honey. Giveaway. Cheers. OK. Maggie Long, she was called. I'll tell you what happened, though I still can't make sense of some of it. You don't really know the Ochils yet, do you? They're not really big hills, but you've got to watch them in winter. Most of the summits are rounded, and it's easy to lose your bearings. And you get plenty of snow some years. Maggie has a cottage just at the start of the hills, near Dollar. Late fifties, I suppose she must be. Good job with the council, something to do with illness and bad housing. How they go together. She's had mental health problems of some sort, though I've never asked her about it. Not married. She has a sister, Angela, couple of years younger. I get on really well with Angela. We've done a fair bit of walking together. She's divorced, Angela, but she keeps her ex-husband's name, still calls herself Angela Christie. Probably because she's got the two daughters living with her.

"Well, it must have been late February. It had been snowing all week, on and off. One night – eight, nine o'clock – I got a phone call from Angela. Had I seen her sister? She said she'd been trying to contact her; they usually spoke once or twice a week. But she'd had no reply. She knew Maggie liked going for long walks on her own, even in winter. But now she was starting to get a bit worried. I could see why. We couldn't work out what was going on. Maggie wouldn't have gone far on a day like this. And if she was just walking nearer home, why hadn't she got back? I remember Angela told me that Maggie had been rather quiet recently, as if there was something bugging her. But she'd no idea what it was. I promised I'd have a look for her. I'd start on some of the low-level tracks near her cottage. If there was no sign of her, I'd have to call out the Rescue.

"I did ask Angela if she had any idea what Maggie might have been wearing, but she didn't. I was hoping she might have had something brightly coloured on. No, I know, I don't like bright colours on the hills either, but it does make it easier to see people.

"Must have been going up to ten by now. The road was really icy, but I drove to where Maggie lived, parked the car, went round the back. There's this track that contours round the lower slopes of the hill behind her house. I'd gone that way with Angela and Maggie a few times – nice circular walk. We'd usually go anti-clockwise. Good two hours. There's a fork about two thirds of the way along. You keep going left to get back to where you started. It was perishing, but there was a full moon. I looked for Maggie's footprints in the snow. There they were, smaller than mine, and I thought, yes, I've guessed right. Maggie must have gone that way, slipped, broken her ankle. Or something like that.

"But when I got to the fork, the footprints stopped. The ground was harder, and you know what it's like, the wind sweeps the snow away when the ground is hard. I went left but couldn't find anything. The other track goes right, up towards the summit. I looked and there were the same smaller footprints, climbing up alongside an old wall. I thought, this is crazy, what the hell's going on? But I followed them.

"I found her about half a mile further on. She was sheltering against the wall, looking back down the track. You can imagine, I was a bit puzzled at what she was doing. A bit mad at her as well. But there was something about her that made me stop. Her eyes were empty; she looked different. She said she'd been there an hour or so. She was shivering and breathing shallow. I took her pulse. It was slow, but no signs of hypothermia. She pointed to her knee, said she'd tripped and twisted it. She could hardly move. I asked her what she was doing, going up the hill in conditions like this. She must have climbed this hill lots of times, why on earth had she come out on a day like this? She didn't answer."

The speaker paused for effect, raising his glass to his mouth. His companion took his cue.

"So you had to build a snow-hole?"

"Correct. First, I thought I'd try and get in touch with the Rescue. I tried a few times, but mobile coverage isn't great in that part of the Ochils. It was looking like we might have to sit it out till morning. Of course, I had my emergency kit. The usual stuff, extra clothing, survival blankets, chocolate, warm drinks. But yes, I could see we'd have to build a snow-hole."

"A tough order, digging one on your own in quick time."

"Right. But we were lucky. For one thing, the snow had just about stopped, and the wind wasn't as strong. The snow had drifted against the wall, and the drifts must have been four feet deep in some places. You were on that course last year, weren't you? You know the drill. I found a spot where there was a bit of a hollow as well, to give me a bit of extra height to play with. I'd seen a ruined shed down at the fork in the track, so I went back to it and got some bits of wood that I could make into a sort of shovel. Two in fact.

"I went back to Maggie and told her we'd have to get cracking. I gave her the extra jacket from my backpack, took off her gloves, put on some new thick ones. Gave her some chocolate, warm orange juice. I told her we were going to dig a snow-hole. I'd start digging the entrance into the deep drift between us and the wall. The entrance would have to be two, three feet long, just big enough for us to crawl through. She'd have to dig another small passageway alongside. Once I could hollow out the snow-hole proper, we'd use this second passageway to remove the snow from the chamber.

"Like I said, she had a bad knee, but she did what she could, sitting on my spare waterproof. I wanted to make sure she had something to do. The snow was nice and soft, but not too soft. We kept digging, stopped every ten minutes or so for a drink and some more chocolate. Eventually the snow-hole was big enough for us both to crawl into. Then I went and found a dead tree by the wall, broke off a couple of branches and stuck them in the snow so that we'd be seen by anyone coming to get us.

"I reckon we did a pretty good job. It's amazing how snug you can be in a snow-hole. Maggie was looking pretty knackered, but the thing was, I wanted to keep her talking. Didn't want her to fall asleep. But it was a bloody funny conversation we had, I'm telling you. I asked her again what she was doing there. This time, she did answer, but I soon wished she hadn't.

"After a bit, she said she could remember the exact moment when she knew that there was no longer a match between her capacities and her circumstances. No, I'm not making this up. That's what she said. No match between her capacities and her circumstances. I mean, I've forgotten a lot of the stuff she came out with. But not that.

"Apparently it had all started a few months earlier when she'd been coming out of a meeting at work. She'd been unlocking the door to her own office, she said, and suddenly it felt as if she was somewhere different. She said it was like looking at somewhere she'd never seen before. And once she got inside her room, the stuff inside, it all seemed unreal, as if it belonged to another person. She had this photo on her desk, she said, her and Angela on holiday in Morocco, and she had to look twice to see who it was.

"She'd tried to do some work, but she'd given up and driven home. On the way back, she'd nearly had an accident. Not surprising, if you ask me. She was coming up to this roundabout, she said, wanting to go left, and for some reason she hadn't looked to the right. Something about being distracted by a dog on the pavement. She'd started to turn, not looking, and had to brake hard to avoid hitting this van. The driver had called her a fucking blind bitch, but he'd managed to miss her, and eventually she'd got home.

"After that I found it hard to make sense of what she was going on about. She said that all the way home in the car, she'd had this image in her mind. She knew it came from an old television programme. There was someone standing in the ruins of a concentration camp, she said, with a handful of dust. When she got home, once she'd eaten, she'd gone to her collection of DVDs and eventually remembered what had stuck in her mind. It was a programme called *The Ascent of Man*, she said, and right at the end the presenter was standing there with dust in his hand. According to Maggie, the guy was saying that what made us human was the ability to imagine ourselves in other people's situations. Something like that. It's something animals can't do. And if we stop doing it, we aren't human any more, we're monsters, like the guards of the concentration camps. That was what had stuck in her mind."

He stopped and finished the drink in his glass. His companion leaned forward.

"What did that have to do with the roundabout? When she..."

"Exactly. It went something like this. She'd been coming up to the roundabout, indicating that she was ready to join it, like she normally would. The cars on the roundabout, they'd been looking at her, expecting her to wait. They'd been in her situation, knew that she didn't have priority. And other times, she'd been in their situation, knowing that they did have priority.

But if you don't put yourself in other people's positions, if you stop seeing things from someone else's point of view, you're going to have an accident. Does that make any sense?"

After a pause, he got his reply.

"OK. Sort of. Spatial awareness, psychological awareness. Moral awareness, if you like. She was beginning to think she couldn't make contact with…"

"Right. Maybe you'd have got through to her better than I did. Thing was, I wanted to keep her talking. If she started losing concentration, drifting off, it was going to be harder to keep her alive. I gave her some more chocolate and warm drink. It was getting cold, even inside the snow-hole, so I went out and collected some blocks of snow from the ditch, kicked them into shape, and packed them round the entrance. Then I tried to contact the team again. Walked round a bit, tried a different direction. Thank God, this time I got through. I left a message, with details of where we were. The team promised to be there as soon as they could. I reckoned it would take them an hour or two, if we were lucky. Sorry, must go for a pee. Back in a minute."

When he returned, there were two more glasses on the table. With a smile, the younger man asked if he could identify the malt. His companion sampled it.

"Ah, you've got me there. Different. Not Islay, definitely not Islay. Not Speyside. Dalwhinnie?"

"No, not Dalwhinnie. Try again."

"Sorry, no. I give in."

"Old Poultney."

"Of course it is. Taste of the sea. Thanks. Where was I? Oh yes, Maggie and her mid-life crisis. She said she'd started to lose interest in what she was doing at work. She still did her job well, like she'd always done. But she felt cut off from everything. It was as if it was all happening to someone else. In the past, she said, when things went wrong, she lost sleep over it. Now she stopped caring. She couldn't be bothered making travel plans, she stopped going to the library to get her books. She began to eat ready-made meals, something she'd never done before. Now, I'm no good at being a Samaritan, and I was getting pissed off with Maggie. So, to keep her talking, I said something like, what right did she have to feel sorry for herself? I know, not very tactful. But it did get a response. She agreed. No right at all, she said. It was true what people said. Our generation, we were the lucky ones. No wars. Lots of diseases dealt with. Free health care, education. More disposable income, more leisure. The usual stuff.

"She said she knew we were living in a golden age. But the thing was, knowing you've no right to feel hard done by, that just makes it worse. She'd said she hadn't understood it before, but now she did. Depression was a disease, just like any other. Like any pain, like a stomach ache. When it's not there, you can't believe it could ever exist. Then it comes round again. Anything can set it off, she said. Just like eating something can make you feel sick. Someone makes a comment that upsets you, though of course they didn't mean to. Or you watch a television programme that reminds you of a time when you were happy.

"We've all heard this sort of thing, haven't we? I still couldn't see why she'd decided to wander into the hills in the middle of a bloody freezing night in February. I took her pulse again. This time, it was much lower. I put her hands between mine and massaged them. I pulled her towards me. I was shocked at how thin she appeared under the layers of outer clothing. I rubbed my hands up and down her back, and she'd seemed to revive a bit. She started talking again. What she said next was a bit of a shock. Apparently she'd been to the doctor for a check-up, and they'd found something. An ovarian cyst. She said her first reaction had been to think how stupid was that? What use were ovaries to her? She wasn't going to have children. They'd told her the tests would take about a couple of weeks, but she shouldn't worry, ovarian cysts weren't usually malignant.

"But she was sure the doctor was wrong. I asked how she knew. She just did, she said. I asked her if she'd told her sister. No, she'd wanted to wait for the results. Then she really started to ramble. Went on about some long-distance sailor who'd gone round the world on his own. Old guy, bit of an oddball. Seems he'd gone out on his boat again. Went missing but got picked up. Everyone made a great fuss of him when he got back to port. None of it meant anything to me, but at least she was talking. She went on about the hundreds of boats that had gone to meet him when he came back home. It had been the big story on the TV news. But later she'd been talking to a friend who'd done a lot of sailing. She didn't know if what the friend had told her was true, but she'd said that the man was terminally ill. He just wanted to let his boat take him off into the Atlantic, not come back. He'd done all he wanted to; it seemed a good way to go. Just go, in your own time. When you're ready. But they wouldn't let him go, she'd said; they had to bring him back. Maggie's words were getting indistinct, and I noticed that she wasn't shivering any more. Hypothermia kills quickly, you know that. So I gave her a bit of brandy, just to stimulate her heart for a while. It did quicken her breathing a bit. Now, of course, she wanted to keep on talking. I told her to conserve her strength.

"I was holding her close, trying to keep her warm, when the

rest of the team arrived. They soon had her in a survival bag and set off down the glen. She was in the Royal by two. Another half an hour, and she might not have made it. They asked me what on earth Maggie was doing there. I just told them she'd got disorientated in the snow storms before she twisted her knee, and that she couldn't get her mobile to work. Tried not to be dramatic. She's OK now."

The barman appeared from behind them and cleared away the glasses. The two men shook their heads: no more whisky.

The younger man asked about Maggie's tests. They had been negative.

"Sounds like you did a good job. Especially with the snow-hole. She was lucky. What was it that Jason didn't want to...?"

"When we got back to the fork in the path, we should have gone right. To get back to the road. Like I said, the track goes round till it gets back to the start. It's a bit quicker to go right. Saves ten, fifteen minutes. But I wasn't thinking properly, took them left instead. If Maggie hadn't made it... But it was a good job we did go left."

"Sorry, I don't get you. If it took you longer that way...?"

"About half a mile from Maggie's house, we came across Angela. At the side of the track. At first I thought she was dead. But she was breathing. Just. That meant there were two casualties to get to the Royal. The guys did a great job. Angela made it as well, thank God. Though it was touch and go for her as well. What had happened was that after she'd phoned me, she'd gone looking for her sister, had a minor stroke, and collapsed. She still can't walk properly, and sometimes she has difficulties talking. But I suppose me not thinking straight, it worked out for the best. We might not have found her until too late if we'd turned right. Though I've thought sometimes, if Angela hadn't survived, I'd have found it hard to forgive Maggie Long."

As his companion was about to speak, the quiet of the room was broken. A group of four entered, led by a heavily built, bearded man sporting a bright yellow SNP badge. He reached the bar and turned to face the two men seated at the table.

"God, Jack, you still here? Drinking in the bar when you could have been at a committee meeting! And corrupting our new recruit. Anyhow, what can I get you?"

"Not for me, thanks, Jason. I've had enough. It's time I was off. Good committee meeting?"

The big man laughed.

"If there is such a thing. Anyhow, thanks for what you've done for us, Jack. And pleased to meet you. Neil, isn't it? Welcome to the group. Keep your nose clean, young man, and we'll have you on the committee in no time. Now come on, you're not going so soon? They've an excellent twelve-year-old Scapa here. Not easy to come across. What do you say, Jack? Thought you might change your mind..."

A Good Example

1

Elaine Allen tried hard not to look at the CD on the kitchen table, but knew she couldn't ignore it all evening. She'd given her word: she'd listen to it and give it back as soon as possible. But she was exhausted. Why was it that the kids were always more excited when it was windy? Primary 3 especially. While she waited for the kettle to boil, she went through to the sitting room and checked the phone for messages. Just one from her mother, a reminder that the Spring Fair was on Saturday; she hoped that this year, her daughter would be able to come along. *This year* seemed to contain a mild reproach.

She returned to the kitchen, poured herself a coffee and picked up the CD. In its plain cover, it looked unthreatening. But she was anxious about the content. Switching on her laptop, she slipped it into the drive and waited. At least it wasn't a DVD; seeing Ari's father's face again after all these years might have been distressing. At first there didn't seem to be any sound, but then she remembered to switch the speakers on, and the familiar voice emerged.

Dearest Ari, you'll no doubt be surprised that I've decided to reach you this way. A bit melodramatic, you'll be thinking. What's wrong with a normal letter? But two things: one, my writing is lousy these days – my hands shake more – and two, I always was a bit of a performer, wasn't I?

She had to smile at that. He'd been a performer all right. A good one. He'd loved to make them all laugh. She could still remember his version of the *Four Yorkshiremen* sketch, *The Four Weegies*. And he could bring tears to their eyes too: "Do not go gentle..." – she felt a lump rise in her throat.

So bear with me, Ari. I've not been the best father in the world, that's for sure. But there are things I'd like you to know. And if I can perhaps explain why I became what I am, then perhaps my life will not have been in vain. Sobs uncontrollably. Well...

She pressed *Pause*. Enough to be going on with; the rest would have to wait. She placed the shepherd's pie in the microwave, poured a small gin and tonic.

Was it only last Wednesday? It must have been. Wednesday afternoon was for creative play.

2

The playground had gone quiet at last; the final convoy of cars was driving away down the hill, past the notices the council had put up directing voters to the polling station in the school's main hall. She could still picture little Rory Roberts peering out of the window of his mother's Toyota. Small he might be, but he was big enough to make a proper nuisance of himself when the mood was on him.

The headmistress must have been reading her thoughts:

she appeared at the door of her classroom and, sitting on one of the few desks whose surface had been cleared of card, paint and brushes, said how grateful she was for Elaine's help in dealing with young Rory.

Elaine rolled her eyes and produced a tired laugh.

"No problem, Jo. Rory's OK really. It's his mum that's the problem. She just wants you to say how hard her little boy is trying. He isn't, but never mind."

They returned to their tasks, the head to gathering the paperwork she would be taking home with her, the younger teacher to tidying up. To her dismay, Elaine noticed Top Trumps World Cup cards scattered on the table under the window. This could be a problem, she knew. She'd have to hand them back on Friday, and there would be the usual difficulties over footballers' names which didn't mean much to her. She noticed that one of the children had decided to join together two open tubes of Pritt Stick in the middle of the Show and Tell table. Kaylee MacIver had forgotten her jacket again.

At least she had tomorrow off. Jo was right: it was a shame they didn't have more general elections.

After a while, she became aware of heels clicking down the corridor. The other teachers wouldn't wear high heels at school; she guessed that they must belong to the woman from the educational supplies company, who had been delivering her sales pitch to Jo and some of the other teachers earlier that afternoon. She heard the head-teacher's door opening, and half-listened to the conversation that followed.

The head was saying how useful the presentation had been, and that she would certainly be in touch once she'd had time to check what needed to be replaced.

Then she heard the head apologise for forgetting the visitor's first name. The reply made Elaine drop Kaylee's jacket just as she was hanging it up.

"Ariadne, Mrs McConnachie," she heard. "I know, it's an odd one. Don't know what my parents were thinking about, but I suppose I've got used to it."

Elaine rushed to the door, knocking over a chair.

"Ariadne!" she gasped. "Ariadne Colquhoun? From... Yes, it is! I'm Elaine, you remember? You used to... We used to..."

A second's delay, then:

"Elaine Allen! This is fantastic! You... you've not changed a bit. So you're a teacher now, Elaine. Good for you."

The two young women looked at each other, stood back a bit, smiled and suddenly embraced. The head-teacher smiled in turn.

"Well," she said. "It seems you two know each other. I'll leave you to it." She shook hands with her visitor and went back to her piles of paper.

Suddenly, they didn't know what to say. The teacher looked towards the briefcase on the floor, with the familiar logo of Strathclyde Educational Services.

"I didn't know you were working in this area, Ari. Didn't you go to Newcastle after school?"

"Yes, I did. Moved back to Glasgow three years ago. I can't believe it's you... So how are you finding teaching?"

"Fine. The kids are good – most of the time. And the other staff are great. What about you? You must do a lot of travelling."

She said yes, she was on the road a lot, and was starting to explain how she'd got into the job. Then she stopped to look at her watch.

"I'm sorry, Elaine," she apologised, "but I really must get the twenty-five past train. We simply have to meet up for a meal or something. What's your number?"

She pulled out a smartphone from her bag and rapidly entered the number Elaine gave her. Then her friend picked up a post-it note and a broken pencil from her desk.

"I'll have to write yours down, Ariadne," she said. "You were always better with technology."

They hugged again and the visitor clicked away down the corridor. At the door, she turned, waved and disappeared.

Elaine went back more cheerfully to her tidying up, though her smile had faded a little by the time she'd finished and was making her way to the staff car park. Her first thought, once she'd driven the two miles to Kirkpatrick Court, opened the door to her flat and gone into the bedroom to change – and immediately she was ashamed of herself for thinking it – was that Ari must have thought that she was a real scruff. Her hands were partly covered in paint. Her shoes were dusty, and the bottom button on her skirt had come undone. Looking in the mirror, she could see playdough in her hair. She kicked off her shoes and changed into a pair of jeans, a sweatshirt and a fleece. What would Ari be changing into, she wondered. In the school corridor, she'd noticed the quality of her trouser suit and the label on her handbag. Ari was clearly doing well. It was certainly a growth area she was working in, and she seemed to be running her own business, or at least a franchise. Thank goodness for young Rory Robert's behavioural problems, she thought with a sigh. At least that had meant she hadn't been able to go the presentation; it might have been unnerving to see Ari in full PowerPoint flow.

Back in the kitchen, she decided that she deserved a

chocolate ginger from the rewards box. She sat on the stool at the kitchen table and closed her eyes.

Ariadne Colquhoun, 36 Campsie Avenue, Bearsden. How close they'd been at school! BFFs all right, though the term probably hadn't been invented then. But since those days, she'd often wondered what had kept them so friendly. Their mothers had gone to the same church, that was true. They'd shared boy band crushes, of course. (Which of their friends hadn't?) Ari had fancied her older brother Tony – or at least she'd said she did. It was in fifth and sixth years that they'd become really good friends, and it had been books that had brought them together. There'd been the usual teenage stuff at first, and then their tastes had got more grown-up. Orwell. D.H. Lawrence (not just for the dirty bits). Then Jane Austen. Elaine remembered how they'd go on and on about the personalities of her heroines. Poor old Fanny Price, what was it about her that Ari had found so ridiculous?

"What a strange pair we were!" To stop herself talking to the radio on the table, she moved it to one side.

Sleepovers. First at Hillend Road, only later at Ari's. Nighttime reading sessions of their favourite novels, until one of them fell asleep.

And sometimes their talks had been interrupted by something else. Ari's father, and the noises from downstairs.

She closed her hands around the mug of tea, thinking that if a woman nowadays was remembering how teenage sleepovers had been disturbed by her friend's father, there would only be one explanation. But no, that wasn't the problem. How long had it taken her to realise what was going on? She'd been a bit naive; she knew that. Her own parents were quite strict; alcohol only on special occasions. At Ari's, it had been different. When she'd helped with the washing-up at their house, there had always been beer mugs and wine glasses. (She looked over at the sink, still full of plates and pans from yesterday's lasagne.)

She could still remember clearly when she knew for sure that Ari's father had a problem with drink. Arriving late one evening, she'd seen him get out of his car, open the boot and help himself from a bottle of something. She'd stopped and waited, hidden behind the privet hedge, until the front door closed. Then she'd walked up the drive and knocked on the door. The little scene had left its mark on her memory, even if at the time it had felt like something from a soap opera.

Gradually she'd started to feel more uneasy at the Colquhouns', though she still went over often enough. Out of loyalty to Ari, she supposed. And Ari's parents – both of them – were so kind. Her dad used to help her with her history Higher. He'd groan and say he'd wasted his time being an accountant. But in the end, it had been a relief, really, when they'd gone their separate ways after leaving school. Then they'd gradually lost touch. Birthday cards had arrived for a couple of years, bits of news passed on via mutual friends. But for a good few years now – nothing. Until this afternoon.

It was starting to get dark. Looking across at the calendar by the cooker, she counted the weeks until the summer holiday. Seven: was it only three since Easter? She remembered that *So you're a teacher now. Good for you.* Had she been right to detect a note of condescension?

She found the post-it note in her handbag and copied Ari's number onto the pad by her phone and dialled the number. It would be good to talk over old times, even if there were some topics of conversation she might prefer to avoid.

3

The Amalfi was hardly busy; some shoppers on their way home from the city centre, and what looked like a birthday party in the corner, judging by the balloons and the popping of Prosecco corks. Outside, a few noisy football supporters on their way home. They found a quiet table away from the window and sat down.

"I'd have asked you round for a meal, Ari," Elaine said. "But I'm a lousy cook."

Ari said she didn't believe her, but that the Amalfi was a great idea. She loved Italian food. They scanned the menu: too much choice. The food was only an excuse, they knew that. Ari said that she was on a diet, and she fancied a bruschetta. What about sharing a plate of antipasti for their main course? Elaine was happy with the suggestion; she'd have soup as a starter. Ari picked up the wine list.

"Oh, shall we just go for the house white, Elaine?"

"Fine by me."

Each waited for the other to start to talk. Eventually, Ari laughed and, looking around the restaurant as if to make sure they were not being watched, asked in a faux-conspiratorial manner:

"So, Elaine Allen, what have you been up to since we last talked? What secrets have you been keeping from me all these years? Oh, for God's sake, how long is it? We left school in '98, didn't we? It must be twelve years."

"You went off down to England..."

"Had to get away." She gave no further details. "What about you?"

"I was a bit stuck, didn't know what I wanted. I did a few boring office jobs, even worked for Tony for a while..."

Ari spread her hands, widened her eyes. "Ah! Tony, Tony!"

"Now, now."

"How is he, anyway?"

"He's fine. Married, two little boys. His wife – Magda – she's Lithuanian."

"Lucky Magda."

A portly waiter came slowly over to the table to take their order. He lit the tea-light, took their order and retreated, promising to bring the wine over *subito*.

Ari grinned and leaned over the table.

"Accent more Milngavie than Montecatini, wouldn't you say? Anyhow, where were we?"

"Tony and his family. Before you ask, Ari, no, not at the moment, I haven't. Josh – he moved out last summer. He was good company, but I think he wanted a bit more... I don't know... adventure? More than I was providing, anyway. Are you...?"

"Am I... seeing someone? I love that expression, don't you? Makes it sound so sweet. No, I'm not either. Though I nearly got married a couple of years ago, would you believe it? Outdoor type, big and hairy. Very big, very hairy. Stop laughing. But twenty years older than me. Had his good points, though it wouldn't have been a peaceful relationship."

Smiling, she removed her napkin from its holder.

"I mean, Ariadne and Jason, it wasn't meant to be, was it?"

"Sounds like a bad animated film."

"Oh, Jason was animated all right."

They smothered their giggles as the waiter returned with

the starters and a carafe of wine. They chatted on as they ate. The rented flats they'd lived in to start with, the mortgages they were stuck with now. Common acquaintances, career plans. What they were reading now – much less than in their teenage years, they agreed. The best part of Ari's job, she said, was getting out and meeting people; she admitted that there was a bit of showing off in the way she presented her stuff. Elaine explained that, though she really enjoyed being with the children, especially the very young ones, she wasn't sure she wanted to teach for ever; she could see what the paperwork was doing to Jo and the deputy head.

They'd finished the antipasti and Ari was debating whether to have a dessert. Elaine slipped out to the ladies', and on her way back could see Ari scanning her mobile. She was suddenly struck by the thinness of the hair on the top of her friend's head and by the wrinkles around her eyes that she hadn't seen before.

Ari looked up, the menu in her hand.

"Hi," she said. "Just checking on Mother. She seems to be getting on OK."

Elaine sat down, poured out the rest of the wine.

"Your dad..."

"He died in March. Just a few weeks ago."

She leaned forward and covered her friend's hand with her own.

"I'm very sorry to hear it, Ari."

Her friend put the menu down and pulled tissues from her handbag. Suddenly, Elaine was back in Campsie Avenue, reading and arguing with Ari, then stopping when they couldn't ignore the noise from downstairs, the noise of bottles being opened, or glasses breaking on the kitchen floor.

"Was it... sudden?"

She was struck at the banality of her question, and relieved that the reply came back promptly.

"No, we were expecting it. His heart just couldn't cope in the end. Though it's always a shock. And it was hard for Mum."

She smiled her gratitude and withdrew her hand. When she spoke again, her voice was less steady.

"The thing is, he didn't help himself, Dad. You know he was an... of course you do. Never really sorted out his problem. We tried to help, and he did go to AA a few times. But he never seemed to want to give up. Really give up, I mean. It was worse for Mum, of course. How does the song go? 'Most of all, you've got to hide it from the kids.' She tried, but of course you can't."

"You don't have to talk about it, you know, if it still hurts. It's so recent..."

"No, it's OK. Helps to talk. You and Dad got on really well, didn't you? That was one of the best things about you coming round. Took some of the pressure off."

"He was a lovely man, you know, Ari, despite everything."

"You're right, he was. And the thing was, he kept on working right to the end. Or nearly. What do they say, 'a functioning alcoholic'? I suppose that's about right. And he never lost interest in the things he enjoyed. He was always reading, history books most of the time. The two of you always had that in common, didn't you? The Tudors, ancient Greece, or whatever. Do you remember when we all went to see *Julius Caesar* at the Theatre Royal?"

"And your mum fell asleep."

"Dad had to keep prodding her. Happy days. We did have some good times. You know, I think he'd have loved it that you've gone into teaching. It was almost like you were another daughter..."

Elaine raised both palms, interrupting.

"Don't be daft, Ari. You meant everything to him."

"I know, you're right. But come on, let's not dwell on all this. Tell me about your parents, Elaine. Still the same, I bet. They must love being grandparents."

The conversation continued, a little stilted, until they decided it was getting late. Ari insisted on paying the bill, beckoning to *Signore MacCafferty*. Elaine promised that she would pay next time and they'd make sure they had time for dessert.

They were both quiet in the short taxi ride back to Kilpatrick Court. Elaine felt uncomfortable; taxis were a luxury, and she would always walk if she could. It was her friend who had called one as she waited for the bill; it appeared to be something she did regularly. But as they approached Elaine's flat, Ari pulled a package out of her handbag and nervously handed it to her friend.

"Can you do me a big favour, Elaine?" she asked. "There's a CD in this. It's Dad's... well, I suppose it's his last letter to me. Except it's a recording, obviously. He made it a week or two before he died. Left it for me in his desk. He must have known he was in a really bad way. But it has some really strange stuff in it. I just don't know what to make of it, Elaine. Would you mind... listening to it and telling me what you think?"

Elaine took the package and said yes, of course she'd listen to the recording. The smile of gratitude on her friend's face seemed genuine. She seemed to be on the verge of tears.

"Thanks so much, Elaine. Since I got it, there doesn't seem to have been anyone I felt comfortable about asking. I couldn't ask just anybody."

Elaine slipped the package under her arm, embraced her friend and rummaged for her keys.

As the taxi pulled away and they waved their goodbyes, Elaine could not help thinking that it might have been easier if Jo hadn't forgotten the name of her visitor from Strathclyde Educational Services.

4

The shepherd's pie was good. The coffee would keep her alert. She inserted the CD and started again from the beginning. She found herself warming to the familiar voice. There was a strength of personality there, a little charisma, even. The first parts of the recording – she checked the timer: five minutes in – were easy enough to listen to.

Funny, anecdotal. She could imagine Ari, for all the emotion she must have been feeling, smiling as she was reminded of the catastrophic sailing lesson on Loch Lomond, or the picnic at Mugdock Park, when the dog had stolen the pork pie. It was flattering to hear herself referred to as *that good friend of yours, Elaine: a quiet girl, but so thoughtful.*

When he began to talk about his alcohol problems, however, she became more uncomfortable. Some of it she half knew already, from talking to Ari in the last year or so of school: how he had learned to drink – really drink – when he'd done a stint in the army, before he'd met Ari's mother, settled down and began to train as an accountant. She wasn't aware of all the background, though. Then he explained how easy it had been to move from drinking a few pints socially with work colleagues to being in a position where he needed alcohol just to get by. He didn't want to look for excuses, or indulge in self-pity. He had known what he was doing.

Eventually the story became a more familiar one and her attention began to drift. One of Tony's work colleagues had gone more or less the same way; television dramas were full of stories of alcohol abuse and the problems they brought. Was there anything different about Ari's father's story? She was beginning to ask herself what she might find to say to Ari when she gave her the CD back.

It was when Ari's father mentioned homelessness that she found herself concentrating again. How did this fit into his story? He was talking about the voluntary work that she and Ari had put in at weekends, when they were in their sixth year. He'd been proud of his daughter, he was saying, and of her friend. But there was something that they perhaps hadn't grasped, something important that he wanted to put across. He was getting to the point, he insisted.

Bear with me, Ari. What the two of you were doing was great. Showed how much you were engaged with the world. But there's a problem. A problem with voluntary work. At least there is for me. I know people complain that the kind of work you were doing is only so that you can have a clear conscience. That doesn't worry me. If you want to have a clear conscience, what's the harm in that? We do enough bad stuff in our lives. I should know. If we can feel a bit better about ourselves, bring it on. It's not that, Ari. If you think about it, are you really doing right by the homeless, in the long run? You can get hold of blankets, make bowls of soup, sell your raffle tickets. But it's not solving the problem. You know what they say, the poor will always be with us. Well, I don't see why. We've enough wealth, enough resources to go round. What we need is the will to change things. Really change things. Stop patching gaping wounds with a sticking plaster, as they say. All right, I'm getting preachy. But you're too bright not to see that things can't go on like this. And think about this: the more you volunteer, the more you do jobs that should be done by the state, paid for out of tax, the happier some politicians will be. No names, but they know who they are.

She paused the recording. Preachy was the word all right. She could see what Ari's father was getting at, but was this what had upset Ari? It didn't seem likely. Could she leave the rest until tomorrow? An early night was tempting. She checked the timer on the laptop; it showed that twelve minutes of the recording had elapsed. Ari had said that her father's 'letter' only lasted a quarter of an hour or so. Why not finish it now?

OK, Ari, punchline coming up soon. Do you remember watching those fantastic BBC versions of I Claudius *and* Claudius the God*? The three of us. Elaine as well. Your mum wasn't keen. But I couldn't wait to get hold of the videos when they came out. Pretty strong meat they were, but we all loved them. What I remember best comes right at the end. The old man is justifying his excesses. Accepts that he's behaving badly. You remember why? Because he wants the Republic to come back, and the only way this can happen is if he creates so much revulsion that the Imperial family he's a part of will be kicked out. It's a brilliant idea, though I doubt if there's much historical justification for it. But the important thing is that the stammering old fool has got the message. He's understood. For Claudius, the way to do good is to be really bad. It has to get worse before it gets better. That's the only way things can get better. No point in fiddling about with little changes, hoping for a gradual improvement. A bit like your volunteering work. Sorry, Ari, that's not fair, but do you see what I'm getting at?*

She paused the recording again. She certainly remembered the programmes Ari's father was talking about. Some of the scenes had given her nightmares, though she hadn't wanted to lose face by admitting it. But there still didn't seem to be anything here to make Ari feel uncomfortable. She surely wouldn't have minded the comments about their voluntary work: it was such a long time ago. And Mr Colquhoun certainly had a point, she thought with a sigh. After five years teaching, she'd seen what parents were expected to provide out of their own pockets, at least those who could afford it.

She pressed *Play* again.

I'll be blunt, Ari. I don't want you to drink. Simple as that. Nothing. Anything else, it's too risky. Like giving soup to rough sleepers, half-solutions aren't going to work. Radical solutions are the only ones worth thinking about. I'm convinced there is such a thing as an addiction gene. In fact, you don't know this, but I had an uncle who went the same way. Nobody ever talked about him. So, like good old Cl... Cl... Claudius, I'm setting you a good example by being bad. That's why I've not tried properly to give up. My parents set me an example which I chose to ignore. Can you see it this way, Ari love? I guess that's about all I need to say. I'll be gone by the time you read this. (Christ, that sounds like a country and western song. I'd never want to inflict that on you.) So I'm stepping off the cliff, knowing what I'm doing. The only thing I regret is that I can't say a proper goodbye, Ari. I loved you more than I ever loved anyone. I'll never understand why we stop telling our children we love them once they've grown up.

5

"It's emotional blackmail, Elaine. That's what it is."

This time, Ari had agreed to come round to Kilpatrick Court. Elaine knew her chicken curry was a good standby, and she'd had plenty of time to prepare it the night before. Ari had been a little late; there had been delays on the Kingston Bridge. She had raised the topic of her father's recording almost as soon as she had given Elaine her coat to hang up and sat down at the kitchen table. Elaine had answered in a non-committal manner and insisted that she had to attend to the food. But by the time the plates had been placed on the table, and the curry and naan bread had been served out, Ari's agitation couldn't be ignored any longer.

"Blackmail. That's what I think."

"I see what you mean."

Elaine poured out water. She'd deliberately not offered wine; if necessary, she'd say it was because she knew Ari had to drive home.

"I do, Ari. He's made it difficult for you."

"Sure has. And do I tell Mum?"

Elaine hesitated, adding too much chutney to her plate.

"I don't know. No, I don't think so. Your dad wanted it to be between you and him."

The naan bread needed more time in the microwave. Elaine was glad of the distraction.

When she same back, her friend was moving the curry around her plate, picking at bits of meat.

"I'm sorry. It's really good, but I don't have much of an appetite."

Elaine moved the plates away. They went into the sitting room and sat in the chairs either side of the television.

Elaine tried to remember the words she'd prepared, knowing that, when she said them, they wouldn't sound so convincing.

"He obviously thought what he was doing was for you. You've got to give him that, at least. It seems to me, Ari... oh, I don't know... that he was prepared to let you hate him, to get across what he thought was most important. I know, it's a strange way of showing your love for your daughter. Maybe you've got to have kids to understand what he was trying to do. One of the things I've learned from teaching is that sometimes you win by appearing to lose. He was prepared to give everything up, because he thought the stakes were high. Sorry, that sounds a bit pompous, but does it make sense?"

Her friend sat forward in her chair, more agitated.

"But I'm not a child any more, Elaine. And you can't prevent your children from making mistakes. You just have to hope they're not catastrophic. What he was trying to do was so controlling."

"He was warning you, in his own way. I think he was a bit frightened."

"Frightened? You mean, all that about setting an example. Like he's trying to be a good parent? Bit late. Christ, we're talking as if he's still alive."

"But he was a good parent, you know that."

Ari nodded, more with her eyes than her head.

"He tried to be, I suppose."

"Look, you must be a bit hungry. I've got some chocolate cake. I'll make some coffee."

Ari followed her friend to the kitchen and began moving the plates to the sink.

"How would you have reacted if it had been your father, Elaine?"

Elaine rested her hands on the edge of the sink. This was what she had been dreading.

"I don't know. I've been thinking about that. I think... I think I'd have... respected his advice."

"And acted on it?"

"I... I like to think I would have. But I don't know."

They returned to their chairs with their mugs of coffee. The conversation stalled while they ate and drank. Eventually, Elaine broke the silence.

"Look, I'm sorry. I'm not being much help. It must be really difficult... Oh Ari!"

The coffee and plate crashed to the floor. Elaine had to lean forward to stop her friend falling.

The tears came in floods.

"It's OK, Ari. It's OK. Just try to breathe slowly. Take your time. It's all right."

She wrapped her arms around her friend's shoulders. Slowly the convulsions eased.

For several minutes, neither woman said anything. Then:

"Thanks, Elaine. Thanks. God, what a mess! I'm sorry. You've said... you've been brilliant. I had to find someone... honestly, I don't know what I'd have done if we hadn't bumped into each other like we did. There wasn't anyone who'd have understood. And you... you *knew* Dad, how lucky was that!"

Elaine found more tissues in her bag; her friend sat back, wiped her eyes and smoothed her hair. Elaine brought a damp cloth from the kitchen, dropped it on the coffee stain.

"You know what," Ari said after a while. "You're probably right about Dad. I think I was starting to see things that way. How he'd been prepared to make me angry, so he could get the message over, say what he thought was important."

There seemed nothing more to be said for the moment. They scooped up the bits of cake. In the kitchen, Elaine allowed Ari to help wash up, tidy things away. She offered more coffee.

"Thanks, but no. You've already done so much. Look, you must have lots to do. I'll let you get on."

Ari collected her belongings. Elaine helped her on with her coat, asked if she felt OK to drive.

"Yes, I'll take it easy."

"So..."

"So... I'm not going to do what Dad asked. I like a drink. Millions of people do. They don't all end up alcoholics. But I respect what Dad was trying to do. And I... I love him for it. The old bugger."

A final embrace, a promise to keep in touch.

As Ari was about to leave, she thanked her friend once more.

"You've been just what I needed. I can't say how much..."

"Don't, Ari. Anyone would have tried to do the same."

"Don't know about that. But one last thing. You know that bit about Claudius. Well, I looked him up online. Couldn't find anything about him wanting the Republic to come back, if that's what Dad was getting at. And the guy who came next was Nero. He was one of the bad ones, wasn't he? So you can try to control what comes after you, but it doesn't always work."

Elaine nodded and closed the door carefully as her friend drove away. Only when she got back to the kitchen did she see the CD still on the kitchen table. Too late to chase after Ari. She'd parcel it up and put it in the post.

The Plagiarist's Tale

First come the hits, then come the writs.

I can't remember who said that, and I suppose that's part of the problem. He – or she – was talking about popular music, presumably, but it could apply to anything. As soon as you try to produce something – words, music, paint, anything – there's a good chance you'll be told that you've got the idea from someone else. One thing I have learned: it's impossible to be totally original.

(Why do we prize originality so much anyhow? I still remember my tutor at Cambridge handing back an essay: "But, Miss Chalmers," he'd said, "if you'd told Shakespeare he was being brilliantly original, he wouldn't have known what you were talking about. It's the Romantics' fault if we think originality is something to be valued.")

If you're a university lecturer like me, you learn quickly that producing your own research is an important part of the job. You can be a lousy teacher – and plenty of academics are – but as long as you have your research published, and as long as it's original, you won't go too far wrong. These are the rules of the game. Everyone knows them, and almost everyone tries to play by them.

In the sciences, they make good sense. Scientists are paid to find things out, to test their findings against hypotheses. What they discover can be important. I had friends in medical research at Aberdeen who helped to develop the MRI scanner.

But research in the humanities is a different animal. My specialism is the history of theatre in London in the seventeenth and eighteenth centuries. A narrow area, certainly, but it can be fascinating. Analysing theatre bills, for example, tells you which dramatists were popular and which styles of performance went down well with the public. This in turn can shed light on patterns of social behaviour at the time. My work isn't going to make the world a better place, but it is a small contribution to our understanding of the past. And it helps to pay the mortgage. University jobs are – or were – reasonably secure, and at the time I was getting along fine.

That was until I was accused of plagiarism.

The article in question – the one that caused the problem – was one I had had published in the most prestigious journal of European theatre history. It's not always easy to have articles accepted by these journals. You submit your paper to the editor and it's passed over to experts, who – you hope – recommend it for publication. These reviewers are therefore powerful people. Most are scrupulously fair, though some have agendas of their own.

I ought to say at this point that I did have issues with the editor of this particular journal. Or rather I didn't. Have issues with him, that is. Let me explain. Malcolm Roberts and I were married for ten years, back in the eighties. He wanted a family, and I didn't, at least not so soon. That's basically why we split up. It probably wasn't quite as simple as that, if I'm honest, but the fact that we had different views of what we wanted from the marriage certainly contributed to its collapse. He came from a big family and loved the idea of having babies around. I came from big family too and had seen what it did to my mother. Somehow, I couldn't see Malcolm making a major contribution towards bringing up any children we might have. I accused him of having a selfish attitude, which perhaps wasn't entirely fair, but he wasn't prepared to see things from my perspective. We also worked in the same department, which didn't help. Academic marriages are not always made in heaven. He already had a lectureship when I started at Bristol as a teaching fellow in 1978. I had to work like mad to get a permanent post and wasn't going to take a step back on the career ladder. Back in those days, things were even harder for a professional woman than they are now. I knew the effect that any break to have kids would have on my prospects of promotion.

It wasn't a particularly bitter divorce. We're 'civilised people', as the lawyer put it. But it's never a pleasant experience. I have to admit that Malcolm took it more personally than I did. He became quite ill for a while, and his Head of Department allowed him to take a term's sabbatical leave a year early. It was a struggle to make Malcolm see the irony of the situation: he was taking time off from teaching as a result of a divorce whose principal cause was my unwillingness to take time off from teaching. Malcolm isn't strong on irony.

A couple of years later, in 1993, I got a job in Edinburgh, while Malcolm stayed in Bristol. That helped to heal the wounds. Malcolm's career took off, and he remarried. Judy is nice enough. We've always tried to be pleasant to each other. But she's not the brightest. Malcolm got his wish, eventually, and Judy had three boys. Ewan's the oldest, just into his teens, then Neil, then Rory. After Rory, Judy persuaded Malcolm to have the snip. She told him that it would increase his sex drive. She probably wishes she hadn't said that.

Malcolm became the editor of the *Journal of Theatre History* a few years after the divorce. It was quite a coup for him. These jobs usually go to Oxbridge people, not academics from the provinces. But he's very knowledgeable and he always gives a good account of himself in interviews. I was pleased for him at the time. And he's very good at the job, puts a lot of work into it, in addition to his teaching and research. In 1996, Malcolm got a chair at Glasgow. Since then, I've seen them fairly often, and get on pretty well with Judy and the kids, though the boys are certainly hard work. The oldest one's a real character, I have to admit, sharp as anything, but with a smile you can't resist. Thoughtful too. Now if we'd just had the one, Malcolm and I, and he'd been like Ewan... I don't know.

Things went well for me too. Soon after moving to Edinburgh, I met Barbara through a local wine-tasting group, and after nearly fifteen years together, we've formed a civil partnership. Then last year, I got a senior lectureship and a reduction in my teaching load because of the research income I was bringing in.

* * *

Things *were* going well. It was in the middle of the summer term, two years ago, that I was summoned to see the Head of School, as a matter of urgency.

"Come in... er, Joanna," he said. (He had to look at his notes to remember my first name.) "I'm sorry to drag you in at such a busy time, but there's something of the highest import I need to discuss with you."

Something of the highest import. That was just the kind

of phrase Phil Grattan would use. He was an ace bullshitter; everyone knew that was how he'd become Head of School. He'd been an indifferent teacher, and had some second-rate material published. But he could talk the talk.

On his desk, I saw that he had a copy of an article of mine which had recently been published in the *Journal of Theatre History*. I was surprised to see that the margins were full of notes. Grattan hadn't put them there, for sure. He's a sociologist, doesn't know much about... anything, really. Certainly not about the content of my paper.

He said that he had been made aware of suggestions of plagiarism in the paper.

I laughed. Of course I hadn't plagiarised anything. I wasn't dishonest, and I certainly wasn't stupid enough to think I could get away with passing someone else's work off as my own. I told him so. Then he brought out a folder from his drawer, opened it – rather dramatically, I remember – and placed another article on the table. He said that there were striking similarities in the contents of the two papers. Automatically, I leaned forward to see who had produced this other paper, but he made sure I couldn't see it well enough to do so. Then he said that he was treating the matter as something very serious, and that two of the members of the School Board had been asked to look into the matter, and that they would be in touch with me as soon as the matter had been *diarised*. I don't know if he saw my smirk at his choice of words. He told me I had to keep this to myself for the moment. And that now I should return to my normal duties.

I stood up and, like a fool, thanked him before leaving his office.

It seemed such a stupid idea – that I had copied the

content of an article by someone else – that at the outset, I didn't take it seriously, despite what the Head of School had said. Some mistake had clearly been made, and Grattan was over-reacting, probably because he was afraid of the Principal, who is a bully. It was frustrating not knowing what it was that I was supposed to have stolen. I had a pile of dissertations to mark, so I tried – not very successfully – to put it out of my mind for the meantime.

A couple of days later, I received an email telling me that the meeting with the members of the School Disciplinary Board – my very own Star Chamber – was scheduled for the following Thursday. In my reply to Grattan's secretary, I insisted that they give me details of the charge against me. But their answer was evasive; for reasons of institutional security, I would have to wait for the meeting.

As I sat down that Thursday afternoon, Grattan introduced me to a professor of anthropology whom I knew vaguely, and a suit from the university office who looked as though he would rather have been anywhere else. Then I was handed a copy of an article in the *Nueva Revista de la historia del teatro*, published in – wait for it – Lima. I had to stop myself laughing. I'd just about heard of the *Nueva Revista de la historia del teatro*. New academic journals are appearing all the time. Their content is usually second-rate. Like many of them, this *Revista* was only available online. The family name of the author of the article in question was Hernandez-Carrero. The name rang a vague bell, but I wasn't given the time to work out who he might be. The article was, of course, in Spanish. My knowledge of Spanish is limited, but I could see from the title of the article that it dealt with the finances of running a theatre at the time of the Restoration; this is a field I have explored over the years. I picked up the article and pushed it away from me dismissively. I said I couldn't read Spanish and that I would need a translation if I were to have an opinion on it. Grattan passed me half a dozen sheets of paper and told me that a member of the Hispanic Studies Department had already provided one, without being told what its intended purpose was.

I drew a deep breath. So this, I asked the three wise men, was the piece I was supposed to have plagiarised? Grattan said that this appeared to be the case. The other two nodded; neither looked me in the face. Grattan than passed to me the annotated offprint of my article and informed me that he would be in touch about further discussions, going forward.

Enough was enough. I picked up the offprint, the Spanish article and its translation, nodded to each of the three monkeys and left the room.

That evening, after a meeting with a colleague to agree on the marks for my dissertation students, I sat down with the three documents. The title of my article – *We Never Closed: How Drury Lane Theatre Stayed Open Despite Everything* – made me wince, but you have to try and make everything sound suggestive these days, even pieces about the history of theatre. I read the translation of the Spanish article. There were certainly similarities between the two. Neither was long – seven or eight pages – and this made the points of convergence more obvious. Roughly the same period was covered, and the same data about takings and expenditure had been analysed. I checked the publication date of the Spanish article: it had appeared three years before mine. I tried to think objectively. If I'd been given the two publications, and noted when they had appeared in print, what conclusions would I have drawn?

I re-read the pieces. At the very least, it looked on the surface as though the author of the article in the *Journal of Theatre History* (me) could well have taken material from the earlier, Spanish article.

But of course she hadn't. I hadn't.

Needing a break, I checked my phone. It was election night, and the first results were coming in. The news hardly cheered me up. It was looking very much as though the Conservatives were going to be the biggest party, even if they wouldn't have a majority. Christ, I thought, Cameron for prime minister! What a shallow, self-regarding young man! And just the sort of Tory that goes down badly in Scotland. Barbara would be delighted, though. She's in the SNP, and had been hoping for a Conservative win, since she's sure that everything Tory governments do helps the nationalist cause. She's probably right.

I went back to the two papers, tried to work out a way of showing that I'm not a plagiarist. For one thing, the sort of information which the articles contained is being digitised all the time, which means that it's unsurprising that data-sets should be analysed by more than one researcher. And it was absolutely clear to me that there was nothing in my paper that couldn't have been written by someone who had not seen the Spanish one. Unfortunately, there were probably too many negatives here for the members of the School Board to be able to grasp what I was trying to say.

I was looking again at the translation of the Spanish article when the penny dropped. Victor! The Spanish assistant we'd had at Bristol, how many years ago? Fifteen? At least. About the time of the divorce. Hadn't he been Victor Hernandez-something or other? A double family name, like all Hispanics. It had to be him. He'd been really keen about the theatre. I remembered the falling-out we'd had. He'd wanted to attend classes in my Master's course, without paying fees. I remembered the Registrar had told him not to attend – quite rightly – and he'd blamed me for it, and then for some reason – perhaps to make life awkward for me – Malcolm had taken his side.

Malcolm had to know what was going on. First thing the next morning, I phoned his number. It was Judy who answered. She sounded dreadful, as if she had flu. But then the snuffles became sobs. I apologised for bothering her, but explained that I needed to speak to Malcolm, as a matter of urgency.

Malcolm wasn't there. Hadn't I heard? He'd walked out on them a month ago.

I said I was very sorry to hear this and told Judy I'd be back in touch later. Poor woman, I thought, after I'd put the phone down, with those youngsters to look after. I hoped Malcolm was providing for them all. (I've recently heard that he's set up house with one of his research assistants, who's much younger than him and thinks he's wonderful. She'll learn.)

The next few days were pretty fraught. More marking, and more depressing political news. However, I managed to get a good idea of how the accusation of plagiarism had arisen, and phoned Grattan's office to arrange to see him. His secretary told me that he had been called away until Sunday. I said that I had to see him urgently. She agreed to text him, and later phoned me back to say that a meeting had been arranged for the following Tuesday.

I had plenty of time to plan my defence – as if I was guilty of anything! – and work out exactly what I needed to say at the meeting. It took a lot more emails, texts and phone calls – some of them distinctly acrimonious – to Malcolm and other former colleagues to get to the bottom of things. Inspector Morse would have been proud of me.

This is what had happened.

Victor Hernandez-Carrero had left Bristol in the late eighties and taken up a teaching post at Salamanca University. He'd done some research into the history of theatre in Western Europe. In 2002, he'd sent Malcolm a manuscript of his article, the one I was supposed to have plagiarised, asking if it could be published in the journal he edited. Malcolm had sent it back, explaining that they only published articles in English, and suggesting that he could either have it translated and resubmit it, or try another publication. Malcolm had thought no more about it.

Then, in 2006, I'd sent my article to Malcolm. He'd read it, remembered Victor's submission and tracked down his article in the Lima journal. He'd seen the similarities in content between the two pieces. Crucially, because he's an expert, he'd also seen the differences. The conclusions which I had drawn were more significant and better formulated than Victor's. His article was basically a matter of adding up the sums involved in the various theatrical activities; his analysis was flimsy.

There were also some factual errors in his article. If I'd been stealing his ideas, I would probably have reproduced these errors, but I wasn't, and I hadn't.

In fact, the similarities the two articles shared were pretty superficial. Once the peer-reviewers had said they were happy with my article, Malcolm had had no hesitation in publishing it.

Victor must then have read it when it appeared in print. He could hardly *not* have read it: the *Journal* is the most prestigious publication in the field. He'd then decided to stir the pot, either because he thought he saw a chance of revenge for the slight he imagined he'd suffered of all those years ago, or because he genuinely believed that I had stolen the ideas in his article. The former has to be the more likely explanation, but I don't really care one way or the other.

My analysis made an overwhelming case that I had done nothing wrong. Malcolm, to be fair, agreed with my assessment of the situation. Naturally, he wouldn't have wanted it to look as though an article published in the *Journal* had been based on another scholar's work.

When I met my three inquisitors again, I was able to persuade them that what we had was not a case of theft of intellectual property, but more the result of an ambitious researcher seeking revenge for what he considered poor treatment earlier in his career. They were quite relieved, I think, to be able to agree with my assessment, and a couple of weeks later, I received a curt email informing me that the matter was closed.

That should have been the end of it. But I was so incensed by the injustice of the whole affair that, after taking the advice of a friend in the Law Department, I informed the Head of School that I was intending to take the matter further and accuse them of damaging my career prospects by the way they had treated me. I was banking on the fact that no institution likes bad publicity.

Then, a few weeks later and quite out of the blue, the university decided to restructure. For only the third time in fifteen years. They were looking for members of staff to take voluntary severance. Out of curiosity, I applied. Amazingly, I was offered an enhanced package. It sounded rather obscene to me, and I suspect some of the enhancement might have been hush money. After taking some time to do the sums, I decided it was a good time to leave the university. The management arranged a farewell meal, and everyone said how sorry they were to see me go. I'd like to think that most of them meant it.

For the last two years, I've been freelancing. It's wonderful. I've taught on some courses that interest me, taking the classes and avoiding the admin; I've done some paid reviews and organised conferences. When I see the weary faces of former colleagues as they pick up their piles of marking or try to think of original exam questions, I realise that Victor Hernandez-Carrero may have done me a great favour.

Between the Showers

It wasn't a voice I recognised. I was on my knees, clearing out the onion rows. When I looked up, it was a second or two before I saw him. He was standing at the other side of the fence. Backlit by sun, I couldn't see him well. For a moment, he looked familiar. I thought of Josie, who's got the plot opposite. Her son sometimes comes to help. But no, it wasn't him.

"You've got a lot of weeds there, Mr..." he said again.

"It's been a good year for weeds," I interrupted. (What's it got to do with you, I thought, but I didn't say so.) "We've had a wet spring; it always brings them out. Er... are you looking for someone?"

He said he was just having a walk round the allotments. Was that all right?

I said yes, of course, though there wasn't much to see. I said there would be more people around by the evening, provided it stayed dry.

He lifted his hand from the fence post and waved his thanks.

I went back to my onions. A few minutes later, I couldn't help looking up. I was a bit curious. People do come to have a wander round the allotments sometimes, but usually later on when there's more growth and more colour. In early May, things are only just getting going.

I saw the man – he'd only be about twenty, I suppose – chatting to Gordon Shepherd, who was working away in his corner plot, spreading something that smelt quite rich. Then he had a word with one of the other plot-holders. I even saw him picking up a bit of litter and putting it in his pocket.

Another half an hour's weeding and I'd had enough. My back was getting stiff. I emptied the bucket into the compost bin, hung up the tools and set off home. I had a quick glance around the allotments but couldn't see anyone I didn't know.

It started raining after lunch, so I got on with tiling the shower room. Another wet day. Just my luck. You take a week's holiday to get the allotment into shape, and then it's never really dry enough to get much done.

* * *

The next day – Wednesday – it had cleared up a bit.

When I got to the plot, I was surprised to see the young man there again. And then I saw that he'd brought gardening tools with him.

"Can I give you a hand with the weeding, Mr...?" he asked.

"I'm Ian," I answered. I was going to say no, I was happy to get on with the job myself, but thought that sounded a bit mean.

"Yes..." I said. "If you really want to."

"Thanks." He smiled. "I'm Andrew, by the way."

I opened the gate for him, and we looked over the plot. Most of the things I'd put in hadn't grown much so far. The garlic and onions that had been planted in November were doing well, but the beetroot and the brassicas were just about finished. But there were plenty of weeds, like he'd said. I asked him if he lived locally, and when he said he was from Bal something or other, I wasn't much wiser. There's lots of places starting with Bal around here. He said he was doing a part-time degree in horticulture at the SRUC. When he'd been at primary school, he'd loved learning about plants. Then, when he'd gone to the academy, no one had seemed interested in things like that. He believed that horticulture was going to be vital to the economy of an independent Scotland, but at the moment what he wanted was more practical experience.

I laughed and said I wasn't sure about his politics, but that if he wanted to tidy up round the blackcurrant bushes, that would be fine.

I went back to my onion rows, thinking I'll give him half an hour, he'll have had enough by then. But he got right down to it, did a proper job. I kept looking over. He pulled out the weeds, roots and all, shook the soil off, and remembered that I'd asked him not to put the couch grass into the compost. I'm not used to having someone working on the plot when I'm there. Some of the other plot-holders have friends and family up sometimes, but I like to do my own thing. When I was still married, my wife would sometimes come up and give me a hand, and that was all right for a while. I suppose I've got a bit possessive about my patch since then. It's not easy to let someone into your own space.

But Andrew, he just seemed at home somehow. As if he knew that you're best not talking much, keeping your energy for the digging, the hoeing, or whatever. He was still at it when I was ready to knock off for lunch. I thanked him, said he'd done a really good job. He straightened up and shook the soil off his hands. Said he'd enjoyed it, but that he had classes in the afternoon, and then he had to get back to Bal... wherever it was. He said he'd be happy to come again another day if I thought he could help. I said yes, if he really fancied it, and I'd be there on and off for the rest of the week. I'd have to be back at the yard on Monday.

He smiled and said goodbye. I couldn't help noticing how he looked straight at me when he smiled, not to the side like a lot of people do.

* * *

I've never been one for taking food and drink to the plot. I'll have a coffee before I go, get on with the jobs that seem most urgent, then go home. It's only a five-minute walk, after all. But when I went up to the plot on the Thursday – it stopped raining soon after breakfast – I thought I'd take a flask and some biscuits, in case Andrew turned up.

No one was there when I arrived. I felt a bit flat, but told myself that he'd obviously found something better to do. I dug in some compost, earthed up the garlic so it didn't get damp, and went home. I had to go to the dentist's in the afternoon.

The next day was Friday, 14 May. It's a date I dread. I suppose as a gardener, I should be pleased when things start to grow properly, but there are too many bad memories associated with that date.

When I got to the allotment, it seemed different, but to start with, I couldn't work out what it was. Then I saw that the old soggy leaves of the strawberries had been removed, and a couple of the raised beds had been hoed.

It must have been Andrew. I didn't know whether to be

pleased or not, but I had to admit he'd done it as neatly as I could have done. Then I noticed the plant pot in the middle of the path. It had a polythene bag wrapped around the top, and inside was a bit of paper. It said: "Hope you didn't mind, but these looked like the next jobs to do. Andrew."

Then I heard him laugh. He was over by the fence, where I'd seen him the first time.

"What do you think?" he asked. "Is it all right?"

I told him it looked fine, and thanked him for his efforts. He opened the gate, and we had a walk round the plot. I had to admit things were looking much tidier, and I was beginning to wonder how it might have been if I'd had someone to help me over the years. Then he explained that he couldn't stay that afternoon. He had a birthday party to go to. "Whose?" I asked. When he said it was his, I felt shaky. I leaned on my spade, hoped he hadn't noticed. But he was already picking up the things he'd brought with him. As he left, he said he'd try to come back the next day, if I thought it would be useful. I said yes, it would be fine, there were still plenty of jobs that needed to be done.

* * *

He worked at the plot most of Saturday. He certainly made a difference. I thought I ought to give him something as a thankyou, but somehow money didn't seem right. And it wasn't as if there was any produce in the plot that I could let him have. When we knocked off for lunch, I asked him if he'd like to go for a pint in the Prince Charlie at the end of the afternoon. I've never really found a pub I like in Dumbarton, but the Prince is OK for a drink in the early evening. Andrew said yes, but then while I was at home having lunch, I remembered that they'd started doing a Happy Hour from five in the evening, and that the place can get really noisy. So instead I took some beer and crisps over and we sat down in front of the greenhouse. It's a nice spot, and it gets a lot of sun late in the day.

I said I was grateful for his help. I told him how I usually take a week off in May to try and get on top of the allotment, but that if it's wet, I can never get everything done and then I'm playing catch-up for the next few months. He asked me how long I'd had the allotment, and if I did all the work myself. I said I'd had it for nearly twenty years, and looked after it on my own, since... I hesitated, but then went on. Since my wife left, I said.

He said he was sorry to hear that.

"You had children?" he asked.

I took a while to answer. In the end, I thought, why not? I was talking more than I usually would. Perhaps it was the beer, but he seemed to want to know. He must have been a good listener.

So I told him about Jamie, and the meningitis. How he'd been such a happy, healthy little boy. How pleased we'd been to have him, since we were already in our thirties. How he loved to mess about outside, in the garden or at the park. Then how he'd come home from nursery one afternoon, not his usual self. How we'd given him Calpol and put him to bed. And then... how sudden it had been. How it was just twenty years ago.

Andrew didn't say anything while I was telling him the story. When I stopped and looked up, it took me a couple of seconds to see him. He was standing a couple of feet away, looking into the distance. Then he turned to me and nodded slowly. Funny thing, I got the impression he wasn't surprised by what I told him.

I was going to say that my marriage to Barbara had never really recovered from the shock, though it had still been hard to take it when she said she was leaving to live with another woman, but I was beginning to feel a bit uncomfortable about telling him this personal stuff. I opened another beer and passed it over. It struck me that he'd still hardly given me any information about himself. So I asked about where he came from, his family, his course at the college. His answers were a bit vague, but I'm not the sort to press people about themselves. He was an only child, he explained, and had spent most of his early life in the area. He'd not been what you'd call an academic kid at school, which was one reason why he'd chosen to go for horticulture. The time he'd spent at my plot had been just what he'd wanted, learning on the job.

I laughed, and said that it wasn't all that difficult, pulling up weeds. No, he said, it was all useful; he'd learned about digging in last year's peas and beans to add nitrogen to the soil, planting things like comfrey to attract pollinators. He'd remember that it was best to split rhubarb crowns in the autumn, that some things are better if they're divided up and allowed to grow on their own.

I told him to stop; he was starting to make me feel good about myself. Then he put his glass down, thanked me for the beer, and said he'd better be going. He wanted to write up a report of what he'd done over the week.

I thanked him again, and asked if he might be coming back. He said he couldn't commit himself, but I could see in his manner that he meant no. I opened the gate for him, and turned to go back and pick up the bottles.

* * *

He wasn't there on the Sunday morning. I think I knew he wouldn't be. I remembered that Gordon had been a lecturer in agriculture – not sure which college it was – and I thought of going over to ask him how I'd go about trying to track down someone doing a degree in horticulture at the SRUC. But I really didn't have much to go on, and I decided against it.

As I was checking the gooseberries for magpie moth, I was caught out by a shower. I sat down on the seat in the shed and waited for it to pass. But it kept on raining. Soon, the other plot-holders were leaving, and I decided it was time to go home for lunch. It's frustrating when the weather makes things difficult for you. Then, sitting there looking out at the plot in the rain, it struck me. All this work I put in – the work we all put in – sure, it's necessary. You can't just leave things to nature. But most of the time, we're not working. We're not even here. But whether we're here or not, it rains, then it stops. The sun shines, sometimes. Things grow. So most of the time, it's not about us.

It must have been because I'd been telling Andrew about Jamie. I suddenly remembered sitting in the lawyer's office when we were sorting out the divorce, a few years after our boy had died.

"It's not about you," Barbara had said. "It's not about us. We have to try to see that."

I'd always thought she meant that we shouldn't blame ourselves for what had happened. Of course, ever since Jamie had died, we asked ourselves what might have happened if we'd called the doctor earlier, if we'd known what was happening. But maybe she meant something else. Perhaps she was trying to say that it was our son's life that hadn't been lived, after all, not ours. We couldn't *own* it.

I looked out of the dirty shed window. The rain had almost stopped. I saw Old Willie leaving and remembered how, just after I'd taken on the plot, I'd told him how pleased I was to have my own bit of land to work. He'd looked at me, then over at the plot.

"Well," he'd said. "Good luck, but don't forget, it's not yours to keep; it's only a loan."

At the time, it had seemed a bit discouraging, a bit unkind. But I could see that he was probably right. We're not in charge as much as we think.

It was time to go. I'd probably come back in the afternoon, get on with preparing the potato drills. But if I didn't, the plot would still be there the next time.

As I closed the gate, I thought of Andrew standing there the evening before. When he left, he'd raised his hand towards me, and for some reason, I'd thought of ministers at the end of church services, giving a blessing, if that's what it is they're doing.

PART THREE

Spring–Summer 2016

The Event Manager

I'm wondering how long I should leave him there. It's nearly eight now. I'll let him stew a bit longer. It's good to think that B 12 will be getting dark. I'm glad I managed to unscrew the light bulb, though my ankle still hurts where I strained it getting off the table. If only I could have made him more uncomfortable, but I wasn't able to think of a way of tying him up – not without getting him unconscious first.

He made me feel uncomfortable enough, though.

This bar has got really dingy. The Crown was never smart, but it seems to have gone downhill since the old days. It was the nearest pub to the Grange, that was its only good point. We could sneak in for an illicit drink after dram soc rehearsals on Fridays or netball on Tuesdays. (I think it was Tuesdays.) I suppose we thought we were really cool. But the magic went out of it that evening when we saw Mr Innes there too, pretending not to see us, just like we pretended not to see him. If teachers liked a drink in the Crown, it didn't seem so cool any more. Tonight the place is very quiet. An old guy at the bar, clearly with no conversation left in him, and a couple in the corner (Mr Innes's corner, I think), finishing their burgers.

On the table in front of me: my bag and what's left of my G

& T. I check my phone. Five to. I'll go in ten minutes. It's only a short walk back to the college. I'm sure the panic button on my phone won't be needed. But I'm glad I told Claire that I'd phone her at 8.30, or soon after; she promised to come over if she doesn't get the call. Best to be on the safe side. Not that I've told her what I'm up to, of course.

It feels strange to be working at the Grange. It's a new venue for us, though I wasn't surprised to see it added to our list. Fee income for schools like it must be getting harder to come by, and it's too close to the south side of Glasgow to have many posh kids locally. It must make sense for them to try to use their facilities for conferences in the Easter holidays. And we got it quite cheap.

"Cyber Security in a Changing World." Not a very snappy title for a gathering of people who reckon they're opinion-formers, and it might change more than they think if we vote to leave the EU. But I was quite impressed with some of the names on the list the Department for Business and Training sent us: the minister, a couple of BBC Scotland journalists, an economist from Heriot-Watt.

Some of the other names were familiar too. Damien Grayson, for example, chair of a seminar on Day 2. Damien Grayson, star of the Grange's science sixth, future start-up genius, occasional contributor to BBC science and technology programmes.

Damien Grayson, my ex-boyfriend.

How long had we been going out for when he ditched me? Nearly a year. *Ditched.* God, that sounds quaint! Now, we'd have been an item, and he'd probably have texted to say we ought to uncouple.

Newton Grange had only gone co-ed the year before. Funny

how I'd forgotten that. I was one of the first girls. We'd joined in the lower sixth. It made the atmosphere pretty febrile at times, and I guess most of us pretended we were more sexually experienced than we really were. I certainly did. But with Damien, it was the real thing. I loved him. He said he loved me. We'd made sure we were applying to the same universities; that way, we'd a better chance of keeping together.

It was at the Christmas party in our upper-sixth year. The college was quite good about allowing social events on the campus. Looking back, I reckon they thought there was less likelihood of us 'letting the school down' if they could keep an eye on us, though they must have known that we wouldn't be quietly going home when we had to leave at ten. They let us use the art room, which was pretty shabby and due to be refurbished, if I remember rightly. The advantage for us was that it was tucked away in the old north wing, and that there were lots of little studios nearby, where we could... brush up on our techniques, if you like.

Damien and I had taken our drinks to B 12, right at the end of the corridor. It was good to get there before anyone else could grab it. We'd made it clear that that was where we were going, and we didn't want to be interrupted.

Except we were. We'd been chatting, discussing plans, pretending for a few minutes that this was what we'd come for. Then the door opened, and Jenny was standing there.

I have to admit, Jenny looked sensational. She usually did. I remember how, in those boring French classes, you'd see the boys' eyes were drawn to her. That evening, she had a long black skirt, a tight-fitting blouse, hair undone.

"Oh hi," she said. "Didn't know this was where you two were heading." Lying bitch. I could feel Damien getting uncomfortable. I was sure there was nothing going on between them, though there had been talk... She asked if she could join us for a minute and sat down in the chair next to Damien. We chatted for a bit, though it was awkward. She seemed to want to find out what our plans were. Then she pretended to drop something, made sure she touched Damien as she picked it up. He seemed uncertain first, but then I suppose the male animal in him took over.

I don't want to remember all the details; it's too disagreeable. Damien did phone the next morning to apologise, tried to say how much he regretted it. The usual clichés. How much I meant to him, how he'd never treat me like that again, etc. But I wasn't having it. So for the rest of the school year, we kept our distance. Christ, it wasn't easy. Not for me. After a while, Damien didn't seem too bothered, and that just made it worse.

So, ever since, whenever I see Damien on the television, it's always painful, and when his name cropped up on the list of participants for this conference, it all came back again. I remembered how hurt I had been. Now I had the perfect chance to get my revenge; after nearly ten years, the opportunity was too good to miss.

Everything fell into place nicely. B 12 has a security code now, and the door at the end of the corridor an old-fashioned key. I'd no difficulty getting what I needed from the office. They must have assumed that, as the event manager, I had a use for them. If only they knew.

The only tricky bit was getting Damien to go down that corridor. But I persuaded him we ought to do a tour of "those hideouts we used to go to at the end of classes". Had he remembered what had happened there? He didn't seem to. I'd make sure he remembered.

Once we were inside, I'd waited until he'd sat down to look at the photo (of our trip to Ibiza the summer before) and start to read the piece of paper on the table in the middle of the room. I'd made sure the only chair had its back to the door, so I could slip outside and close the door before he could notice. Then I quietly went down the corridor, locked the door and got away. The note reminded him of what had happened here all those years ago, and informed him that later in the evening, the janitor would be checking all the doors. He'll be surprised to find the one at the end of corridor locked, assume someone at the conference had forgotten to tell him, unlock it and leave. No locked doors at night – that's a fire hazard. This bit is all made up, of course, but I'm sure Damien will swallow it. The note also promises Damien I'll text him with the code to B 12 once the janitor has finished his rounds, and he'll be free to go.

All perfectly planned. That's my job, after all.

I'm sure I can rely on Damien not using his mobile to get in touch with anyone. He won't want the indignity of requesting rescue from a woman who has kidnapped him.

Time to go and let him out. He won't be expecting anything to happen just yet. I'll quietly unlock the door at the end of the corridor, then send him the text when I'm back in my car.

* * *

For all that, as I climb the stone staircase, I am a bit nervous. The Grange is an old building, despite the attempts to modernise parts of it. At least the corridor is well lit. I'm glad I remembered to bring trainers to change into; heels would have made too much noise.

After I've unlocked the door, I decide to go down the

corridor and have a quiet look at Damien in B 12. I want a moment to enjoy my revenge. Once I reach the door to the room, I stand to the side so that I can't be seen through the glass. I look inside, but I can't see Damien. He's not sitting at the table where he ought to be.

Cautiously, I put in the code and open the door. Inside it feels chilly. For a moment, I am puzzled, then become aware of cold air blowing from my left. I turn and see the window... it is open. I spin round the room, again looking for the man I locked in. The corners are dark, with a pile of old desks in the one on the right. But I can't see any sign of life.

I force myself to go to the open window and look down into the quad. I peer into the gloom for a few moments, dreading the sight of a body spread-eagled below. Nothing. Then I hear a movement behind, turn and see Damien seated at the table, facing me. His face is in shade, his expression hard to see. He stands, gestures to the chair.

"Brigitte," he says. "Come and sit down." As I move to the side, the faint light from outside shows his face more clearly. He is smiling, but I cannot tell what kind of smile. I wish I hadn't removed the light bulb.

"I'd like to talk to you, Brigitte," he says. "I do remember what happened here, you know. We never had a proper chance to..."

I stay by the window. This isn't how it's supposed to work out. Damien stands up and walks towards me.

"You're bloody good at your job, Brigitte. The conference has gone so well. But... oh, come on, no janitor is going to unlock a door and just walk away, is he? Assuming there is a janitor."

I can't think of what to say. I'm frightened. Damien was

never violent, but he might have changed. He won't like being tricked. He nods towards the window, and then turns back towards me.

"I was pretty sure you'd come back to have a look, Brigitte. You'd want to make the most of the moment. And I knew you'd have to look out of the window. Nasty moment, that, eh? So let's..."

My phone vibrates in my bag. We both start. I check the screen: it is an unknown number. But my memory has been jolted. I pretend to look at the call details, but am speed-dialling Claire. Looking straight at Damien, I speak into the phone.

"Claire. It's me. I'm in B 12. There's... someone here... Right... Good, thanks."

The expression on Damien's face changes. He is serious now. I think I can see him reflecting, calculating what course of action to take. Then he stands and, looking me calmly in the eye, pushes the chair under the table, turns and leaves the room.

I wait a minute or two, also calculating. Damien will have assumed, won't he, that Claire – accompanied by others? – will be making her way to this room. His best bet will be to hide somewhere and then slip out of the building. Shivering, I go to the window and close it. It is not long before I hear voices, including Claire's.

I know I'll have to tell her what I've done, or most of it, later on. I can trust her. I'll have to think of a story to tell the others. Damien won't want to report me for my actions, will he? That would just make him look stupid.

Tomorrow is the last day of the conference, thank goodness. I can't call in sick, but I really don't want to face Damien. I'll have to play it carefully, find a job that keeps me away from him.

I can't help thinking that the Grange has let me down again.

The Old School

The invitation came months ago. Out of the blue. I thought it had to be a joke. I couldn't see why they'd want someone like me handing out the prizes at their Founder's Day. But then I realised it had to be to do with the NNR. My name did get into the papers when it reopened in the autumn. "Local Environmentalist Does the Honours at Refurbished Reserve." Someone at the school must have noticed my name and recognised it from when I was there. But it's over thirty years ago. If it was a teacher that made the connection, he must be nearly retired by now. When do they retire these days? As soon as they can, I reckon. It's a tough job.

I've had one or two of their pupils coming to the field station over the years, doing projects for their biology Highers, but that's about all the contact I've had with the place. I pass the school if I have to go Glasgow for anything, and I noticed they'd put up a new sign. "Newton Grange School, HMC. The Best Preparation for a Fulfilling Life." Why does everything have to have a slogan these days?

In the end, I decided I had to say yes, even though it's not my kind of thing. When I was there, it was usually local councillors, businessmen, people like that, who gave out the prizes. Always men. The school must have thought, now it's 2016 and the planet's up shit creek, we'd better ask someone with an ecological background. I was going to have a word with Colin about the invitation, but his school doesn't have a prize-giving day as far as I know, and he's certainly no fan of private education. I bet he'd take a job at the Grange if he had the chance, though.

When they wrote back to me, they said how delighted they were – and honoured – that I'd agreed to give the oration on Founder's Day. (It'll be a talk they're getting, not an oration.) Any topic that might be of interest to staff and students. But I was sure they'd want something environmental, otherwise why would they have asked me? No doubt they'd want me to mention the solar panels I saw on the roof of the new science block.

It took me a while to decide what to talk about.

When I saw the date, I thought, that's the Saturday after the EU referendum. So I'll start by saying that there have been some improvements in the environment, that it's not all bad news. Cleaner rivers, restrictions on pesticides, things like that. And that a lot of this is down to the EU passing laws that UK governments would never have done.

Then the main point of the talk will be about the need to be untidy. That should go down well. But before getting on to that, I'll ask them to name any famous scientists they can think of. Einstein, I'll bet. Stephen Hawking. (Will they get his name right?) Darwin, possibly. Newton, if I'm lucky. Then I'll ask them if they can name any famous Swedish scientists, tell them that one of the most important of them all came from Sweden. (Wait five seconds, just enough to create an embarrassing silence. Dare I ask if any of the teachers knows the answer?) Then give them the name of Linnaeus, spell it for them.

Then I'll show them a picture of an animal, or an insect. A butterfly, perhaps. Give them the name, in English, then in Latin. Point out that it has a genus name and a species name. Explain that everything identified by scientists has to have a name that everyone uses, and that everyone has to agree on which categories it belongs to. A neat and tidy system, that's what the Swedish scientist is famous for. (Can anyone remember his name?)

But I'll say we've become obsessed with having everything neat and tidy, that we're all control freaks. That this isn't good for the natural world. Big square fields, no hedgerows, and so on. I'll ask them what they have in their front gardens. Tarmac or paving blocks I'll bet, parking for the four-by-fours.

Next, I'll ask how many of them have been to the reserve. No doubt they'll have been primed. ("The speaker at Founder's Day is the manager of the Lochburnie Reserve, so he'll probably talk about it, and he might ask you some questions.") I'll tell them that when we refurbished it, we deliberately left lots of untidy corners, because wildlife loves untidiness. They might even have seen some of the changes, piles of wood at the edges of the trails, things like that. We don't cut off the seed heads of the flowers straightaway. We leave most of the broken branches where they are. (Do they know that a dead tree is a richer habitat than a live one?) I'll show them some pictures.

Then I'll suggest that they can do their bit for nature by making their own untidy piles, starting in their bedrooms. (Pause for a laugh, if I haven't lost them by now.) Suggest that their dads might cut the grass less often. (Another laugh, maybe.) Say it's a good idea to dig in some of the garden weeds, and not to sweep up leaves as soon as they fall. I've got a great photo of a toad looking out from a pile of leaves we'd left under the willows behind the visitor centre.

If it looks as though they're interested, and haven't got their phones out yet, I'll go on a bit about wildlife corridors, rewilding. Say there's a plan to reintroduce wolves to Cumbernauld, and see how they react. Would they like that? What about lynxes in Greenock? Bears in Bearsden? (Wait for the groans.)

Probably that will be enough. I'll thank the school for inviting me, say that they're lucky to have such a good school to go to, with teachers who do a lot for them outside lesson time. That was certainly the case in my day. Then give out the prizes, and sign off.

* * *

It went down fairly well, I think. I kept it short, and they were pretty attentive. I had to cut out the stuff about the EU, of course. But the kids laughed at the right points, and the head seemed pleased. At least there were no flowers. Someone must have worked out that there isn't a Mrs Rogers any more. The Waitrose voucher is a good idea and the chocolates look quite classy. There was some polite small talk afterwards with a few of the parents, though when one of them said how good the school had been for her boys, and how "We all want what's best for our children, don't we?", I had to bite my tongue.

It was only when I got back home that I started to feel really uncomfortable. It was the head's closing speech that did it. It brought back memories of my time at the school, and some of the things they used to say to us. About the ethos of the place, I suppose, though they might not have used the word then. In those days, it was all captains of industry stuff, how we were the people to lead, set the example. They've got to be a bit more subtle now, but some things don't appear to have changed. One comment in particular got me thinking. The head talked about former pupils who'd died in the past year. Most of them were old, obviously. Older than me, at any rate. But there was one guy who'd died young, of cancer. Not really the Newton Grange sort. He'd got elected to the city council on a hard-left ticket, representing somewhere really run-down. But the head spoke approvingly of him. He'd rebelled against the schooling he had had, but that was all right. The important thing was to have principles, ideas, even if they were different ones from the school's. I must admit, this rankled. It struck me that they've got you by the balls whatever you do. Either you're one of them and you accept their ethos, or else you show how great the school was by not being one of them. You can't win.

Maybe I'm overreacting. But when I look at the difference between a school like Newton Grange – and their new science block is fantastic – and the sort of place where Colin teaches, it's clear how unfair everything is.

I tried to put it out of my mind, think of something else. I checked to see if there were any decent films on Film 4.

It was uncanny. The first one I saw listed was *If...* I've seen it before, more than once. I remember being quite disturbed the first time. It's pretty sexy. That naked motorbike ride certainly stuck in my teenage mind. But it's the ending that you really can't forget, when they get on the roof and use the guns and the grenades they've found to attack the party of teachers and posh parents. Suddenly it's not a game. And the woman who grabs a machine gun and turns it on the kids on the roof, screaming "Bastards, bastards." I suppose I was uncomfortable then at the violence, in the setting of a school which wasn't all that different from the one I was going to. I must have felt that this wasn't the way to do things, that peaceful change is possible. I wish I was still so sure.

Watching the film again, I was trying to guess how the head might have reacted to the ending. "Revolutionary violence is clearly something we cannot condone, but these boys have at least learned to think for themselves." Perhaps not.

* * *

Sunday morning was bright but chilly. I'd not slept well, still a bit stressed about the prize-giving. And the bloody referendum. What the hell have we done there? I can't get my head round it. Some clown tosses a coin, it comes down heads not tails, and we go back to the Dark Ages. Makes no sense.

I got up early and decided to pass by the reserve on my way to do the Sunday shop. I hadn't checked the pond levels for a time, and they can get a bit low at this time of year. When I arrived, I was surprised to see someone sitting on one of the benches, near the visitor centre. I said hello, and he said something about it hadn't been a bad night. I could see he was pretty badly dressed, and then realised he was saying he'd been there on the bench all night. He was sitting alongside a large, tattered backpack. I don't really like the thought of people spending the night at the reserve, though there's not a lot we can do about it. It's not exactly a secure site. We've had a bit of trouble over the years – mostly pot-smokers – but no real problems.

But he seemed unthreatening, and I half-recognised him. I asked him if he fancied a bite to eat; I keep some food in the reserve office, in case I get hungry when I'm there on my own.

As he was eating his microwaved toastie, we got chatting. His name was Peter Field. He seemed happy to talk. It was when he mentioned that he'd worked as a school technician that I realised where I'd seen him before: at Dalton High when Colin worked there, before he got his promoted post. Peter said he just about remembered me.

His story was typical in a way, I guess. A broken marriage (he admitted he was mostly to blame), a couple of years living at his mother's. Then she'd died suddenly; he had to leave her flat, nowhere to go. No home address, no job. He'd been promised temporary accommodation by the council, starting in August. In the meantime, he was on the streets. It wasn't too bad, he said; he could usually find somewhere not too cold at night, and there were meals of a kind to be found. But he was sure he wouldn't be able to hack it in the winter. He said that I'd be surprised at how many people like him were sleeping rough: people with an education, not addicts, but there because of a mixture of bad luck and bad judgement. He did know some rough sleepers who had killed themselves, though. The welfare system was brutal, he said. He didn't want to go on about it, except to say the people who had set up Universal Credit should roast in hell.

He finished his toastie and looked at the clock on the wall. He said he'd better be going. He asked me when the reserve opened on Sundays, and I said not until ten. Suddenly I saw how thin he looked. Somehow his bushy dark hair made him appear bulkier than he was. I made some more coffee and asked him if he wanted anything else to eat. He said no, he was fine, and that it was surprising how little food you needed to keep going. He'd be OK, though it made him sick to think of parents who didn't have enough to feed their kids. I told him to keep the packet of biscuits, at least.

He'd been very calm, matter-of-fact until then, but suddenly he stood up, looked out of the window and shouted:

"You know what, eh? I'll tell you. This society of ours, it fucking stinks. My mother was a primary school teacher. She once told me that if you go into a classroom of thirty kids round here, nine of them will be living in poverty."

Immediately he sat down and apologised for his outburst. It wasn't easy to know how to react, but I said something about social inequality, how it was clearly getting worse, but what could we do about it, start blowing things up, throwing grenades?

He looked at me in a strange way as he swept the crumbs off the table onto his plate.

"Why do you say that?"

It was my turn to feel uncomfortable. I told him about the film I'd been watching the night before, and how it ends.

"I know," he said. "I saw that film years ago at the cinesoc your son used to run. I was a real film fan in those days. That one certainly made an impact. He was great, your son. That club was really popular."

I thanked him for the compliment.

After a few seconds, he stuffed his hands into the pockets of his scruffy coat and looked through the entrance door to the seating area outside the reserve.

"I remember another film from those days," he went on. "Can't remember what it was called. But it was about a family and how their kids got taken away because the parents couldn't cope."

He looked at me as if he was asking if I knew the film. I said it rang a bell.

"When they'd seen the film, your son asked the kids what they thought about it, tried to get them to react."

I laughed. "Just like Colin," I said. "Always was good at asking awkward questions."

Peter said that was how he remembered him too.

"Some of them came out with practical suggestions, how the parents might borrow from friends until they could get things sorted, how they might look for a smaller flat. Things like that. I remember Colin saying to me afterwards that he was disappointed none of them seemed to think there was something fundamentally wrong with a society that did that to families."

I thought he was going to say more, but he stood up, drained his cup and slipped the biscuits into his backpack.

"Look, thanks for the food and the coffee. It's good of you. I'll let you get on with what you're doing. It's a lovely reserve."

I wished him good luck, said that I hoped he'd get the accommodation he'd been promised. I said that if he managed to be discreet at night, I wouldn't look too hard for him in the morning.

As he was opening the door, I had a thought.

"Look, when you've got sorted out, use this for something special."

I pressed the Waitrose voucher into his hand. He looked a bit puzzled, then said thanks, smiled and went on his way.

An Afternoon at the Reserve

In front of the visitor centre, groups of children and adults were enjoying the afternoon sun. At the table nearest the gift shop, where the sun was brightest, an elderly woman was sitting on a plastic chair, looking into the distance. Her handbag was in her lap, her walking stick leaning against the table.

After a while, she got up slowly, collected her belongings and crossed over to a table under the shade of a blossoming hawthorn. Two of the seats were occupied, one by a young boy finishing his ice cream, the other by an older man. Grandfather and grandson, she assumed. The man smiled and gestured at the other seat: yes, of course, it was free.

They watched as the youngster picked up a fishing net and ran off towards the pond.

The man picked up a well-used book from the table and wiped ice cream from the cover.

"We don't often have to move into shade, do we? Even in June," he said with a laugh. "I'm Eric, by the way. Pleased to meet you."

The woman removed her sunglasses and placed them carefully in her handbag. In a soft voice, she said her name was Joan; her daughter and granddaughter were following the nature trail through the reed-beds. She rummaged in her bag until she found her regular glasses, and put them on. She leaned over to look at the title of the book on the table and asked,

"He must be keen on frogs, your... grandson?"

"Yes, right on both counts," Eric laughed, picking the book up and smoothing its covers. "He's Alistair, and ponds are his big thing. He was eight last week. Lovely age. Don't know where he finds the energy. I bring him here when I can. It's a great place for kids, isn't it?"

Joan nodded her agreement, and added that she and her family often came over from Linlithgow for the day.

"Eileen and Kirsty usually come at the weekend. It's nice to be here on a weekday for a change. Kirsty's school has an in-service day. They've been here for a couple of hours now."

For a few moments, they sat quietly looking over to the pond and the woodland, listening to the sound of the birds and the occasional cries of excited children.

Eric broke the silence by offering to put up the umbrella which was leaning against the table.

"No, thank you," Joan replied. "I'm fine over here. It's lovely to have a warm day for a change, isn't it? I make sure I move into the shade before they come back for me."

Eric laughed.

"Do they tell you off too? We'd struggle to get sunstroke in Scotland, wouldn't we?"

His grandson waved at him from the pond: he'd caught something in his net. A volunteer in a green fleece was examining it with him, and then helped him return it to the water. As they watched, another volunteer approached their table with three differently coloured bags. She cleared away the rubbish, telling them that since the reserve had been reopened, they were keen to recycle as much as possible. She proudly pointed out the plants growing on the roof of the visitor centre and the compost bins at the entrance to the car park.

Eric was about to ask her something when they were interrupted by a child's voice, breathless and excited.

"Hi, Gran. Look what Mum's got me."

The new arrivals collected two chairs and sat down.

The girl placed a small cloth bird on the table. Brown wings, a speckled breast. Joan picked it up and looked at it carefully, deciding that it was probably a thrush.

"And Gran, if you press it here" – the fair-haired girl took the bird back from her grandmother's hands and squeezed it hard – "it makes the right noise."

A short burst of song emerged from the bird's interior, repeated twice in a slightly altered form.

"That's lovely, dear. It's a thrush, isn't it? Did you find anything on your walk?"

Before the girl could answer, her mother had picked up the umbrella and inserted it in the hole in the middle of the table.

"You sure you're not too hot, dear? It's really quite warm today."

"Thanks, Eileen. I'm fine. I've been talking to..." She paused, embarrassed, searching for the name.

"Eric. Nice to meet you." He laughed. "I'm just as bad. Until I've heard a name at least three times, it doesn't sink in. That thrush has got the right idea. You remember things if you say them over and over again."

It was clear that the girl wanted to get away. She took a leaflet out of her mother's hand and asked if there was enough time to go on the Fen trail. He mother seemed reluctant, but her grandmother insisted that she would be happy sitting waiting for them, and that the two of them should make the most of the afternoon.

Joan held out her hand and asked, "Shall I look after your thrush for you, Kirsty?"

"Yes please, Gran."

Eric leaned over and whispered in the girl's ear.

"And I'll make sure your gran doesn't fall asleep in the sun. How about that, Kirsty?"

The girl looked up at the strange man but after a moment's hesitation took her mother's hand and pulled her towards the start of the track.

Her grandmother watched her leave. A few minutes later, her reverie was interrupted.

"Excuse me a minute."

Eric stood up and walked to the pond, where his grandson and the volunteer were busy examining another catch. When Eric returned, he sat down heavily and said it was still very warm.

"I'm for another ice cream. Can I get you one?"

Joan hesitated, but then agreed with a smile.

"Thank you. That would be very nice."

When Eric came back, he found Joan sitting quietly, eyes half-closed. He eased himself into his plastic seat.

"Here we are. Sorry, the shop was busy. They only had choc-ices, I'm afraid."

"That's lovely, thank you very much. Your grandson still appears to be enjoying himself."

Eric nodded.

"Alistair thinks Hamid's wonderful. I'm sure he's right. Hamid is brilliant with the youngsters. Knows such a lot much, but never talks down to them. He's a student at Strathclyde, comes over to help out when he can. He's very good on frogs, toads and so on. Bumble bees are really his speciality, though. When we were here last week, he was saying that he thought he'd found a rare bee in the bushes over by the pond. Today he's brought along his good camera to get a better picture of the bee. He says he gets some funny looks when he's peering into the undergrowth, trying to see what's there. Some odd comments too. That's why he called me over just now. So I could keep an eye on Alistair while he takes some photos. He's going to show them to an expert at Edinburgh University."

They chatted about families, about their children's busy lives and the efforts they made to spend time together at the weekend. Alistair's parents both had full-time jobs, Eric explained, so he was happy to look after his grandson when he could. They both agreed that the reserve was a wonderful place, that the volunteers were so good with the children, that it was important for the next generation to spend time outside, away from their computer screens and their mobile phones.

When Eric stood up to drop the ice-cream wrappers in the litter bin, the volunteer with the three bags was passing. Eric obligingly placed the wrappers in the black bag. Once he had sat down again, he closed his eyes and leaned back in his chair.

"We're not going to save the planet that way, are we?"

"I'm not sure I..."

"Sorry, not making myself clear. Recycling, solar panels, all that. It's just to make us feel a bit less guilty. Jamie and Lorraine – that's Alistair's parents – keep telling me I must remember to rinse the plastic milk bottles and put them out with the newspapers every Thursday. Shouldn't use the car when I go bowling. Do some exercises instead of putting the heating on. They think it's all right for them to fly to Berlin for a weekend break as long as they use low-energy bulbs. Anyhow, they shouldn't be plastic in the first place. The milk bottles, I mean. Sorry, shouldn't go on. It's a bit of an obsession with me."

Joan picked up the thrush and smoothed its feathers.

"My children are always telling me I must protect the environment as well. But they don't see the value in sitting still. Eileen told me the other day that she often drives more than a hundred miles over a weekend. I wonder if they're trying to make up for Monday to Friday. They're both so busy. But then they do so much on Sundays that they're exhausted again."

"Sounds just like Jamie. Tires himself out. Then he'll say: you ought to get out more, Dad, find things to do. But I've got enough on. And I quite like watching television in the afternoon, sometimes. And you're right. About lifestyles, I mean. We've been told we can have it all. Sometimes I tell Jamie that our generation was the really thrifty one, we reused things before the eco-warriors told us to. Just to annoy him."

He picked up the bird book and cleaned its cracked covers. He gestured towards the three coloured wheelie bins at the side of the visitor centre.

"I'll tell you what happened to us once, when we were in Florida on a family holiday. Sorry, you've probably heard enough by now."

It was Joan's turn to laugh.

"No, go on. I'm all ears."

"Well, you know how wasteful that kind of trip is. It's not just the flights; it's all the things you throw away, the size of the food portions, everything. Well, we went to a diner – all-you-can-eat breakfast, for $3.99 or something ridiculous – and there was a sign at the counter, by the pile of napkins. "Please just take one napkin per diner. We can save the planet one napkin at a time!" I'm sure it wasn't a joke. Who are we kidding? I couldn't get over it. We think we can continue living the way we do, with a few little adjustments but no real changes, no sacrifices. It's not going to work, and we owe it to... Sorry, promise I won't preach any more."

He broke off, thinking the conversation had run its course. They waited for their grandchildren to return. It was Joan who broke the silence.

"I remember, my parents would often sit all evening, reading, doing the crossword, sometimes playing a game of solo. Not very exciting, maybe, but they didn't think they were missing out. Keeping still, doing nothing, there's a lot to be said for it. And they weren't wasting resources. The best way to use less energy is to keep still."

Eric gave a polite clap.

"That's very good, Joan. Can I use that with Jamie and Lorraine?"

They looked up to see Alistair returning from the pond, shorts filthy, face streaked with mud. Hamid handed him over with a smile, saying he was amazed how much Alistair managed to remember. His grandfather thanked the volunteer for his patience with Alistair, adding that he hoped the experts would confirm his identification of the bee.

Hamid said he'd had a great afternoon and walked towards the reserve office. Alistair touched his grandfather's arm.

"Grandad, have you seen Hamid's backpack? It's really cool. Look, it's stripy like a bee. Can I have one?"

Eric was saved from having to deny his grandson's request by a shout coming from the end of the Fen trail.

"Gran, we're back. It was fantastic. We saw some ducks, and a heron. It just took off, looked like a dinosaur."

Mother and daughter reached the table in the shade. The thrush was returned to its owner, and once the bags and other belongings had been gathered together, the two small family groups made their way towards the exit. The car park was beginning to empty. Eric put his grandson's muddy trainers into the boot of his car and walked over to where Eileen was fastening her daughter into the back seat of her people-carrier.

"It's been really nice meeting you, Joan. I'll tell my son I've been advised to spend more time sitting still. Who knows, we might meet up again some time."

"That would be good. I owe you a choc-ice. Goodbye now."

Eileen held open the passenger door for her mother. Then she hesitated:

"You're sure you don't need the toilet before we go, Mum."

"No, I'm fine."

The driver looked over her shoulder as she reversed out of her parking space.

"He seemed very pleasant. What was he called again? Oh yes, Eric. What did you talk about?"

"Oh you know, families, the reserve. How to reduce our carbon footprints."

"That's nice, dear. OK, Kirsty? All set for home?"

People-watching

She has a quick look at the map above the seats on the other side of the bus. Not that she needs to; the names are familiar enough. Broxburn, Maybury, Drum Brae, Haymarket. Terminus for the X18: St Andrew's House. She decides she'll get out at Princes Street and walk. It only takes ten minutes, and she can call in at the shop.

She closes her eyes. It's been a tiring day. She's not getting any younger, and the girls were as lively as usual. Still, it's always nice to spend time with them. And Deirdre appreciates the help; the dialysis wears her out.

The bus pulls up sharply and she opens her eyes. Broxton post office. A good half hour to go. The journey seems slow somehow, but she doesn't mind. She always enjoys travelling by bus. Especially now she doesn't have to use it in the rush hour. She sits back to enjoy the rest of the journey. Buses might be old-fashioned – Lothian buses certainly are – but there's still something human about them. The new tram's fine, though God knows it's cost a fortune, but it is a bit... clinical. (A good word, she thinks, for an ex-nurse.) Paddy doesn't rate it highly either. "No character. Too clean."

But really it's the passengers that make bus journeys

enjoyable. Longer journeys are better, when passengers stay on the bus long enough for you to work out who they might be, what their backgrounds were. Their 'back stories', that's what Gavin calls them when he jokes about her fascination with her fellow passengers. Though she can never see what the *back* has to do with it; it's just their stories, as far as she's concerned. But then he's done a degree in media studies, so he must know about these things. (She remembers Paddy's dismissal of their son's choice of subject; he thought Gavin watched too much television already.) But Paddy has never shared her delight in people-watching either. It's too vague for him; you can never be sure whether you're on the right lines. But that doesn't matter; it's using her imagination, that's the point of it.

The time of day does make a difference, though. It's better in the evening, when things are starting to get quiet, but before they're too quiet and you can get a bit nervous. In the old days, coming back from the Royal at eight at night, you used to wonder what sort of work the other passengers had been doing. You could sometimes get an idea. From their clothes, from what they were reading (if they were reading; most people nowadays either have their eyes closed or they're staring at their phones), from the colour of their skin. Were they pleased to be going home? You'd hoped so. It wouldn't always be the case. There might be troubles at home. Broughton's all right. But there are plenty of rough areas in Leith. Gangs of kids (feral, Paddy calls them), families with not enough money for a decent meal. And noise everywhere; it seems to get worse all the time.

She looks around without letting the other passengers notice her. She's got quite good at this over the years.

Opposite, older man in some sort of uniform – traffic warden, off-duty? A couple who'd been there when she got on – fifties? early sixties? – looking through photos, passing them to each other. A bit farther back, a younger man, a bit fidgety, brown-skinned, bearded. Student, perhaps. On his right, a dozy-looking schoolgirl, lost in her phone. Behind them, a youngish guy in a black puffer, shaved head, looking out of the window. Another woman, middle-aged, smart blue jacket, reading from what looks like a Kindle. The sort you'd hardly notice.

Who to start with? OK, the couple. She can't see what the photos are of, but the couple are smiling as they look at them. Wedding photos, perhaps. So... daughter's wedding, a few weeks back; she's asked them to come over and choose some. The man has a scar on the side of his throat; she can't help noticing it. Cancer operation, presumably. Daughter and son-in-law had brought the wedding forward in case he got worse. But now he's in remission. (How many times has she seen patients going home from Oncology, relieved at the prognosis they'd been given? It was awful to see those who had to come back later.) They look quite well-off. The woman in an expensive-looking trouser suit. She's been... what? Teacher, civil servant? Maybe still is. (Paddy uses 'civil servant' as a bit of an insult; for him, they're people who haven't had to work too hard, but who've got a good pension ahead of them.) The daughter might be an only child. Maybe her mother had her fairly late.

She becomes aware that they are looking at her. But there's no hostility, just a smile and a slight nod of the head. The man looks at the map above her head; she hears him say something about getting out at Haymarket. (It's not true that people aren't so friendly any more. And they do offer their seats to older people; it happened to her last week, for the first time. She must be getting on.)

What about the single guy nearer the back? Not so easy, this one. Asian, judging by his appearance. Good-looking. What's the book he's looking at? Backpack by his feet. He takes a camera out of it, looks at it and then puts it back. Now he has his phone in his lap. When he closes his eyes, he seems to be trying to memorise something. Keeps looking at his watch.

The man raises his head from his book and looks out of the window. She turns her head away. But he doesn't seem to see her. He's trying to work out where he's got to, counting the stops to... where? He puts the book in his backpack.

She thinks: wouldn't it be funny if the other passengers were trying to work out who I am? They'd get quite a bit wrong. A bit too well dressed for a retired nurse, for one thing. (I've always liked nice clothes; Paddy used to call me a 'Dedicated Follower' back when we were first married.) I'm supposed to look young for my age; they'd probably say mid-fifties. Local, though, that's pretty obvious. Certainly not a tourist, too relaxed, too much at home. Mind you, Edinburgh's such a mixed place these days. You can't tell who might have been born here. I like it that way; more interesting stories. I suppose I can see what Gavin means when he talks about his back stories; how you've got to be where you are, where you've come from.

Oh, the guy with the backpack has dropped his phone. It's on the floor in front of him. Someone might stand on it.

She stands, a little stiffly, and walks the three or four steps to where the young man is sitting. She taps him on the shoulder, smiles and points to the phone at his feet.

He seems rather startled, but when he realises what has happened, he says, "Thank you very much", retrieves his phone and puts it carefully into the front pocket of his backpack. An odd colour for a backpack, she can't help noticing. Black and yellow stripes, red zips.

She goes back to her seat. The man in the puffer at the back is looking up, the first time he's moved since she saw him.

At Haymarket, most of the passengers leave the bus. The couple smile as they pass her. The schoolgirl gets out too. The two men and the woman in the smart jacket are still there. More people get on, but there's no time to work out who they might be.

* * *

At the end of Princes Street, she gets out and sets off up Broughton Street. It is starting to rain. She'll call in at the shop for an apple pie. Paddy's good with pasta, but he won't have made a pudding. It'll be a chance to have a word with Tomas as well. It's good that they're making such a success of the shop. It was certainly getting too much for Paddy. All those long hours. But Tomas and his brother both work so hard. Even Paddy is beginning to accept that *his* shop can be run by immigrants.

When she gets to the shop, she looks at the Polish food they have started to sell. Lots of pickles, judging from the pictures on the jars. Sausages, odd-looking vegetables in tins. She collects a ready-made fruit pie and joins the short queue at the checkout. She is pleased that Tomas recognises her, asks about the family. He even remembers about Deirdre and the dialysis.

Just before she turns into McDonald Road, she notices several police cars and ambulances speeding towards the city centre.

* * *

"Thanks, Paddy. Tasty as ever. I'll get the pie. Custard or ice cream?"

Ice cream. It's easier. They leave the washing-up for later, take their puddings into the sitting room. They settle back on the sofa and put the television on.

On the Scottish news bulletin, commentators are still analysing the EU referendum result. Paddy groans. Then, dramatically, the discussion is cut short. The newsreader announces a major incident in Edinburgh city centre, and the screen is suddenly full of flashing lights, armed policemen, ambulances. People are being held behind metal barriers. The reporter says that so far she has little to go on, except that the police believe that they may have thwarted a terrorist attack.

Shocked, they turn the sound up and lean forward.

They recognise St Andrew's House. There is a number X18 bus, hurriedly parked on the pavement.

She is about to say something, but she holds back.

The reporter is providing more information. It appears that the bus had been stopped by police cars just before its destination. Counter-terrorism officers had stormed it and seized one of the passengers.

They become aware of how close all this is. Then:

"The bus, Paddy! It looks like the one I was on. The one I got off. I could have been..."

She half rises, almost knocking over her bowl. It takes a moment for her husband to follow her train of thought.

"All right. I get you. But Margaret, the X18s, they come every..."

The phone rings. It is Deirdre. She is watching the news: have they heard?

She picks up the receiver.

"I'm fine, love. I'm fine. Got back an hour ago. Yes, we've just seen it. I know, it could have been my bus, but I walked from Princes Street."

She realises she must get in touch with her son, reassure him that she's all right.

"Thanks for ringing, Deirdre. I'll phone you back later."

There is no reply from Gavin's mobile; she leaves a message. They return to the television.

Paddy asks why she got off before the terminus. Was the bus crowded?

"No, not really. People got on at Haymarket, but..."

She stops, remembering the passengers.

"Oh heavens, Paddy. There was this young man. Muslim, I suppose. Reading from a book, looked a bit edgy. Kept looking at the stops on the map. You don't suppose...? Oh, the mobile! This man, Paddy. He'd dropped his mobile. I went over and told him, and he said thank-you. Don't they use mobiles to... you know...?"

"Set bombs off? I don't know. But why should he...?"

"He kept counting the stops."

"People are always counting the stops. Perhaps he didn't know the city. Sit down, love. It's just a coincidence."

They look again at the television. They focus on the bus, but flashing lights make it difficult to make sense of what is happening. The reporter is repeating herself; it appears that a lone terrorist has been apprehended on a bus heading for the city centre. The police are still not allowing people to leave the scene.

"Let's switch this off, Margaret. Come back to it when we've done the dishes. Why not try Gavin again?"

He isn't able to finish his question.

"That's him, Paddy! The man with the mobile. That's his backpack. I remember the colour. Black and yellow stripes. And if he's just standing there, it can't have been him, can it? I mean, the police would have taken him away by now, wouldn't they?"

She looks over at her husband, reassured, though she can't quite work out why.

On the screen, the reporter abruptly moves in front of the camera, announces that the police are removing the suspect. There is a glimpse of a man in a black puffer jacket, handcuffed, being pushed into the back seat of a police car.

It takes a moment for her to make the connection.

"Paddy, *he* was on the bus as well. I was looking round at the passengers, trying to work out who they were. You know what I'm like when there are people to work out."

"I know, I know. Look, it looks like no one's been hurt. Let's put the kettle on."

"OK. But let me try Gavin again first."

But as she picks up the remote, she stops and points it at the set once more.

"The woman in the blue jacket. I saw her at the back of the bus. I'm sure it's her."

Her husband tries to hide a sigh. They watch as the woman, who seems to be in charge, gestures to one of the policemen. He reads out a statement to the camera. The authorities believe that the suspect, who was armed with a knife, but probably no firearms, was probably acting alone. His motivation is unclear, but he had shouted anti-immigration slogans as he was taken away. He may have been suffering from mental health problems. Residents are thanked for their patience and understanding. They can be reassured that the neighbourhood is safe.

The phone rings. She picks it up and begins a long conversation with her son. The television is switched off at last.

An hour later, they are finishing the washing-up. As she puts the plates away in the cupboard, she replays the bus journey in her imagination. Some of the participants in the drama now have their roles: the young man in the puffer, the Asian student, the woman in the blue jacket – who must be Special Branch, according to Paddy. But these are not the roles she had given them.

She turns to her husband.

"So much for my people-watching," she says. "You can't tell, can you?"

"No, you can't," he replies. "But it won't stop you trying, will it?" he adds with a laugh. "I'll go and lock up now, shall I?"

Doctor Emma

The bell to my flat is one of the old-fashioned types; I can't persuade the other residents in our block to pay for a proper security system. When it rang, just after seven, it startled me. I was trying to stay awake until later in the evening, to get over the worst of the jet lag. I was so dopey that I waited for Stefan to see who the caller was, but then I remembered that, since it was Friday, he'd be working late and that I'd have to answer it.

When I opened the door, at first there didn't appear to be anyone. The building faces north, towards Leith Walk, so even on light evenings, you can't always be sure who the caller is. Then I saw someone coming back from the side of the house; whoever it was must have been looking for a back door. It wasn't until the person was standing in the light from inside the house that I saw that his face was black.

He asked if he was speaking to Dr Emma McAllister. I nodded, and he held out his hand, giving me his name. I had to ask him to repeat it: the surname, Falola, was one I had come across often enough, but I didn't make sense of his first name. I apologised for my drowsiness, explaining that I had just come back that morning from a long flight. To my surprise, he said that he knew that I had just got back from his country. He smiled and said he was sorry for disturbing me. Handing over a business card, he explained that he had been sent on behalf of his country's embassy in London. Now that he was standing fully in the light, I could see how handsome his face was: strong features, dark brown eyes, a neatly trimmed beard.

He explained that the embassy wished to convey their thanks for my medical assistance. Rather than simply phoning me, they preferred to convey a personal expression of their gratitude. And they would be delighted if I could come to a reception the following Wednesday. The reception was to show appreciation to me and the other young Scottish doctors who had helped with the emergency. They had hired a venue on George Street. His business card, he explained, also had the number of the venue; if I phoned it, they would give me further details. I thanked him and said I would certainly consider it. He shook my hand, again said how grateful he was, and walked back down the path towards the road. Then he stopped and caught my attention just as I was closing the door.

He said he'd nearly forgotten, but the embassy had also asked him to collect a few bits of information. Could I just tell him my full name, how I expected to be addressed, where I had stayed while in his country and the details of the flights I had used to return. The people out in the field hospital, he explained, were not always very good at storing data or replying to requests from the embassy, and over the weekend, it would be difficult to get in touch with them. So it would be quicker if I could allow him to jot this down so that the embassy would have the information first thing on Monday.

I don't know why, but I hesitated. My name, he obviously knew it. Surely they had a record of where I had been living.

And why did he want to know the flight details? I said I was really tired, and that I'd find the information for him and phone back. Did his face show a little frustration? He was no longer in the light; it was hard to tell. But he smiled, said that would be fine, and thanked me again for all I had done for his fellow countrymen, and for Africa as a whole.

I closed the door and locked it. In the kitchen, I put the kettle on and placed the business card on the pile of mail next to the toaster. Now I felt hungry but didn't have the energy to prepare a proper meal. A cup of tea and two slices of toast was all I could manage. I couldn't face tackling my recorded messages or emails. When I tried to call my mother again, there was no reply. Then I remembered she'd be at her conference at St Andrews. One of her former students was giving a talk.

I was in bed before eight. It was good to be back in my own bed after all that time.

* * *

I woke up before it was light. I tried to get back to sleep, but couldn't. Eventually I crept out of the bed, trying not to disturb Stefan. Then I noticed that his side of the bed was empty. He must have gone to the spare room when he'd got in so he wouldn't wake me up. Quietly, I picked up an extra fleece from the chair by the bed. They'd told me that Edinburgh had had a mild spring, but it felt cold enough to me. In the kitchen, the clock said 5.10. I made a cup of coffee and opened the curtains. It was already daylight; the foot of Arthur's Seat was still in shadow, but the sun was glinting on the roofs of the tall buildings beyond Calton Hill.

I suddenly realised how much I had missed the city. African sunrises and sunsets can be pretty dramatic, but they're over so quickly. I'd got used to the hot sunshine and the torrential downpours, to the primary colours and the vitality, which nearly makes you not see the poverty. But after nearly ten weeks of six hours of daylight and six hours of darkness, with no variation, I knew I'd appreciate the unpredictability of Scottish weather, the slow changes of light and shade.

Stefan's lightweight jacket was on the back of the sofa in the lounge. Suddenly, I welled up at the thought of being with him again when he woke; the occasional emails we'd managed to exchange had made the separation worse. I wondered how long it would be before he came round. I knew how much he needed his long lie-in on Saturday mornings. It wasn't just Edinburgh's muted colours that I'd missed.

I sat down on the sofa and thought back to my visitor of the night before. The recollections were fuzzy. Would the card he had left make things any clearer? Why had I been a bit cagey, unwilling to trust him? It certainly wasn't because of the colour of his skin; I'd spent enough time in Africa to know that there are as many honest people there as in Scotland, and as many dishonest ones. It did seem an odd approach, though. But what use could anyone make of an address and a flight number? There was hardly enough there to let them steal my identity, for goodness' sake. And their embassy had always been helpful, more so than the Foreign Office.

A proper breakfast, that was what I needed. More coffee and then... I wondered if Stefan had had time to restock the fridge. Oh, good man! Bacon, eggs, mushrooms, tomatoes. Even some of the lovely Polish bread his brother bakes. I decided I ought to wait a while – you can't fry quietly – but by seven o'clock, I'd given in. The smell of the bacon must have woken Stefan. He came sleepily into the kitchen and put his arms around me. I put on more bacon, more bread. It was the best breakfast I'd had for a long time. After we'd finished, we put the dishes in the sink.

"I really missed you," Stefan whispered. "Tomas can manage without me until this evening. But you must still be tired."

"Well, you know. I did get a decent sleep. What about you?"

* * *

Hours later, as we lay warm and content under the duvet, I began to tell Stefan about my visitor. Before I could make much sense, we were both fast asleep again.

* * *

When we woke, it was already early afternoon. We put on some clothes and went into the kitchen, where we sat at the breakfast bar. Neither of us fancied cooking. We ordered a pizza for later on.

I picked up the business card from the pile and gave it to Stefan, and asked him what he made of it.

The visitor had been polite and friendly, I told him, and I had been pleased about the invitation to the reception, since it would give me a good chance to talk to the other doctors on the project, away from the hospital. But I told him I was uneasy about being asked for my personal details and the flight number. And it had been an odd time of day to call. Was I right to smell a rat?

The look Stefan gave me reminded me that, although his

English was really good for someone who had been in the UK for only three years or so, there were sometimes idioms that I had to explain.

I laughed. "Not a real rat. I meant, was I right to be suspicious?"

"Well, possibly. You never know. I think I'd have done like you. Promised to contact him later. There's the number on the card, the one for the venue. Let's phone it, see if it exists."

He went back to the lounge and returned with the laptop. There were several venues on George Street that could have fitted the bill, but none of their phone numbers matched the one on the card. We decided to phone the number anyhow.

The person who answered our call said that, yes, they did know about the reception, and that they would pass on our enquiry to the administrator responsible, who would be in touch, though possibly not until Monday morning.

It sounded genuine, but we still weren't getting very far. Who else could we contact? I was reluctant to phone other doctors who had just returned. They might still be jet-lagged.

I collected my work files from my suitcase – still unpacked on the kitchen floor – and found the web address of the embassy in London. When we clicked on it, there didn't appear to be anything about a reception in Edinburgh.

"Do I smell a rat?" asked Stefan with a smile. But we decided that there could be a reasonable explanation, and that they perhaps hadn't got the reception organised yet.

I wasn't keen to phone the other number on Mr Falola's business card, even though I'd promised to, since that would mean giving him the information he'd asked for. How were we going to find out if he was genuine? Stefan interrupted my train of thought.

"Don't be cross. Can I ask, perhaps you are not trusting him because of..."

"No, no," I insisted. "Certainly not. Remember, I was dealing with people of different backgrounds all the time I was over there. I was in their country, after all."

The doorbell rang, and I jumped again, but this time it was the pizza delivery.

We ate the food sitting down on the sofa. We were hungrier than we'd thought.

Neither of us wanted to make any more phone calls or do any more googling.

"I'm dead beat," I said. "Let's sleep on it."

Another quizzical look, another English idiom to explain.

We decided we'd climb Arthur's Seat in the morning, assuming the weather was good enough. A good walk was what I needed. It's funny, but each time I come home, I feel the need to climb the hill. Reconnecting with my roots, I suppose.

* * *

It was an odd dream, which is not surprising after the experiences of the last weeks. I was rushing to reach the door of the hospital, then found it was blocked by a man with a big poster. I was trying to read what it said, when someone called me over to the other side of the street. There was a queue of people, but they were being prevented from crossing the road. One of them called my name, Doctor Emma, Doctor Emma. When I walked over, I saw that it was Mr Falola. Another voice: "When are you going home, Doctor Emma?" Then the man with the poster stepped aside and I went into the hospital. But the patients weren't the ones I'd been treating. My mother was in one of the beds, Stefan in another. I was desperate to find what was wrong with them, but no one would answer my questions. I started to shout...

"Steady, steady, Emma. You all right?"

I turned over and buried my head in Stefan's shoulder.

* * *

It was a bright morning, with gusty winds from the west blowing patches of cloud over the city. We set off after a late breakfast, past Easter Road – Stefan always likes to go that way; he says it reminds him of going to matches in Warsaw with his father – on to Holyrood and up the path along the Crags. I've always loved this way up Arthur's Seat – which other city has a Radical Road, I wonder – and the views over the Old Town are the best. There were kite-flyers, family parties, joggers, dog-walkers. Gulls cruised above us, a kestrel hovered above the crags on the right. In the distance, the profiles of the bridges showed above the horizon. I was glad to be home.

At the summit, the wind was strong. Those who had made it to the top looked pleased with themselves, smiling at the other groups, moving to keep warm. I took out my phone and photographed Stefan against the backdrop of the city.

"I'll treat you to a late lunch at the Museum, Stefan. To celebrate. It'll only take you a few minutes to the shop from there. And I can tell you about this weird dream I had."

We went down the same way, strolled up Canongate, turned left then right to Chambers Street. It was nearly three by now, and the café in the basement was quiet enough.

While we waited for our soup and quiche to arrive, I told Stefan about my dream. It was still vivid in my mind. After I'd finished, he thought about it for a few minutes, and then asked if I'd ever had the impression that the medical staff in Africa felt unhappy about all the western experts arriving to help them out. I said I didn't think so. We all worked well as a team. It had been made clear before we left the UK that we shouldn't expect a high level of health provision, and that we should be careful not to be negative about what we did find. But no, I wasn't aware of any real antagonism, if that was what he meant.

The food arrived; we ate it without saying much. After we'd finished, Stefan put his fork down and looked at me with his keen blue eyes. He said that he knew how hard it could be to get things right when you've got people from different backgrounds working together. He told me how, a few months after he'd arrived from Poland, he'd volunteered to help with an integration project for immigrants who didn't have much knowledge of the British way of life. I'm sure he'd mentioned it once before, but I let him go on. It had been tricky, he said. The professionals from the Social Work Department had wanted to do things their way, but the volunteers had been unwilling to take too many orders; after all, they had the first-hand experience of the problems, and they were giving their time freely. In the end, there had been a bit of a stooshie (Stefan loved to use the Scottish words I'd taught him, even when they weren't entirely appropriate), and the volunteers had left the project. Was this at all like the job I'd been doing?

"OK," I said. "It can be tricky. But, anyhow, we did get along. Most of the time. And what do you do? Not get involved, even when you know you can be helpful?"

"Of course not," he replied, putting down his knife. "If I was a doctor, I'd have done the same, I hope. But... I don't know. If you were one of the African doctors. You'd be glad of help, sure.

But you might feel... well, I'm trying to say you have to tread lightly."

"Carefully," I corrected him. "Tread carefully."

I looked at my watch. It was time to go. Stefan started at five and worked at the shop until it closed at eight. As he turned towards the Grassmarket, he said he'd be back as soon as he could. I promised to try and stay awake until he got back. The euphoria I'd felt in the morning, climbing the hill, was starting to fade. On South Bridge, there was a number 14 coming; I was pleased not to have to walk all the way home. I sat down and closed my eyes. Some of the things that Stefan had told me about his early years came back to me: how his parents had survived in the years when everything that happened in their country had to be approved by the Russians, how they had learned to be suspicious of everyone, even people who acted in a friendly manner – especially people who acted in a friendly manner. On our way up Arthur's Seat, Stefan had said how worried he was by the EU referendum result. He was sure it would make it harder for people like him to feel that they belonged in the UK.

Then noises from the street woke me up as the bus passed the Playhouse. There were two policemen trying to calm down a couple of drunken youths. I thought of the time when I'd been out with Stefan and his brother, and we'd been pulled over by the police, who were looking for witnesses to a road accident. Stefan had become very uneasy; afterwards, he'd tried to explain that it was difficult for him not to feel frightened of authority figures. He'd convinced me how lucky I was to live in a society that was well ordered but not too... my concentration was starting to wander; I nearly missed my stop.

* * *

Again, it was getting late when the bell rang. *Please don't let it be Mr Falola*, I thought. It wasn't. It was the police.

There was a sergeant who looked to be in his thirties and a younger female police constable. They had tried to contact me earlier, they said; it was a fairly urgent matter. Had I had a visit from someone of African appearance inviting me to a reception at a venue on George Street?

I invited them in.

Yes, it was a scam. They explained it carefully, with as much detail as they had managed to put together. Basically, the group checked the media, looking for news of people returning from long-haul destinations, especially if they could find several people who had been abroad for the same purpose. Then they got someone to call with the kind of story which my Mr Falola had spun me. If they could speak to people who were still jet-lagged, so much the better. As usual, it was bank details that they were after.

I suppose I had half wondered if this was what they'd been after, but it still seemed hard to believe. I asked them how the information which Mr Falola had requested could possibly allow them to access my bank account. The sergeant's smile implied that this wasn't the first time he had to talk to people with my degree of naivety. Apparently, flight details could be used to get into the airline's computer – some basic hacking was all that was required – and then into the account which had been used to pay for the ticket. "Nothing sophisticated needed, Dr McAllister. Entry-level stuff," the sergeant added with just a note of glee. Could I believe that some people would even hand over their boarding cards, if they were asked.

But what about the venue, and its phone number? I didn't want to seem completely gullible; I said I had been suspicious about that, especially when it didn't appear to have a website. The policewoman explained that, naturally, the venue didn't exist. The number I'd phoned belonged to one of the group. The non-existent venue was just to make things seem a bit more plausible, though she agreed that it wasn't the best thought-out part of the scam. The sergeant nodded.

It seemed that one of my fellow doctors had been suspicious like me, but she had done something about it and contacted the police. The police had recognised the scam. It wasn't the first time they'd come across it, or something similar. The sergeant advised me to be especially careful when I booked my flights; some airlines' websites were more secure than others, apparently.

I was starting to feel pretty miserable. The policewoman probably spotted this; she said that it would be a mistake to feel that I'd been let down by people I'd tried to help. Mr Falola, she said, had an address in Edinburgh ("He's no more African than you or me, Dr McAllister" – an odd thing to say, but I let it pass), and had only been a runner for the gang, which was in fact based in the north of England. I suppose that came as a kind of relief, though I'm not sure why.

They could see that I'd had enough. I thanked them for calling, and promised to be more circumspect next time. As they were leaving, they arranged to return early in the week, to keep me in the picture. At least they said I'd done the right thing in not giving my visitor the information he'd asked for on the Friday evening.

I put the television on, hoping that it might keep me awake. More dissection of the referendum result. The commentator was stressing the fact that Scotland had voted to remain in the EU, unlike England. That made me feel a bit better. I was starting to drop off when I heard the sound of a key in the door. In my drowsy state, I thought at first that it could be an intruder, but of course it wasn't.

Stefan came in and dropped his jacket over the sofa. The shop had been quiet; he'd got away early. I started to tell him about the visit from the police, but then we decided it could wait until morning.

The History Student

1

Rodney looked across to the Ochil Hills on his right. At Easter, they had still been covered with snow; now they looked very dry. Who said Scottish summers were always wet? His new English friends were always teasing him about the weather *up there*. He'd ask them if they meant Glasgow, Aberdeen or Lerwick, but they didn't really get it; beyond Carlisle, everywhere was the same for them.

As the train left Gleneagles, he checked the timetable he'd picked up at Queen Street. Perth in fifteen minutes. That reminded him: Aunt Cecily had told him to phone for a taxi, since the doctors had advised Uncle not to drive any more. He got out his mobile, dialled the number she had given him and arranged to be picked up just after eight. He looked at his watch. He'd be in Pitlochry in less than an hour. He'd have to read the document again, but he put off getting it out of his holdall. It would be better if it was fresh in his mind before he had to discuss it with Uncle George.

He closed his eyes and thought back to his early visits to Uncle George and Aunt Cecily at the Lodge. That very first time, how old had he been? Seven, eight? Uncle's chauffeur had been there to meet them at the station. His mother had been embarrassed when, as the big house came into view, he'd jumped up excitedly and knocked off the chauffeur's cap. How many times had she explained that Uncle George and Aunt Cecily lived in the country, that Uncle George was quite a few years older than she was, that they had no children, and that Aunt Cecily thought boys were dirty and tended to break things? He smiled. His mother wasn't to know how well he'd get on with his rich relatives. He thought back to all the afternoons they'd spent in the enormous kitchen baking chocolate cakes and gingerbread, or the marathon sessions of Monopoly in the summerhouse. Once they'd even gone out late at night to look for badgers.

Sure, the visits had become shorter over the last year or two. He had assumed that they might not invite him now that he was at university, but his uncle and aunt still seemed keen to see him. He was still very fond of them, but it was true that their conversations were often awkward. So it had been a surprise to be invited to visit at Easter, and he'd been shocked to see how frail Uncle had become, walking with a stick and spending more time alone in his study. And Rodney had been relieved that, with his end-of-year exams coming up, he'd had a good excuse to get away after the weekend.

And then there was the document he had given him to read. Rodney closed his eyes and remembered the melodramatic way his uncle had handed it over, so out of keeping with his normal matter-of-fact way of doing things.

It had been after Sunday lunch. Uncle had taken him aside and said he wanted to show him something important. They'd gone slowly up the main staircase to the second floor.

At the end of a corridor, they'd entered a room Rodney had never been in before. He could still picture the chaotic jumble. There had been books, chairs, old clothes, a rocking horse and a stuffed owl, pictures leaning against the walls. Then Uncle had opened one of the chests and taken out the two large envelopes. They'd gone back down the staircase and into the study. Once they were seated at the desk, Uncle George had passed the envelopes over.

What had he said? One envelope contained the original document, which was in Latin. He'd come across it when he'd been clearing out that room earlier in the year. He didn't know how long it had been in the chest. He thought it must be more than four hundred years old. The other envelope contained two copies of an English translation, done by a classics lecturer that Uncle knew. The translator had returned the papers to Uncle the week before. He'd said something about trying to produce a translation that reflected the personality of the writer of the original, who was verbose and solipsistic. "Self-regarding," Uncle had explained.

His uncle had asked him to read the document – the translation, of course – and tell him what he thought of it. Rodney had said yes, of course he would, and asked him who had written it. His uncle had pointed to the last page, and the initials W.M., saying that he was sure the author was William Melbray. Apparently there had been Melbrays in the family in the sixteenth and seventeenth centuries, and one of them was supposed to have worked at the court of Queen Elizabeth.

"As a history student, Rodney," his uncle had confided, "you should find it interesting. I would like you to give the second copy to your tutor, and ask for his opinion. Or her opinion."

The train was pulling out of Perth. He couldn't delay it any longer. He reached for his holdall and opened the envelope. Fourteen pages, plus Uncle's notes at the start. Fortunately, he knew he wouldn't have to read it all.

The refreshment trolley came round. He bought a coffee, settled down and began to read. The first sheet was in his uncle's immaculate handwriting:

Rodney,

The original document, of which this is a professional translation by Dr Grieves of Aberdeen University, relates a journey in Southern France, undertaken by an Englishman, probably in the early 1580s. His mission was manifestly secret. The traveller was in all probability William Melbray. He had been given the task of making contact with the followers of Henry King of Navarre, a Protestant, and find out how England could support them. Given Queen Elizabeth's reputation for parsimony, it's not easy to imagine what form this support might have taken. The report is addressed to 'My Lord Secretary'. Judging by the author's references to 'your worship's means of persuasion', this is likely to be Francis Walsingham, who was in charge of Elizabeth's spies.

Our traveller makes it clear at the start that he has had little success in his contacts with those French people whom he was sent to help. He speaks little French, he tells us with pride. He has no knowledge of the area or of local customs. He is scathing about the food, which cannot have made him popular.

It is obvious that Melbray's mission has been a failure. He says he has spoken to a number of Huguenots, but none of them seems to have provided him with any useful information, or to have given him any encouragement. He is returning home, rather crestfallen, when he relates a meeting which seems to me the most interesting part of his report. Don't bother with the other parts of

his story, Rodney. I've indicated which pages I'd like you to read. I'm looking forward to hearing what you think.
Good luck!

Rodney leafed through the first six or seven of the densely typed pages until he came to those which his uncle had clipped together for him, and began to read.

I feel obliged, your worship, to inform you of an encounter I had with one of the noblemen of the region. He was no lover of God's word, yet without his support, my return to England, and the delivery of this account, would have been more hazardous. Such are the mysterious workings of the Lord, sometimes to use his enemies as servants of the truth.

I had journeyed some two miles from C... where I had witnessed barbarous massacres of God's elect, perpetrated by the Catholic forces led by the Duke of Guise. May Her Gracious Majesty continue to bring succour to those who desire to see Henry of Navarre restore the one true faith to this wretched country.

I fled most precipitously. After three days on foot, I found myself somewhere to the east of the town of Bordeaux, whence it was my hope to seek a ship to take me back to England. I had had nothing of substance to eat since the capon I had shared with the family of honest believers who had given me shelter after the massacre.

Towards the end of the afternoon, exceedingly weary, I came to a handsome, square-built castle, well placed on a small hill and overlooking a river valley to its north. Only berries had sustained me since morning, and I was very hungry. I climbed to the top of a high wall which ran from a round tower on my left towards a smaller tower some sixty feet to my right, and saw a well-kept garden, tended in silence by two peasants and their brood of three or four children.

When evening came, my hunger made me bold. But after I had climbed over the wall, I heard voices approaching. As you know, sire, I have little knowledge of the confusing language of the French, so I could not understand their speech. To attempt to climb the wall again would have made my capture certain. Accordingly, I hid myself in the shade where the wall joined the large round tower. Access to the tower was given by a wooden door. Praying that the Lord might look kindly on his faithful servant, I lifted the heavy metal bar. Surely, the door must be locked, but no, with an effort, I opened it and found sanctuary in the tower.

Inside, I rested, my back against the wall, waiting for my eyes to accustom themselves to the gloom. It became apparent to me that I was in a chapel, private and Papist. The Holy Book was nowhere to be seen; indeed, its presence here would have surprised me.

Since this chapel seemed to contain nothing to sustain the soul of the believer, I asked myself if the remainder of the tower might contain food for the body. It appeared unlikely, but, driven by fear and hunger, I had little choice but to explore further. To the left of the door by which I had entered, rough stairs ascended to the floor above. If I had hoped to find stores here, I was disappointed. Instead, I encountered a room with a comfortable bed and a fireplace, and other pieces of furniture suited to a gentleman's occupancy.

Then I recalled seeing, before climbing the garden wall, that the tower had three windows. Indeed, beside the door to the bedroom, a further set of stairs led up to the second floor of the tower. On reaching this highest level of the tower, what a surprise awaited me! Never had I seen so many books! The faint light of the low sun illuminated shelves of books of all sizes in all corners of the room. In the middle, a wooden desk covered in more books, opened seemingly at random, and great tumbles of written sheets. As I looked up to the ceiling, I saw the strangest feature of all in this strange place. On the beams were inscribed phrases in Latin, Greek and I think Hebrew. A few also in French. I began to be fearful that I found myself in the lair of some diabolist. My fear increased as I became conscious that I was not alone in the tower. I heard a voice, coming from I knew not where:

"Qui va là?"

The question was repeated; this time, I sensed that the voice came from behind me. I turned. To the side of the library was a small room, containing nothing but a desk and a chair. Seated in the chair, facing me, was a man of a certain age, unimposing of stature, quite bald. He appeared to be unarmed. But if he feared the intruder, he showed no sign of it.

"Je suis voyageant," I told him.

His subsequent question was not comprehensible to me, so I told him, in Latin, that I was making for Bordeaux. He replied, likewise in Latin, that I was still twenty Gascon leagues from the town, and that it would be dangerous for me to continue my journey at night. I expected him to call his men and have me placed under guard, but to my astonishment, he offered me lodging. I was clearly in need of repose and sustenance, he said: if I chose, I could sleep in the room below, where his servants would bring me bread and fruit. Astonished, I expressed my thanks at his generosity. He informed me that, on his departure, the door to the tower would be locked; escape would be impossible. He gave me leave to peruse his books if I wished, and showed me where I could find candles. The papers on the table, he insisted, were to be left as they were. Promising to return the next morning, he wished me a good night and descended the stairs to quit his tower.

After expressing my gratitude, I descended to the floor below, ate the food provided, said my prayers and fell into the bed.

In the morning, his servants delivered a welcome breakfast of hams, bread and good wine. Once my host had returned, and we were seated in his library, he informed me that he assumed I was English, and that my intention was to make contact with those of his countrymen who had embraced the Calvinist heresy.

I was speechless. What had I said to reveal my purpose? And what would become of me? My mind filled with images of the means of persuasion which your worship must employ to extract information from those who would plot against the life of Her Gracious Majesty; I knew the French possessed torments as excruciating. I had no choice but to admit, in Latin (our shared tongue), that my purpose had been to provide succour to those of his subjects who adhered to the word of God.

He smiled. He said that he had matters to which he must attend but that I was to remain his guest. Again, he offered me use of his library. He wished to be more fully acquainted with me, and – this perplexed me – to converse with me, if I desired, on questions of faith.

Who was my jailor? Why did he wish to have conversation with me? I reasoned that, if I were to persuade him to release me, I must be better acquainted with him, and that the books might tell me what kind of man he was. I climbed to the second floor of the tower and inspected the volumes that filled his library. Now that the room was flooded by sunlight, I was able to comprehend the extent of the library. I saw books on shelves, piled on the floor, on the desk. They were in Latin and Greek for the most part, with some in French, Italian and other languages. Their owner had read widely. Orators, rhetoricians, philosophers. Tragedians, writers of comedies. Doctors of the primitive church. An abundance of Latin poets and historians. I glanced at the sheets on the desk – written, I presumed, in my jailor's hand – though I left them untouched, as he had insisted. These were in French, but hard to decipher, with many deletions and insertions.

I heard footsteps on the stairs. The French lord re-entered his library and asked me to be seated. Looking at me with eyes which seemed to speak of firm authority, he informed me that he had sent messengers to the King of Navarre, to ascertain whether he had knowledge of an Englishman seeking to make contact with his followers. I did now know how to respond. I was clearly in the company of someone of importance. I asked if I might know his name. He replied that he would furnish it later. I was amazed to find a Catholic lord on good terms with one who must be his enemy, and commented, as politely as I could, on this paradox.

"Is this so strange?" he asked in turn. "Are you so sure of your friends and your enemies? To be thus certain must be comforting in our troubled times, but do you not find that men change sides, that a friend can become an enemy?"

I replied that those who truly believe will remain steadfast to the end.

"Yes," he answered. "They are indeed to be admired. But to be martyred is not proof that one's beliefs are true."

I answered as our divines would have instructed me. "The Word of God alone is true, and he who abides..."

Slowly raising his hand, he interrupted me. "But even among your fellow believers, are there not different interpretations of the Word?"

I knew my reply to this. "Sir, you may dispute the authority by which we believe, but wherein lies the authority of the Roman Church?"

His answer astounded me. He said that he believed as he did because he was born in a Catholic town, to a father whose honesty and affection left him no choice but to remain true to his faith. He then asked me what were my impressions of those who worked in his garden and his castle. Confused, I replied that I had none, only that they seemed hard-working and loyal.

"It will doubtless surprise you," he continued, "if I tell you that I am unaware of which faith they adhere to. What they may have learned from their ministers concerns me little; they may believe it as honestly as I believe the lessons taught me by my father and our priests. It matters more to me that my servants know when the grapes are ripe than that they should understand the mysteries of the Holy Trinity."

"But Sir," I protested, "if faith is then merely a matter of chance, do I not therefore have as much right to my beliefs as any? And is this not also true of those of your countrymen who are cruelly persecuted by Guise and his men?"

"In France," he replied, "those who rise up against the King do indeed suffer. But it is not only Catholics who murder and destroy. All sides have their martyrs. All sides have their inquisitors too. In your country, Catholics are cruelly persecuted, I believe."

I was ready to answer that Papists in England were in league with foreign powers, that their conduct was treacherously directed against the legitimate monarch, but on reflecting that he might view my presence in his country in a similar light, and accuse me, however unjustly, of treason, and seek appropriate punishment, I desisted. Instead, I said I was convinced that those who do not believe strongly enough to die for their beliefs are not true believers, and that being a true believer obliges you also to bring the light of your convictions to others.

"We may indeed choose to die for our beliefs," he concurred, "but to kill for them is another matter. We shall need absolute

certainty if we are to take the lives of those who disagree with us. Such certainty is not to be found in our human state. I think those who would conduct a Holy War are dangerous men. But I fear that it is they who will triumph. Because they are strong in their convictions, they will never lack for followers. The doubter has fewer disciples, I fear."

I observed that I held my beliefs with all the certainty it is possible for a man to have, that my intentions were pure and that, if our intentions are pure, we are not at fault.

After a few moments' pause, he asked me what intelligence I had gathered. Ashamed, I told him I had little of import to take back to England. My truthfulness saved my life; he said he hated dishonesty above all things. He offered to release me in the hope that I might return to England with a more favourable view of those whom I had come to destroy on account of their beliefs. He advised me to seek a boat at La Rochelle. This would mean a long and hazardous journey, but he assured me that it was safer than attempting to find passage at Bordeaux. He provided me with a safe-conduct. My gentleman was clearly of some consequence; I asked his name again, but when he pronounced it, it meant little to me. What was it? Ayken? Aykem? I was too confused to ask him to repeat it.

I departed the next morning. When I asked my host, as I quit his tower, about the handwritten folios to be found on his desk, which had so perplexed me, he seemed, for the only time during our conversations, uncertain of his answer.

After much reflection, he answered me thus:

"They are... an account of my life, a record of my thoughts, to which I wish to bring clarity by setting them down on paper. This I do before old age dims my memory, and I do it for the eyes of none but myself."

"You say you write for no one else's eyes!" I cried. "But, my lord,

what you write about yourself will be seen by God! How can you confess, not to a priest, but to paper?"

My surprise was perhaps abruptly expressed, but he maintained his courteous tone.

"We live in harsh times," he said. "Yet I find there are many ways in which we can enrich the life we are privileged to live. We may enjoy conversation with our fellows, the company of women, the pleasures of the table. But for me, the most satisfying dealings are those which I have had with the wisdom to be found in these ancient books. So I have recorded on paper my responses to the thoughts of these minds, greater than ours, who lived long before us. To engage in humble conversation with these writers cannot be considered a sin, do you not think?"

Once again, my Socrates had answered a question with a question.

On my journey to La Rochelle, I was to find that he was indeed well respected; on two occasions, my safe-conduct was assured when I spoke his name, as best I could. I admit that our debates had left me with a greater sense of the man's merit than I would have imagined possible when I first climbed the wall of his castle. Though his views were manifestly mistaken, he was not without intelligence. And I had reason to be grateful for his generosity of spirit.

Rodney put the document back in the envelope and closed his eyes. He'd no idea what he'd be able to say to his uncle about the meeting between the English traveller and the French nobleman. All the talk about faith and martyrdom, it was hard to know what to make of it. He'd have to let his uncle lead the conversation and see what came up. It was unfortunate that Professor Carmichael had not been in touch with him since he'd lent her the other copy.

With a start, he opened his eyes. The train was pulling into Pitlochry. He quickly dropped the envelope into his holdall, slipped on his jacket and left the train. The taxi ride to the Lodge took half an hour; the driver said he'd never been that way before. Aunt Cecily opened the door and led him to the study, where Uncle George stood up and attempted a smile. Rodney was shocked to see how much he had declined since his visit at Easter.

"Thank you for coming, Rodney," he said. "It's good to see you. You must be hungry. Cecily will bring us some supper."

As he cleared away papers to make a space on the desk in front of him, his wife beckoned to her nephew, who followed her into the corridor.

"Try to avoid discussing the referendum, Rodney. It's been preying on his mind. He just can't understand how we've turned our back on Europe."

Rodney nodded and returned to the study.

They exchanged family news. Asked about his first year at London, Rodney tried to sound enthusiastic. His aunt arrived with cheese and biscuits and tea. She smiled at Rodney, discreetly placing a finger on her lips as she left the room. Rodney inclined his head to show that he had understood.

The older man leaned back in his chair and folded his arms across his chest.

"Bowel cancer," he said simply. "They gave me six months back in the spring; it seems they were optimistic. But let's not dwell on it. A rich life. A good innings, if I can permit myself a cliché."

Rodney searched for the right words. He realised that he'd known at Easter that his uncle was seriously ill, but hadn't expected anything like this. His uncle waved away his clumsy attempts at sympathy.

"Don't worry, Rodney. There really is nothing to be said. It's good in a way to have a chance to set things in order. Closure, I believe that's the term they use. And I'm really pleased that you've been able to come. Now, tell me what you think about my ancestor and his secret mission."

Rodney walked over to the doorway, where he had left his holdall. He unzipped it and extracted the envelope. Seated again, he placed it on the table between himself and his uncle. He was uneasily conscious that his response to his uncle's invitation might fall short of what was expected of him.

"I see what you meant when you said our ancestor was self-obsessed and... what was the word?"

"Solipsistic."

"That's it. Are you sure you don't need anything, Uncle?"

"I'm fine. Please go on. I'm eager to know what you think."

Rodney explained that he had enjoyed reading the account, but that he found the author unsympathetic. The translator had been right about Melbray's personality; no wonder he hadn't gone down well with the Huguenots.

His uncle laughed. "You're right, Rodney. He was certainly no diplomat. What about the conversations in the castle?"

Choosing his words carefully, Rodney said that Melbray seemed to be a typical product of his times, strong in his opinions, but narrow-minded. The picture of the French nobleman, on the other hand, somehow didn't ring true; his mindset appeared too modern for someone living in the sixteenth century. Studying the Reformation period, he said, had taught him how passionate the people of the time were about their faiths, and how intolerant this made them.

His uncle nodded and leaned forward, looking at Rodney with his keen eyes.

"Yes, it is intriguing to find someone so different from what we're expecting. When he tells Melbray that our beliefs are decided by an accident of birth, it takes us by surprise, doesn't it? He never manages to shake Melbray out of his prejudices, but I do like the way he tries. I appreciate what you say about the period, but I'm not sure I agree entirely. We always assume that we're wiser than people who lived in the past, but are we, really? Why do we find it so hard to believe that the French nobleman could have been open-minded? And I sometimes wonder, Rodney, if our attitudes aren't sometimes closer to Melbray's than the Frenchman's. Our times certainly produce plenty of bigots. Melbray's kind of certainty will always have its appeal. What is it that the Frenchman says? 'The doubter has fewer disciples.' I'm afraid he was speaking the truth."

Rodney carefully folded the papers and looked across the table.

"Do you know what happened to Melbray in the end, Uncle?"

"He must have returned safely to England and submitted his report. Then he disappears. He's never mentioned again in our family records."

Once his uncle had started to talk about the French nobleman's 'strange autobiography', Rodney had difficulty in appearing interested. He was relieved when his aunt appeared. She was clearly anxious that her husband shouldn't overtire himself, and told him that she had his medication ready.

Rodney stood up and collected the papers. He remembered the question he had prepared when he'd finished reading.

"Do you know who the French nobleman was, Uncle?"

"Ah, you're the historian," his uncle replied with a smile. "Or you're going to become one. Keep the document, Rodney.

See if you can find out who he was. There are clues, I think. If you succeed, you could try to have the original published, with the translation perhaps. Have another word with your tutor." Rodney promised to do his best.

The following morning, Rodney accompanied his uncle to the door of the Lodge, though it was clear that the older man had difficulty moving more than a step or two. They shook hands – Rodney knew it would be the last time – and then, awkwardly, embraced. Rodney stepped out in the bright sunshine and got into the taxi. At the end of the drive, he looked over his shoulder at the elderly couple, supporting each other and waving goodbye.

2

The restaurant was almost empty and the staff were clearing the tables. I still had work to do on my paper and knew that I couldn't put it off any longer, though the thought of returning to the cramped student flat they had given me – how can they call them *studios*? – was hardly an incentive. Like everything else nowadays, it seemed that the conference was being done on the cheap.

I was just about to stand up and leave when a tall man in a leather jacket sat down in the chair next to mine and looked at the book I had been reading.

"Excuse me, do you mind if I ask? Are you enjoying it?"

This is an unsavoury approach, I thought. I gave him what I believed was a dismissive look, closed the book and turned to pick up the bag with my notes in it. But before I could slip the book inside it, he leaned over and handed me his passport, open at the page with the photo and the personal details. He was pointing to the name below the photo. It took me a second or two to make the connection. I glanced at the book again. He did the same and, with a smile, pointed to the name on the front cover of my book.

"The same," he said. "I hope you don't think I'm being intrusive."

"Ah," I said. "You're Alistair Black."

As soon as I'd spoken, I realised what an inadequate reply it was. I wished I had been able to think of something rather more effective: *You mean you're really called Alistair Black? I'd assumed it was a made-up name*, or *Wait till I tell my mother I've met Alistair Black – no, not Sir Alistair Black the actor, Alistair Black the author of popular history books*. But you can never think of the right riposte at the time, can you?

I gave him his passport back, and gave him a hard stare. He looked about fifty, with dark hair a little too long for his age. He said he was extremely sorry for interrupting me, but he'd always wondered what he would do if he ever found himself talking to someone who was reading one of his books. Would he be brave enough to ask them what they thought? It had never happened before, he said. Once in an airport, he'd seen someone – someone much older than me, he insisted – buy a novel of his, but this was the first time he'd actually had the chance to sit down next to a reader. He hadn't been able to resist the temptation to ask me for my opinion of *Salamanca*. What did I think?

I said something non-committal, but obviously I wasn't non-committal enough. He was not to be put off. Would I mind if he asked my name? I said it was Professor Carmichael. He offered to buy me a drink, "to make up for spoiling my afternoon". I said no, but when he persisted – and only to delay my return to my rabbit hutch and my unfinished paper – I succumbed. I'd have preferred a gin and tonic, but, to show him I wasn't just a naive Englishwoman, I asked for a Bunnahabhain. I think he was quite impressed with my choice.

After I'd thanked him for the whisky and added a little water to it before taking a sip, I pointedly picked up the book off the table and placed it on the floor beside my bag. I had no wish to discuss Mr Black's book with him, so instead I asked him if he was in St Andrews for the conference. Rather to my surprise, he said that he was. He was looking forward to it, he said; it would be a new experience for him. He assumed it wouldn't be new for me.

I laughed. Oh no, not new for me, it was part of the job. I'd been coming to conferences for twenty years or more.

He took out a copy of the conference programme from his pocket. I was afraid that he was going to look for my name on it and ask me about my contribution, but instead he said he knew that the kind of book he wrote didn't usually result in invitations to serious academic conferences, and that he was only here because when he was an undergraduate, he'd shared a flat with Charles Symons.

They went back a long way, he said. When Charles had said he was organising a conference on biography and autobiography and asked him if he fancied coming back to St Andrews, he'd jumped at the chance. He liked the idea of spending some time with 'proper' writers and academics.

Rather than react to his flattery, I told him that conferences had become as competitive as everything else in the academic world, that biography was a broad subject, and that I could understand why Professor Symons had gone out of his way to entice a range of writers to his conference.

"Even my kind!"

The wrinkles deepened when he laughed; I guessed he was a smoker, or had been once.

He placed his malt on the table, looked over my shoulder at the golf course behind me and said that he'd always loved St Andrews. He told me he was from Methil, a mining town in Fife ("in the days when we had a mining industry") and had found the university and its wealthy students intimidating at first. But he'd come to love the place.

It was my first visit to St Andrews, but I decided not to admit it, in case he offered to show me around. I had to agree that the town had a charming atmosphere and that the hotel's restaurant had a fine view. It was a warm, sunny afternoon, typical conference weather. He asked if I was staying at the Russell. I told him I was staying with a former colleague (not true, obviously, but I didn't want him to think I was staying in a hall of residence) and had just come over for lunch. I insisted that I really had to get back to my paper. He asked me if I would mind telling him what its subject was.

I answered that it was about Michel de Montaigne and watched for his reaction. I was ready to explain that Montaigne was an influential sixteenth-century French nobleman who wrote semi-autobiographical *Essays*. To my surprise, Mr Black said that he knew a bit about Montaigne. When he'd done English honours, he explained, his tutor had persuaded him to read extracts from some of the major European authors, in translation. And he'd enjoyed sampling the *Essays*, though sometimes it was difficult to follow the thread. He said it was easy to get seduced by the personality of the author. That was one of the dangers of writing about yourself; like Montaigne, you could be tempted to give yourself pardonable vices. His tutor had called it pre-emptive self-criticism.

It wasn't a bad response. So, I asked him, what would he be talking about?

Of course, he wasn't giving a paper as such. The organisers had been looking for someone who might add a bit of non-academic glamour – he laughed at his own words – and get the conference a bit of media coverage. It would be good for the department. He'd been invited along to attract publicity, and maybe sell a few copies of his latest book at the same time.

He must have seen the look on my face, and claimed that he shared my distaste at the depths to which serious academic work had had to stoop.

"Still," he said, "what's sauce for the goose. You still haven't told me what you think of my book."

What should I have said? That I often read lighter historical fiction like his account of the Peninsular War? That Spanish history had always fascinated me? That the couplings of his characters were portrayed with a certain verve?

I told him that I'd enjoyed it so far and that he had a certain gift for narrative. He laughed again, and said that if what I really meant was that creating characters wasn't his strong point, he had to agree. So I asked him about the inclusion of real people in his novels. It's a bit of an obsession of mine. I conceded that it was acceptable for a novel like his *Salamanca* to feature historical figures such as the Duke of Wellington. After all, Napoleon plays a major part in *War and Peace*. But what about his novels where some of the protagonists were still alive? (I had to admit to having read Mr Black's opus on the Falklands War, *The Islands at the End of the Gun*: what a ridiculous title!) Wasn't this dishonest? Wasn't he taking advantage of his readers' familiarity with some of the figures in his narrative, and saving himself the trouble of having to invent his characters? One of the characters in the book was a real-life British military commander. Presumably he had obtained permission to include him in his novel (he nodded at this), but perhaps there might be members of his family who were uncomfortable with it. And General Galtieri had a walk-on part in the novel too. I assumed he hadn't been able to contact him. I'm not sure whether I believed completely in what I was arguing. I was trying to provoke Mr Black.

His reaction wasn't the one I was expecting. He agreed with me. It *did* save time, he admitted, choosing people who had really lived, and putting them in a fictional context. He wasn't sure that it was dishonest, however. There was trickery in all writing, he'd decided, and readers and writers were all in on the game.

I decided to change the direction of the conversation. I asked him what his motives were in writing books like *Salamanca*.

"Money," he said nonchalantly. "The big M. And using my imagination. I'm in the business of making things up and entertaining people, and that's what I enjoy."

It was the cheerful way he put it that struck me. He'd chosen historical fiction because it appeared to be a profitable niche. A well-populated niche, he agreed, but still with room for a few more. The research could sometimes be a bore, but once you had a couple of successful titles to your name, you could usually pay for someone else to do the tiresome bits for you. But he enjoyed visiting the locations, especially when the trip was paid for by his publisher. He'd even enjoyed the Falklands;

the penguins were wonderful. Occasionally he'd been to some of the European locations featuring in his books with parties of readers; the trips were organised by travel firms and paid well.

He asked if I'd managed to read any more of his books.

Just those two, I said, as casually as I could, adding that I found it was useful sometimes to read other kinds of biography so that I could..."

"Come on," he laughed. "You're slumming. Let me buy you another malt."

No, I said, I really had to go. I told him that there is never enough time to write papers during the summer term, and that June was a ridiculous time to arrange a conference. My paper needed polishing; it had been a last-minute choice of subject, and I'd written it in a rush.

We shook hands, and he said that he hoped we'd meet again some time over the next few days.

* * *

My paper was to be delivered on the Monday. It was scheduled for six in the evening, which, for a conference, is very much the graveyard shift. I was uneasily aware of the fact that my contribution wasn't quite in the conference mainstream. It wasn't straight lit-crit, whatever that is nowadays. It didn't have a feminist take on the practice of writing autobiography. It didn't tackle it from a *nouvelle critique* point of view. I leave that sort of thing to people who understand what they are talking about, or claim to do so. I'm more of an historian; it's the history of ideas that really interests me.

Then, at lunch, I was told to my horror that the chairperson slated for my talk, an expert in the field, had had to return to London at the last minute, and that she had been replaced by... Alistair Black. I protested to Charles Symons that a serious paper required a serious chairperson, but he wouldn't budge. It was obvious that he was repaying Mr Black a favour of some sort, or using the situation to get some of the non-academic glamour that the popular novelist was supposed to bring to the conference. I had to concede, but I did manage to get Charles to promise to be ready to ask a proper question or two after I'd given the paper, since I wasn't sure that Alistair Black would be capable of directing a weighty academic discussion.

On the whole, I was pleased with the way the paper was received. Alistair Black made a good job of introducing it, and I started with some generalities about Montaigne. How the modest way he presents himself is calculated to endear him to his readers, and how this is reflected in the apparently artless, unstructured nature of the *Essays* themselves; how it is the scepticism in his writing that appeals most to our conflicted times. The current orthodoxy, in other words.

Subsequently I explained that I was working on a document which had come to me in a roundabout way. It was something which could turn out to be of great interest to Montaigne scholars, but which needed more research before it could be presented to the academic world. I spent some time filling in the historical background to the document, on the assumption that this would not be familiar to most of those in the room. I summarised the early years of the French Wars of Religion, explaining how attacks against French Protestants had culminated in the Massacre of Saint Bartholomew's Day in 1572, and how in England, the government of Elizabeth I had come under pressure to find ways of supporting the French Calvinists.

This, then, was the context of the material I was working on. I hoped to arrange its publication once I was convinced of its authenticity. The document recounted a meeting between an Englishman, clearly a spy, and a French provincial noble. I had fairly compelling reasons for believing that the latter was Montaigne. The opinions expressed by the nobleman echoed those of the essayist, and most of the topographical and historical details which it contained were consistent with this assumption.

I concluded by saying that I was still investigating the provenance of the document, but that I was confident that the world would soon be in the possession of new material relating to the most intriguing autobiographer of them all. I offered to answer any questions.

I looked for Charlie Symons and his promised friendly observations but, with a shudder, realised he was nowhere to be seen. No one spoke. There was the usual embarrassed shuffling of papers, and the sound of chairs being manoeuvred to allow their occupants access to the corridor. Eventually a younger member of the audience – a postgrad probably – raised her hand and nervously made an asinine query about Montaigne and Alzheimer's. I answered it with as much respect as it deserved.

It was Alistair Black who eventually broke the silence. He knew a little about Montaigne, he said, and remembered being intrigued by the *Essays* when he was an undergraduate at St Andrews. He was sure the revelations in my paper would have a tremendous impact once they were published, though he could understand why I was reluctant to commit myself before I was sure about the document's authenticity. Then he laughed and said that what he personally had liked most about the conference had been the chance to mix with people who had a much deeper knowledge about the past; by contrast, he was only a jobbing hack who tried to make a mostly honest buck from those two everlasting human concerns, sex and violence.

The audience loved him, and his comments brought proceedings to a neat conclusion, though I did feel that he had rather stolen my thunder. As we left the platform, I went over to Alistair to thank him for his help. He smiled his sly smile and said it was no trouble. I offered to buy him a drink. He thanked me, but said that he had promised to go to Kirkcaldy to see his sister and her family. He made me promise that I would send him a copy of my article on Montaigne once I had got it published. We shook hands; he turned and left with a wave. One of the other speakers must have seen our parting. She came over and asked in a surprised voice if I knew Alistair Black. I told her we had spoken briefly a couple of days earlier.

Then I noticed that I'd left my papers on the table. When I picked them up, I saw a card lying on top of them. It was Alistair's, with his address and phone number. Over it, he'd written *Thanks, Stephanie. Keep in touch.*

I was going to throw it away, but I slipped it inside my bag. As I was leaving the room, I passed the table where Alistair's books were on display; they were being packed away into boxes. I hesitated, then selected a copy of his effort on the American War of Independence, *The Colony Strikes Back*.

If I ever do get in touch with him, I suppose I could ask him to sign it.

3

The train climbed slowly out of Inverness and up to Slochd Summit. Rodney watched his mother gaze through the window at the hills, their summits lost in cloud. The funeral had gone "as well as these things ever do". She took out the two bars of chocolate from her bag and offered Rodney one. He thanked her and said something flippant about food being comforting at a time of stress. She smiled silently. Rodney didn't think his mother had been particularly close to her older brother; but his death had clearly upset her. She had done her best to be supportive towards his aunt; they had agreed that Uncle's widow was a strong woman and would cope.

Now they were having difficulty finding things to say to each other. Rodney had noticed how, since he had left home a year ago, his mother had become much quieter; living on her own seemed to have made her lose interest in things. On the journey up from Glasgow, she hadn't been forthcoming when he'd asked her about Uncle George and Aunt Cecily. What precisely was it that he had done for a living? Why had he had to go to Edinburgh so often? And who were the important visitors he and Aunt Cecily used to entertain at the Lodge? Trying to lighten the mood, Rodney had reminded her about the time he'd been told to keep away from Uncle's study because a 'man of letters' was coming on a visit, and how he'd said to Aunt Cecily that he didn't understand why they were making so much fuss over a postman. His mother had smiled. When he had tried to talk about the document his uncle had given him, she had admitted that she knew something about an ancestor who was supposed to have been a spy: this must have been the man.

It would be late by the time they got back to Glasgow. He'd promised to help his mother sort through some of the clutter that had accumulated over the years, and which she had no room for in her new flat. He still hadn't found the courage to tell her that next year he was planning to give up history and study accountancy instead. He'd come to realise that he wasn't the kind of person who wanted to communicate with the past, its dead men and women. He kept thinking of the last time he'd seen his uncle. He hoped that the interest he'd shown in the story of the family ancestor hadn't appeared too unconvincing. Uncle had been an intelligent and sensitive man. Had he seen that his nephew wasn't going to be the enquiring, bookish adult he had hoped he would become?

Better to remember the good times at the Lodge, the card games, the walks through the grounds late at night, watching *The Simpsons* together.

Travelling with a Conscience

First of all, thank you so much for inviting me. June always seems to me the best time of year to be in Scotland. And this must be my favourite book festival, away from the big cities. With people who love books for the right reasons, not for all the media attention.

This afternoon – just like everyone else, I suppose – I'm here to talk about my new book.

I've always argued that travel writing ought to focus on the view and not the viewer. The writer's ego shouldn't come between him or her and the reader. Who wants to know about the writer's digestive troubles when you're reading about Angkor Wat? Or, to come nearer home, you don't want to know about someone's sore ankle when you're trying to imagine what it's like standing on the Black Cuillin with a cloud inversion below you? But for this book, I've thrown my principles out of the window. It recounts some of my early experiences as a travel guide – as a courier (yes, I go back a long way) – before I got going as a travel writer. So for now, I'd like to give you a flavour of the first couple of chapters, hoping that it will whet your appetite and perhaps encourage you to open your wallets.

* * *

I suppose my parents were what you'd call left-wing intellectuals. Some of you might remember them. I was born in 1964. Believe it or not, in those days, you could belong to CND, support Cuba and so on without being considered a freak. At least in the enlightened parts of Nottingham where we grew up. Mum and Dad believed in rational argument, the power of the written word. Can you believe it, we didn't have a television until the year I did my A-levels! But we had newspapers and books all over the house. Dozens of kids' books for me and my sister, shelves full of novels, plays, poetry that Mum and Dad were always reading. And it wasn't just in the house. Every Saturday morning, they used to take us along to the local library. It was a real ritual. The library cards were taken out of the kitchen drawer, and we had to make sure we had all the books we'd borrowed the Saturday before. They didn't like taking books back unless we'd read them. I remember asking Mum and Dad how we got all these books for nothing. Dad said we were very lucky, living when we did and where we did. And they weren't really free; they were paid for out of everyone's taxes. As if I didn't know.

Although my parents were committed to social justice, they weren't what you'd call militant; it was all very reasonable, very British. They'd write letters to the paper, badger their MP about the arms trade. Their intentions were honourable enough, I suppose, but at the time, I couldn't help thinking they were a bit sad. I once told them it was just our good luck, being born at the right time in the right place. You can't really change anything, that's what I said. It's just how things are. Dad asked why other people shouldn't share our good fortune, so I told him I reckoned there was only so much to go round, and that if everyone had fair shares, we'd have to give something up: we could start with the free library books. I pointed out that the things they were fighting for were a long way away. And they could campaign as much as they liked, but in the end, it wasn't as if they were really suffering for their causes.

As you can see, I could be pretty charmless when I was a girl.

After school, I spent a number of years working in an office and getting in my parents' way. We'd call it boomeranging now, wouldn't we? The money I earned was spent on inter-railing with friends in the summer months. You could do it so cheaply, and you certainly felt quite adventurous, visiting places like Yugoslavia and Morocco. Eventually my parents persuaded me to get a proper qualification, and I came to Scotland to study economics at Heriot-Watt. I could have gone to somewhere in England, of course, but Edinburgh had the advantage of being different. Abroad, almost. Dad had advised me that economics would be a good subject to do. But it's not called the dismal science for nothing, and I couldn't stick it. I dropped out at the end of my first year. It didn't help that the guy I was in love with left for a job in the States.

In those days, leaving university without a degree was quite a brave thing to do. A lot of my friends at Heriot-Watt weren't too keen on what they were doing, but they stuck it out because they had been told how fortunate they were to have got into university in the first place. So, brave or ungrateful, take your pick. But at the time, I'd simply had enough of books. Looking back, I have to say I was amazed at how supportive my parents were when I told them I wanted to leave university. I suppose they could see there was no point forcing me to do something

I hated. And it helped that my year in Edinburgh hadn't cost them a penny.

I decided to look for a proper job in the travel business. This was the mid-eighties, when all sorts of different travel opportunities were opening up. People seemed to have had enough of package holidays in the Med, at least some people had. They wanted a different kind of holiday. And countries in the developing world – we could use that term in those days – were starting to realise that they could bring in foreign currency if they offered western tourists a new kind of holiday experience. Sorry, I'm sounding like a brochure, I know. It's hard to kick old habits. A boyfriend I had at the time was keen on scuba diving, and he tried to convince me that if he spent half the year showing well-off Europeans how to explore the coral reefs off some island in the Indian Ocean, then it would be good for the local economy. Diving was much too scary for me, though. But I took up his suggestion and applied for a job with one of the companies that were just starting up. When I look back, I think I was perhaps trying to prove something to my parents, show them that I'd found a more effective way of being helpful. Some of their guilt must have rubbed off on me, despite what I'd said to them.

In those early days, adventure holidays went to India, Mexico, Peru, places like that. Inca trails, Mayan ruins, they were the things that sold best. The more exotic, the better. Ritual violence was always a good selling point. The organisation of the trips could be pretty shambolic. Some companies were making it up as they went along, and a lot didn't survive. Still, it was a great time to be involved. You could help set up the holiday, find the right locations, deal with the local people. You felt you were into something new and exciting. And you were getting paid to travel. It came just at the right time for me, and it did me a lot of good to get away from my parents for a while. I know what you're thinking, they were probably pretty glad to see the back of me. And you'd be right too.

* * *

I originally applied to go to Mexico, but someone who spoke fluent Spanish beat me to the job. So I started off in the Middle East. Tours to the Holy Land were getting very popular. I suppose you could say ritual violence was part of the attraction there as well. They were good trips on the whole. But some of the groups could be hard work. Often it was the church groups that were the worst. They saw the holiday as a pilgrimage; they seemed to believe that going to Jerusalem would make them better people. As you'd expect, part of my job was to find out about the countries we were going to, so that I could answer questions. I was amazed to find out how important Jerusalem was to other religions. But our holiday-makers weren't interested in this side of things. For them, Jerusalem was a Christian city, and that was that. Nothing else mattered. Who was it that said travel narrows the mind?

There were one or two exceptions, often the church ministers, funnily enough. I remember once on a trip to Jordan having a conversation with a vicar who was sitting in the shade, having a quiet fag. I was needing a breather too. He said he sometimes despaired of the group he'd brought with him. He must have latched on to the fact that I was finding it hard to keep smiling and laughing with some of his people. He called them his flock, though he had a weary look on his face when he said it. The further they travelled from Newcastle, he reckoned, the more narrow-minded they became. At home, they'd get on happily enough with more or less anyone, but once they arrived here, it was Arab this and Arab that, and why can't they understand that I asked for *white* sugar.

I laughed and told him not to worry; most of the groups were like that. Perhaps he could point out to his party that the local people belonged to a civilisation that existed even before the Tyne Bridge had been built. You can see I hadn't got any more tactful. I told him how my boss had once complained to our Jordanian contact about the local guides he provided, saying they weren't good with the paperwork. His contact had politely pointed out that his ancestors had built Petra when the British were still living in wooden huts.

After three or four years, I needed a change. I wanted to go somewhere which might appeal to the more adventurous holiday-maker. Sorry, brochure-talk again. I asked for India, but while I was waiting to hear, a job came up in Egypt, and I ended up doing the pyramids and the temples on the Nile. Not all that adventurous, perhaps, but it worked out well. People who went there did seem to have different reasons for going. On the whole, they were more open-minded, I think. The best part of the Egypt job was the people I worked with. Ahmed for one – I'll come back to him – and Craig, my new boss. Craig Everson was a real character, the sort of guy you'd always want on your side. He got on well with everyone, colleagues, customers and crucially the people we dealt with for hotel bookings, accommodation and so on.

For a long time, business was good. By this time, Nile cruises weren't just for the rich. And anyhow, there were a lot more rich people around. Not filthy rich, perhaps, but middle-class

Brits who'd done well out of the Tory tax cuts and who'd made a packet from privatisations. They'd more disposable income, and we were happy to help them find new ways of disposing of it. But one thing you can't do in the holiday business – like any other business, I guess – is stand still. We found we had more and more competitors offering similar holiday experiences. The company decided it wanted to offer something which the other tours didn't have. If we could attract a different clientele, we might be able to establish our own niche in the market. The company decided to add what they called an ethnic dimension. I know what you're thinking. It is a ghastly expression, but we couldn't come up with anything better. We started to arrange visits where our customers could meet local people in their own villages, their own homes. Bringing our customers into intimate contact with a centuries-old way of life, offering them enriching insights into a different culture. That's what the brochures said.

You could do something similar in Scotland, couldn't you? Get parties up from England, the States or wherever, and give them the full ethnic experience. The Americans would love it. I once floated this idea to Craig. We'd both had a good bit to drink, and in the end, it got rather silly. We decided that when our punters got off the bus in the middle of nowhere, they'd get some coarse cloth to make plaid from. They'd be taken to a ceilidh, and told that local custom obliged them to perform their own regional dances. In the morning, they'd have herrings and oatmeal for breakfast. After that, they'd play some shinty, and then we'd tell them to go and do some cattle rustling before tea. We'd say the local farmers knew about this and fully approved. It was when we had them re-enacting the Massacre of Glencoe that we knew we'd gone too far.

Anyhow, back to Egypt, and guess who got the job of setting up the ethnic dimension? Basically this was what I had to do. Our groups would be given the chance of spending an evening with a local family. They'd eat what the family ate. It had to be away from the cities, on the edge of the desert. We sold it as something different, a visit to a part of the country which other tourists didn't go to. You'll probably say that if they really wanted to see how Egyptian people lived, we should have taken them to the slums of Cairo, but I don't think we'd have sold many holidays that way. It would have been the wrong sort of authenticity. The company insisted that these visits had to be optional. I could see that some of our customers might find the ethnic thing a bit condescending and might want to pull out. Very few did, in fact. I know the whole idea sounds pretty hackneyed now, but at the time, it was quite innovative. We also decided that some of the money raised by these visits would go directly to the villages. That way, our groups could feel that they were doing something for poor countries while they enjoyed themselves.

It wasn't easy to arrange these visits. I hadn't reckoned with the antagonism between those Egyptians who made a living from tourism and the rest of the population. Did you know that when the Egyptian government built the Aswan High Dam and flooded the Nubian Valley, they had to resettle the people who'd lived there? Fifty thousand of them. They put them in villages on the other side of Aswan, and gave them concrete houses to live in. They tried to get them to grow sugar cane, as well, which they'd not grown before. Makes it easier to understand the hostility you sometimes come across.

I didn't know any of this to start with. I learned it all from Ahmed, my main contact in Aswan. Must have been in his mid-thirties. Oh, a lovely man, Ahmed. I do miss him. The first time we met, he told me how he'd been invited to visit an Englishman he'd become friendly with at university in Cairo. He'd gone to see him in Maidenhead. But when he'd bought his ticket at Paddington, the guy in the ticket office hadn't understood his accent, and had sold him a ticket to Minehead, told him which platform to go to, which train to get. When he ended up in Minehead, the people at the station had taken pity on him, found somewhere for him to stay the night and arranged for him to get the train back to London the next day. He'd been really touched by this. Hospitality just like in Muslim countries, he said. He reckoned he could pay it back by being especially helpful to British tourists when they came to visit his country.

Eventually, between us, we got the visits set up, and for a number of years they worked well. There was a camel ride to a village, in the dark – remember it gets dark quickly at about six o'clock most of the year – then a glass of tea, a visit to a typical family house, basic food, music, dancing, the chance to play games with the children. Actually, it was quite interesting watching the reactions of our customers. Some of them – usually the women, you won't be surprised to know – entered into the spirit of the thing, joining in the songs, drawing pictures with the kids. Others looked a bit uncomfortable. There'd always be a few who asked questions – about food, clothing, the way of life, though they'd been told to keep off religion.

As I said, there weren't many who didn't go on them. I do remember one woman who said no, it was degrading, people should be allowed to keep their dignity. Funny, she reminded me of my mother a bit, wore her liberal heart on her sleeve. Anyhow, she got a shirty reaction from one of the other members of the group, who accused her of being patronising in a different way. She told her she was just trying to show everyone on the tour how much more sensitive she was. It was just as insulting, she said, to let the villagers see that you knew they didn't want to perform, but that they didn't have much choice. I let the two of them sort it out themselves. Life could get complicated.

We decided to go to a different village every year, so that the money we were bringing in could be spread around as fairly as possible. At the end of one season, I went to discuss things with Ahmed at his home in Luxor. He said he'd made contact with a couple of men from another village. He'd arranged for us to go and meet them later that evening. He stressed that we'd have to tread very carefully. There was a lot of tension in some of these areas, he said, and a lot of rivalry between different communities. I said I was keen to make the visits as inoffensive as possible.

We got into the taxi at about six. There's a wonderful light in the evening, just for half an hour or so. I used to feel it was the best time of the day. The buildings seem to soften as the sun goes down, and you can almost imagine what it must have been like for an ancient Egyptian to see the sun set over the west bank of the Nile. All their myths, all the obsession with death and the afterlife seem to make a kind of sense. If their society was so well organised that the elite had no physical work to do, isn't it natural that they should become fixated on the one thing they couldn't control, and try to find a way of conquering it? At least that's how it sometimes appeared to me.

As the taxi took us through the potholed streets to the place Ahmed used as his office, it looked as though all of Luxor knew him. He waved to just about everyone we passed. The office was through the back of one of the shops that had been set up to sell spices to tourists. There were two men already in the office. They were reading from the Koran as we arrived. They rose, greeted Ahmed with kisses. *Salaam Alaykum*, I said. They shook my hand, without much enthusiasm. The men were wearing the *djellaba*, with open sandals just visible below the hem. One was smoking. It was still extremely hot. Fortunately, there was an ancient fan clattering away above our heads. Ahmed introduced me to the two men, and they started talking. My Egyptian Arabic was quite reasonable by now, and I could follow the gist of what they were saying. It wasn't a particularly friendly conversation. I'm sure I caught words to do with animals and circuses. The two men came from a village further upstream and were willing for our groups to visit on certain conditions. It was clear that there was no chance of using camels to get there; it was much too far. We'd have to use four-by-fours.

Ahmed explained to me the conditions the men were insisting on. First of all, the women in our groups would have to be modestly dressed. I was more than happy with that. In fact, we always made sure there was extra clothing with us on these visits. There always seemed to be someone who ignored the warnings about the need to cover up shoulders and legs. It wasn't just a matter of courtesy; by late evening, it would become quite cool.

Then they started to talk about what we could and couldn't see. I sensed Ahmed getting uncomfortable. He explained to me that they weren't keen on their women being seen by the tourists. I said it wouldn't really work if the only villagers our groups saw were the men and children. The whole point of the visit was for them to see what village life was like. One of the two men – the smoker, I think it was – said that they'd be prepared to let the women be seen, but only if they were wearing their hijabs, and they wouldn't be allowed outside their houses. I reluctantly agreed to this.

They also insisted they didn't want anyone visiting at times of prayer. I said this might be difficult, since we could never be sure of our exact time of arrival. The men said they could offer tea, but no food. I was starting to get exasperated, and I guess it showed. Ahmed was getting a bit agitated too and started to speak faster, and my Arabic couldn't cope. In the end, I agreed to have a look around the spice shop while they tried to sort things out.

A few minutes later, I heard shouting. Then a real argument broke out. I heard a piece of furniture being pushed over, the sound of broken glass, then a cry from Ahmed. Then the two other men rushed out of the shop and into the street. I ran into the back room, expecting I don't know what.

Ahmed was sitting on the floor, against the wall. Blood was coming from a cut on his left arm, just below his elbow. He pointed to the broken glass on the floor.

He was white and muttering things I didn't understand. The wound looked pretty deep. By now the owner of the shop had come into the room. I sent him for a bottle of cold water and a clean shirt. I rinsed Ahmed's wound as well as I could and tore a few strips off his shirt to make a bandage. I held his arm above the level of his heart – he said it wasn't painful, but he was still probably in shock – and we took turns pressing the strips down on the cut. By the time we got him to the doctor, the blood loss had slowed, but he was starting to feel faint.

I went to see him in his home the following day. He insisted that he was OK and tried to play the whole thing down. But he was clearly still shaken, and I said we'd obviously have to drop our plans to set up visits to that particular village. I told him I'd need to put in a report explaining what had happened, but he said he didn't want the police informed. Before I left, I asked him to tell me what had happened.

He said his first mistake had been saying that the people from the previous year's village had always been keen to meet visitors, that the children had loved showing them their games. He'd also told the two men that he didn't think it was possible to shield their women from all contact with outsiders; in the cities, these contacts were happening more and more. He'd tried to persuade them that westerners should be able to see some of the real Egypt, not just the pyramids and the temples.

He hadn't convinced them. They had asked Ahmed if he wasn't ashamed of what he was doing. Of course he wasn't ashamed, he said; he was making a living for himself, yes, but also trying to help people who had a hard life. One of the men had accused Ahmed of lacking loyalty to his own people.

After a while, Ahmed decided that there was no point in continuing the negotiations and told the men that he thought they were wasting his time. After that, his memory was unclear, he said. There had been some pushing, he had stumbled, the glass had broken. The rest I knew.

I told him how sorry I was about what had happened. I really meant it. Not just about his injury, and the argument. It was more than that. I said how grateful we were for all the work he'd put in over the years, told him how much I enjoyed working with him.

Then he really surprised me. He said the two men had made him think. He wondered if perhaps he was being disloyal to his roots. Should he really be working as a procurer? I had to laugh and said I didn't think it was the right word. But did he really think we were exploiting local people? We'd always tried hard to respect their way of life, to present it to our holiday-makers in a dignified way. We weren't forcing the Egyptians to imitate a western way of life, after all. Ahmed didn't seem to want to take it any further, and he was clearly getting tired.

A couple of days later, Ahmed wrote to me saying that he'd decided to look for another job. I went to see him, to thank him and say goodbye. I said I'd help him in any way I could.

Eventually the company did find some more willing villagers and I managed to set up the visits. It's funny, but it was about this time that the kind of holiday-makers we were attracting was beginning to change too. There were more and more young people who had just finished university. The trip they were taking with us was often just one part of a world tour they were going on before they started some ridiculously well-paid job in financial services. I began to be all nostalgic for the middle-aged phonies we used to get. Craig had seen the way things were going, and he'd decided to get out.

Soon afterwards, I got out too. For a couple of years, Craig and I organised holidays in locations where historical novels are set. Places like the battlefields of the American Civil War or Granada at the time of Ferdinand and Isabella. They were always popular, especially if you could get the novelists to come along. Some of you may have been on one of them. Once I had a bit of money behind me, I went freelance, starting with pieces for travel magazines. Gradually I built up a career as a travel writer. I kept in touch with some of my old colleagues, including Ahmed. I did feel a bit responsible for what had happened to him. A year or so after he left our company, he wrote to me for a reference. He was still looking for a job in tourism. He did have misgivings, he said, about the way tourism affected ordinary people, but it was the only thing he had any experience of. He had decided to train as a guide, showing visitors around the monuments, including the Valley of the Kings in Luxor. I told him he'd be brilliant at it. His English was good, he got on well with people, and he already knew a tremendous amount about his country.

Many of you will know what happened at Luxor that morning in November 1997. Ahmed was one of the Egyptian guides killed when the terrorists opened fire at the Temple of Hatshepsut just before nine o'clock; he died trying to protect the people in his group. Perhaps he was still repaying the kindnesses shown to him at Minehead. I don't know. But I do know that he paid a terrible price for sharing his love of his country and its past. We were all stunned, and for a while, I didn't want anything to do with foreign travel. But in the end, you just have to pick up the pieces. People still wanted to go to Egypt, to see the sights. After a while, I got in touch with Craig and between us we raised money for a scholarship in Ahmed's name, which pays for a student from Cairo to spend a year in London, taking courses in hospitality and tourism. I can't shake off an image I have of Ahmed. It's not of Hatshepsut and how terrible it must have been there. It's of the confrontation in the office behind the spice shop. I see not so much the cut on his arm; it's more the pain in his eyes, the deep lines around his mouth. He seems to be asking *Why should it be like this?*

After so many years in this business, I've learned – from people like Ahmed – that it isn't easy to go to other places without contributing to the corruption of the people who live there. I suppose that's why I called the book *Travelling with a*

Conscience. For all that, I do believe that our need to experience different countries and their cultures is a healthy one. Especially at a time when our rulers seem to thrive by encouraging insularity. I'm sure that we'll continue to travel. The secret must be to do it as responsibly as we can. As sustainably as we can. And without limiting travel opportunities to the rich. In later chapters of the book, I look at the progress the travel industry is making in these areas.

When we travel, we cross boundaries. We have to do it with an open mind. It doesn't matter if these boundaries are dramatic or barely noticed, the Bosporus or the Solway, the Israel-Jordan border or Coldstream, we must learn to leave as much as possible of ourselves behind.

We have to accept that white sugar might not always be available.

Thank you so much for listening to me.